The H

"I though[t] [...]
reformed *rake*."

Sam's lips curved into a grin. "Even a reformed rake slips now and again." Cupping a hand at her cheek, he touched his lips to her, withdrew with a low hum of pleasure, then returned for a second taste.

"Sweet," he murmured, tracing his tongue along her lower lip. Angling his body more fully towards hers, he pushed his fingers through her hair and took the kiss deeper.

God help me, she thought weakly. Though every nerve in her body demanded she respond, intellectually she knew what a mistake that would be. Any kind of intimacy, no matter how innocent, could jeopardise their business relationship.

If that wasn't reason enough for her to put an end to this foolishness, he was a virtual stranger. She didn't know him. Not in the sense a woman needed to know a man before making love to him.

Yet in spite of the reasons pointing her away from Sam, she found herself melting against him, until every thought leaked from her mind, save one. Him.

The Honour-Bound Promise
by Peggy Moreland

I thought you said you were a
gentleman.

Bedded *Then* Wed
by Heidi Betts

ᐸᔦᕽᐯᕽᐯᐸᐯᕽᐯ

"Emma," he said slowly, his eyes dark and solemn as he stared into her own. "Will you marry me?"

Emma had heard of being struck speechless before, but she'd never actually experienced it until this moment.

He'd just asked her to marry him. Mitch. Had asked her. To marry him.

"It may not be a love match," he said, running his hands up her arms to cup her shoulders. "I know that, but we get along well enough to make a marriage work. There's no doubt we're good in bed. And I'll take care of you, no matter what."

Maybe he didn't love her. Maybe he never would. Or maybe he just didn't love her *yet*.

The Honour-Bound Promise
PEGGY MORELAND

Bedded *Then* Wed
HEIDI BETTS

MILLS & BOON®

Desire™

DID YOU PURCHASE THIS BOOK WITHOUT A COVER?
If you did, you should be aware it is **stolen property** as it was
reported *unsold and destroyed* by a retailer. Neither the author nor
the publisher has received any payment for this book.

All the characters in this book have no existence outside the
imagination of the author, and have no relation whatsoever to anyone
bearing the same name or names. They are not even distantly inspired
by any individual known or unknown to the author, and all the
incidents are pure invention.

All Rights Reserved including the right of reproduction in whole or
in part in any form. This edition is published by arrangement with
Harlequin Enterprises II B.V./S.à.r.l. The text of this publication or
any part thereof may not be reproduced or transmitted in any form
or by any means, electronic or mechanical, including photocopying,
recording, storage in an information retrieval system, or otherwise,
without the written permission of the publisher.

This book is sold subject to the condition that it shall not, by way of
trade or otherwise, be lent, resold, hired out or otherwise circulated
without the prior consent of the publisher in any form of binding or
cover other than that in which it is published and without a similar
condition including this condition being imposed on the subsequent
purchaser.

® and ™ are trademarks owned and used by the trademark owner
and/or its licensee. Trademarks marked with ® are registered with the
United Kingdom Patent Office and/or the Office for Harmonisation
in the Internal Market and in other countries.

MILLS & BOON and MILLS & BOON with the Rose Device
are registered trademarks of the publisher.

First published in Great Britain 2007
Harlequin Mills & Boon Limited,
Eton House, 18-24 Paradise Road, Richmond, Surrey TW9 1SR

The publisher acknowledges the copyright holders of the
individual works as follows:

The Honour-Bound Promise © Peggy Bozeman Morse 2006
(Original title: The Texan's Honour-Bound Promise)
Bedded *Then* Wed © Heidi Betts 2006

ISBN: 978 0 263 85025 3

51-0807

Printed and bound in Spain
by Litografia Rosés S.A., Barcelona

THE HONOUR-BOUND PROMISE

by
Peggy Moreland

Dear Reader,

Sometimes life is stranger than fiction. From the moment I decided to write this series, focusing on the lives of six fictional Vietnam soldiers, my husband and I have experienced several real-life encounters that seemed to hauntingly parallel the events of the book I was writing at that particular moment. This book was no exception.

In this story, the soldier mentioned in the prologue is listed as MIA (Missing in Action). That, in itself, isn't strange, as the list of MIA's is, sadly, very long. What *is* strange is that while at a cocktail party, my husband and I were visiting with several of the guests and the topic somehow segued to tattoos. Several of the men had tattoos, including my husband, and all confessed that they had got them while serving in Vietnam. From there, the conversation drifted to what branch of the service each served in. When my husband told the group that he was a Green Beret, one of the guests said that her son-in-law's father was a Green Beret, too, and was still listed as MIA. Curious to discover if he had known her relative, my husband asked the soldier's name...and this is where the "life is stranger than fiction" phenomenon steps in. Not only did my husband *know* her relative, he served in the same unit with him in Vietnam.

In spite of all the stranger-than-life encounters that have occurred during the writing of this series, all of the characters and the stories I've created around their lives are entirely fictional...but who knows? Maybe there is a soldier somewhere out there who wanted his story told and used me as his medium. Like I said, life is sometimes stranger than fiction.

Peggy Moreland

PEGGY MORELAND

published her first romance in 1989, and continues to delight readers with stories set in her home state of Texas. Winner of the National Readers' Choice Award, a nominee for *Romantic Times BOOKclub* Reviewer's Choice Award and a two-time finalist for the prestigious RITA® Award, Peggy's books frequently appear on bestseller lists. When not writing, you can usually find Peggy outside, tending the cattle, goats and other animals on the ranch she shares with her husband. You may write to Peggy at PO Box 1099, Florence, TX 76527-1099, USA, or e-mail her at peggy@peggymoreland.com.

This book is dedicated to all the wives, children
and families of soldiers listed as Missing In Action
while in the service of our country.

Prologue

I can't promise you that I will bring you all home alive. But this I swear before you and before Almighty God: that when we go into battle, I will be the first to set foot on the field and I will be the last to step off and I will leave no one behind. Dead or alive, we will all come home together. So help me God.

—Lt. Colonel Hal Moore
(from the movie *We Were Soldiers*)

July, 1972

The mood around camp was subdued. Those soldiers who had ventured from their sleeping quarters sat in silence, their heads down, their expressions somber, their thoughts focused on the previous day's events and their chances of making it home alive. For some, this war was a joke, a part in an elaborate play they acted out each day, under the direction of their supervising officer.

Not so for Jessie Kittrell.

To Jessie—or T.J., as he was called by his friends—this war was his one chance to escape poverty, to give his family the kind of life he'd never known. With a wife and child to support and another baby on the way, enlisting in the army had seemed the only way out of the financial rut he was trapped in. Besides the training it provided, once he fulfilled his years of service, the army would pay for his college education, courtesy of the GI Bill.

If he survived this hell, he thought grimly. Like most of the men he fought alongside, before arriving in Vietnam, he hadn't given survival much thought. He'd been too caught up in the we're-gonna-whip-some-butts mentality ingrained in them all during boot camp. He'd carried that cockiness with him into his first battle...and left it there, along with the contents of his stomach.

Desperate to block the images that pushed into his mind, he reached inside his shirt pocket for the photo he kept close to his heart. Dirty and creased from frequent handling, the photo was his anchor, his reminder of what he fought for, his reason for being here, his need to survive.

Tears burned behind his eyes as he stared down at his wife and daughter. God, he missed them. Three months was a long time for a man to go without seeing his family. Leah had turned two last week, a birthday party he'd missed. Would she remember him when he returned home? Would she wrap her arms around his neck and plaster a wet kiss on his cheek when she saw him, as she had in the past? Or would she cringe away and cry for her mommy?

The dull *whop-whop-whop* of helicopter blades overhead had him looking up. Knowing the chopper's purpose, he slowly tucked the picture back into his pocket. He watched silently as the Huey landed and two bagged bodies were loaded onto the deck. He gulped back emotion, aware that a third soldier should have been making that ride. Buddy Crandall.

But Buddy wouldn't be making the trip back home.

A wide hand landed on his shoulder and he glanced up to find Pops—the nickname given Larry Blair by T.J. and the rest of the guys—beside him, his gaze on the helicopter as the pilot prepared to take off.

"It's not right," T.J. said, shaking his head. "Buddy should be on that chopper."

"Yeah," Pops said quietly. "But some things just aren't meant to be."

"MIA," T.J. muttered, squinting his eyes as he watched the helicopter slowly rise into the air. "Can you imagine what getting that news is going to do to Buddy's family? Why can't the Army list him as Killed in Action rather than Missing in Action? Hell, we all know he's dead! We were there. We saw what happened. There's no way he made it out of there alive."

"You know the rules," Pops reminded him gently. "If a soldier's body isn't recovered and his death not positively verified, he's MIA."

"I don't want my family put through that," T.J. said furiously. He glanced up at Pops. "Promise me something, Pops."

"If I can."

"If what happened to Buddy should happen to me, promise me you'll let my family know. Tell 'em I fought and died like a soldier. Tell 'em I won't be coming home."

Pops hesitated a moment, then nodded soberly. "Consider it done." He gave T.J.'s shoulder a comforting squeeze. "Check your gear. We'll be pulling out in a couple of hours."

T.J. sat a moment longer, then dragged a hand across the moisture in his eyes and stood. He patted his pocket and the photo he kept there, then strode for his tent and the pack that held his gear.

One

The Craftsman-style two-story house Sam parked his truck in front of was situated in an older neighborhood near Tyler, Texas's downtown area. A breezeway connected the house to a carriage-style garage and served as a pass-through to the garage's rear entrance, discreetly hidden in the backyard.

The house was owned by Leah Kittrell. Mack McGruder had provided Sam with the woman's name, as well as her address and telephone number. An Internet search had provided him with a few more details. According to the information he'd found, Ms. Kittrell owned her own business—

Stylized Events—had gone through a messy divorce three years prior and currently served on the boards of several civic and charity organizations. The photos he'd found of her in the archive section on the Tyler newspaper's Web site provided an image of a woman who appeared to be in her late twenties to early thirties, with long dark hair, classic features and legs that seemed to stretch forever.

More facts than he probably needed, but Sam preferred to know as much about a person as he could before entering into negotiations.

Now all he had to do was squeeze what he wanted out of the woman and he could call it a day.

Confident that he'd be back on the road within the hour, he punched the doorbell, then stepped back, smoothing a hand over hair the wind had rumpled earlier while he was changing a flat tire on the interstate.

The door swung open and a woman appeared. Leah Kittrell, he thought, easily recognizing her from the photos he'd found on the internet. But the pictures hadn't done her justice, he thought appreciatively. While attractive in the photographs, in person she was drop-dead gorgeous. What the pictures had revealed as dark hair was in fact a sleek raven-black. But the image of her legs had been right on target. They did seem to stretch forever.

Mesmerized by eyes the color of aged whiskey,

it took him a moment to realize that she was frowning at him. He quickly extended his hand.

"Sam Forrester," he said, introducing himself.

She glanced down at the hand he offered and her frown deepened. Following her gaze, he saw the grease that stained his palm and yanked it back to drag across the seat of his jeans. "Sorry. Had a blowout on the way here. Haven't had a chance to clean up."

Her gaze met his again. "How many are you expecting for dinner?"

He blinked. Blinked again. "Excuse me?"

Rolling her eyes, she angled her head and pointed to the minuscule headset attached to her ear.

"Oh," he murmured, realizing that her question hadn't been directed to him but someone she was talking to on her cellular phone. "Sorry."

She stepped back and motioned for him to come inside. "Forty guests," she said thoughtfully as she closed the door behind him. "To be safe, I'd suggest we plan to serve thirty-five. Some won't bother to RSVP but will come anyway. Others will say they're coming and not show up."

She turned for the rear of the house, curling her finger in a signal for him to follow. With a shrug, he trailed behind her, glancing at the rooms they passed through. Neat as a pin, he noted. Not a thing out of place. Not even in the kitchen. The woman either had a full-time housekeeper or was anal as hell.

She opened a rear door, stepped out onto a patio and led the way to the garage. *It's in there,* she mouthed, indicating a side door.

Wondering what "it" was, he eased past her and opened the door. Like the rest of her house, the garage was hospital-clean and neat as a pin. An SUV was parked in the slot nearest him. In the other, a vintage Ford Mustang.

He pressed a hand over his heart. "Oh, man," he murmured and headed for it.

He walked a slow circle around the car, then stopped in front and popped the hood. Behind him he could hear Leah talking on the phone, but he was more interested in the vintage set of wheels in front of him than her discussion of food and flowers.

Bracing a hand on the radiator for support, he stuck his head beneath the hood in order to check out the engine. "Two hundred and fifty ponies," he said with a lustful sigh.

"So? What do you think?"

He jumped at the sound of her voice and bumped his head on the hood. Muttering a curse, he straightened, rubbing a hand over his head.

She winced. "Ouch. Bet that hurt."

Grimacing, he dropped his hand. "I've had worse." He turned back to the car and lowered the hood. "Sorry for being nosy, but I couldn't resist. Is it yours?"

"My brother's," she replied, then amended, "Or it was."

He glanced back, a brow lifted in question.

"He was killed in Iraq about six months ago. He promised my nephew, Craig, he could have the car when he turned sixteen. They were going to start restoring it when my brother returned from Iraq." She glanced at the car, drew in a steadying breath. When she faced him again, her jaw was set in determination. "I intend to see that at least part of his promise is kept, which is why I advertised for a mechanic to do the restoration."

And she thought he was a mechanic who'd come in response to her ad, Sam deduced. Though he knew he should correct her mistake, he decided, for the moment at least, to keep the purpose of his visit to himself and said instead, "I'm sorry for your loss."

"*I'm* sorry he ever enlisted."

Surprised by the bitterness in her voice, he began to circle the car again. "How long had he owned it?" he asked curiously.

"Forever."

He shot her a glance over the roof of the car and she shrugged. "My father was the original owner. I guess you could say Kevin inherited it from him."

He turned his gaze back to the car and saw the Army decal on the rear window, it's edges curled and brittle, and knew, by its age, her father was the one who had put it there, not her brother. Thinking this might be the opening he needed, he asked, "Your father was in the Army, too?"

She followed his gaze to the decal. "MIA, Vietnam."

"Your family made a considerable sacrifice for our country."

She flattened her lips. "Not by choice, I assure you." She flapped a hand, dismissing the subject, then glanced at her watch. "My nephew should be here soon. He wants to help with the restoration. Do you have a problem with that?"

Again he felt he should correct her mistake and tell her the true purpose of his visit. But he had a feeling if he did, she'd toss him out on his ear.

"Can't see why I would," he replied vaguely.

She smiled, seemingly relieved by his response. "Good. Craig really needs this."

Before he could ask her what she meant by the statement, the door opened and a young voice called, "Aunt Leah? You in here?"

Leah turned, her smile widening. "Come on in and join us, Craig. How was school?"

Head down, a boy—somewhere between twelve and fourteen, judging by his size—shuffled toward them, one hand cinched around the strap of a backpack he had draped over his shoulder, the other stuffed in the pocket of jeans at least a size too large for his thin frame. "Okay, I guess."

Sam yearned for a pair of scissors so that he could whack off enough of the kid's hair to see his face.

"Craig, I'd like you to meet—" She stopped short, then looked at Sam in embarrassment. "I'm sorry. I can't remember your name."

"Sam Forrester."

Smiling, she extended her hand. "Leah Kittrell."

He held up his palm, reminding her of the grease that stained it.

She tucked her hand behind her back. "Uh, right." She turned to her nephew and, smiling again, wrapped an arm around his shoulders and drew him to her side. "Sam, this is my nephew, Craig. Craig, Mr. Forrester."

"Sam will do," Sam offered, then smiled at the kid. "Nice to meet you, Craig."

Craig mumbled a barely audible, "Yeah. You, too."

"Sam is here to discuss restoring the car," she told her nephew.

He glanced up at Sam through the mass of bangs he hid behind, then dropped his gaze and turned away with a mumbled "Whatever" and headed back toward the house.

"Hey!" Leah called after him. "Where are you going?"

"Homework."

"But don't you want—"

The door slammed, cutting her off. Heaving a sigh, she turned and gave Sam an apologetic smile. "He really is a nice kid. He's just been having a tough time. Losing his father hit him pretty hard."

"Tough blow for a kid his age."

"Yes, it is."

He frowned, remembering the boy's reference to homework, as well as her mention earlier about school. "Isn't school out for the summer?"

"For most students. Craig failed two classes, so he has to go to summer school."

He nodded, wondering if the kid's father's death had anything to do with his failure.

She opened her hands. "So? What do you think? Are you interested in the job?"

You've really stepped in it now, Sam thought, realizing too late his mistake in allowing her to go on believing he was a mechanic. He supposed he could tell her the restoration would take more work than he'd first thought and make a fast exit.

But that would mean leaving without getting the information he'd promised Mack, which didn't settle well with him at all. He owed Mack. Big-time. And he was determined to honor that debt.

Pursing his lips thoughtfully, he studied the car as if considering whether or not he wanted to take on the job while buying himself some time to figure out what he should do.

Getting the information for Mack wasn't going to be the easy-in-easy-out mission he'd first thought. Mack had warned him about Leah's obstinance in refusing to discuss her father, but Sam hadn't taken him seriously until he'd gotten a taste of it himself. It was going to take some time to finesse her into telling him what he wanted to know.

And restoring the car might be just the ploy he needed to gain that time.

But if he agreed to work on the car, he'd be saddling himself with a troubled teen. Sam had seen the resentment, as well as the grief, that shadowed the boy's eyes and suspected it was the loss of his father that had put them both there. Sam had lost a father, too, at a fairly young age. Not to death, but a loss just the same, and he understood what the boy was going through…and where he'd end up if someone didn't intervene.

He had a month, he reminded himself, with nothing to do but puzzle out the direction he wanted to point his future in. He could think as easily working on a car as he could lying on his back on some sun-drenched beach surrounded by bikini-clad women.

Decided, he said to Leah, "Yeah, I'm interested."

He would swear he felt her sigh of relief from five feet away.

"I have no idea what kind of payment to offer you. I know nothing about this kind of thing or how long it would take to complete the job. I guess it would simplify matters if you'd simply tell me what you'd charge for the restoration, then I could determine whether or not I can afford to hire you."

"Since you want your nephew to help with the restoration, I suppose the work will need to be done here?"

"That would be best. He comes here after school each day."

Nodding, he began to circle the car again. "I've only got a month to devote to the job, but I think I could get it done in that length of time. Most of it, anyway."

"Are you saying you'll do it?"

Smiling, he stroked a hand over the Mustang emblem on the hood. "Hard to say no to a beauty like this."

"We haven't decided on a fee yet," she reminded him.

He hitched his hands on his hips and looked up at the ceiling. "Most carriage houses like this have an apartment overhead. Does this one?"

"W-well, yes," she stammered as if wondering why he'd ask. "Although not a full one. Just a bedroom, sitting room and bath."

Lowering his chin, he met her gaze. "Tell you what. Provide me with room and board for the next month, and we'll call it even."

"Room and board?" she repeated dully.

"I'm not from around here. In order to do the work, I'd need a place to stay."

She nervously wet her lips. "I suppose that would be okay. The apartment's furnished. I keep it ready for relatives and friends who come to visit. But I don't cook," she was quick to inform him. "Not regularly, at any rate."

"As long as I'm allowed access to your kitchen, I can see to my own meals."

She eyed him suspiciously. "And that's all you want in exchange for doing the work? Room and board?"

He hid a smile. "If you're worried I'll demand sexual favors, I won't." He waited a beat, then added, "Although I wouldn't turn them down if offered."

She jutted her chin. "I'll want references."

He shrugged. "Fine with me. None will be local, though. Lampasas is where I call home."

Her brows shot high. "How on earth did you hear about the ad I placed? Lampasas is hours from here."

He shot her a wink. "I guess some things were just meant to be."

As he pulled away from Leah's house, Sam punched in Mack's phone number. His friend answered on the first ring, obviously awaiting the call.

"Did you talk to her?" Mack asked anxiously.

"I did," Sam replied. "And the answer to your next question is no. I haven't gotten the information you need. But I'm working on it, which is why I called. I need a favor."

"What?"

"Personal references."

"Why?"

"I'll explain later. Right now I need you to call Lenny, Pastor Nolan, Bill and Jack Phelps. Tell them that Leah Kittrell might be calling and asking questions about me. If she does, tell them to keep whatever information they offer to a minimum and not to mention anything about me being in the Army."

"Why not?" Mack asked in confusion. "Your service record is nothing to be ashamed of."

"No," Sam agreed. "But if Leah finds out I'm in the military, it'll kill whatever chance I have of getting the information you want."

Leah frowned in concentration as she fussed with the strands of ivy draping the tiered crystal pedestal centered on the sample table setting she had arranged. Once satisfied with the design, she would photograph the table, note the style and color of linens used, as well as the other accessories, and record them all in the client's file to reference for the wedding reception scheduled for October.

"Looks good."

Leah glanced over at Kate, her assistant, then back at the centerpiece and worried her lip. "You don't think the ivy will obstruct the guests' views?"

"You're just obsessing because Mrs. Snotgrass is the client."

"*Snod*grass," Leah corrected. "If you're not careful, you're going to slip and call her that one day."

"It would be worth it just to see the expression on the old biddy's face."

"Easy for you to say. It isn't your business she'd send down the toilet."

Kate snorted. "As if she could."

Leah lifted the digital camera hanging from her neck and moved around the table, clicking off shots of the table from different angles. "Though I appreciate the vote of confidence, Mrs. Snodgrass's opinion carries a lot of weight in this town. One derogatory comment from her and my business would suffer the reverberations for months."

Satisfied that she'd taken enough pictures to record all the accessories used in the design, she headed for her office to download the photos into the appropriate file.

Kate trailed behind. "How's the search going for the mechanic?"

"I found one."

Kate dropped down into the chair opposite Leah's desk and lifted a brow. "Really? Who?"

"Sam Forrester."

"Never heard of him."

"He's not from around here."

"Then how's he going to do the work?"

"He's staying in the apartment over the garage."

Kate sat bolt upright. "A complete stranger? Have you lost your mind?"

"I checked his references," Leah said defensively.

Scowling, Kate slouched back in the chair. "Which doesn't mean squat. The references he gave could all be his friends."

Leah caught her lower lip between her teeth, having thought the same thing, then shook her head. "No. He seems like an honest guy. He even agreed to allow Craig to help with the restoration."

"He's probably cleaning out your house as we speak."

"Would you stop?" Leah cried. "You haven't even met the man."

Kate rose. "Then introduce me."

Leah looked up at her blankly. "Now?"

Kate shrugged. "No time like the present. We can grab some lunch on the way back."

"And who would mind the shop while we're gone?" Shaking her head, Leah plucked her purse from beneath her desk and headed out.

"Where are you going?" Kate asked, following her.

"I—I forgot something at home."

Kate bit back a smile. "Liar. You're going to check on the mechanic."

Leah opened her mouth to deny the statement, then clamped it shut and marched out the door, her chin in the air.

Settling into the apartment above Leah's garage took Sam all of about five seconds. All he had with him was crammed into his duffel bag, which consisted of about four changes of clothes, his toiletries and an extra pair of boots—all civilian wear, since he was on a monthlong leave from the army.

He'd just dumped his underwear and undershirts into a drawer when he heard a tap on the exterior door.

"Come on in," he called. "It's open."

Just as he stepped from the bedroom and into the sitting room, Leah was bumping the front door closed with her hip. And a nice curvy set of hips at that, he noted.

She lifted her arms, indicating a stack of towels and washcloths. "Thought you might need these. My cousin and her husband were my last guests, and I forgot to restock the linen closet after doing the laundry."

"Thanks." He took the linens from her and set them

on the antique trunk that served as a coffee table. "And speaking of laundry…do you mind if I use your washer and dryer? I'll supply my own detergent."

"Help yourself. It's off the kitchen. The controls are self-explanatory, but let me know if you have any problems."

"I'm sure I can figure it out."

When she didn't make a move to leave, he looked at her curiously. "Was there something else?"

Avoiding his gaze, she picked up a pillow from the sofa. "About your references…" she began uncertainly as she plucked at its corded edge.

"Is there a problem?"

"No. No problem. In fact, they were all glowing." Huffing a breath, she tossed the pillow to the sofa and turned to face him. "Yes, there *is* a problem. Not a one of the men I spoke with mentioned anything about your past work history."

Though he knew he was treading on dangerous ground, Sam wasn't worried. He'd gotten himself out of tighter spots in the past. "Probably because I've never worked directly for any of them." He gestured to the sofa. "Have a seat," he invited. "I'll answer whatever questions you might have."

She hesitated a moment, then sat down at the far end of the sofa. "Just for a minute. I need to get back to the shop."

Dropping down on the opposite end, he draped

his arm along the back of the sofa and opened his hand. "Fire away."

"You might start by explaining how you have a month available to devote to this project."

"That's simple enough. I'm taking what might be called a sabbatical while I consider a career change."

She looked at him curiously. "You don't like working as a mechanic?"

"Oh, I enjoy working on cars well enough," he replied, neatly avoiding a lie. "Always have. In fact, I think I was about fourteen when I rebuilt my first engine."

Her eyebrows shot up. "*Fourteen?* That's not even the legal age to drive a car!"

Chuckling, he shook his head. "No, but it's legal to work on one. My dad was a rancher, but his first love was cars. Especially vintage models. While most of the boys my age were playing with baseballs and bats, I was pulling engines and rebuilding carburetors." Before she could ask another question about his past, he shifted the conversation to her. "Did you have any weird hobbies when you were a kid?"

She blew out a breath. "I didn't rebuild cars, that's for sure. My only hobby—if you would call it that—was arranging flowers."

"Your mother was a florist?"

She snorted a breath. "Hardly. Our neighbor was.

She ran a floral business out of her home. I hung out there while growing up."

Hoping to take advantage of this opening to learn more about her, as well as her family, he angled a leg onto the sofa and faced her. "She let you help her make floral arrangements?"

"Not at first. In the beginning I was more like a gofer. Fetching supplies, sweeping up the cuttings, that kind of thing. I eventually graduated to making my own designs, but that was years later."

"Do you remember your first?"

Her face softened at the memory. "A baby gift for a new mother. The vase was a ceramic baby carriage. I filled it with pink carnations, baby's breath and greenery." She shot him a sideways glance, her expression sheepish. "Not very original, huh?"

He shrugged. "Everybody has to start somewhere."

"Well, that was definitely my defining moment. I was hooked from then on and never looked back."

Although he knew about the business she currently owned, she wasn't aware he did. "So you're a florist?"

"In a sense. I own my own company. Stylized Events. We handle all the details of a party, from invitation to cleanup and everything in between, including floral arrangements, depending on a client's preferences."

He shuddered. "Sounds like a lot of work to me."

"It is," she agreed. "But I love it." She wrinkled her nose. "Or I do most of the time."

"Uh-oh. Contrary clients?"

She laughed softly. "Only one, really. Mrs. Snodgrass—or *Snot*grass, as my assistant refers to her."

He laughed. "Obviously your assistant believes in calling a spade a spade."

Grimacing, she grumbled, "Which is why I'm here."

He lifted a brow. "And why is that?"

She dropped her gaze, obviously embarrassed that she'd let that slip. "Kate thinks I was a little...well, hasty in allowing you to move into the apartment."

"A cautious woman," he commended with a nod of approval. "But in this case misguided." He slid his hand from the sofa and laid it on her shoulder, drawing her gaze to his. "I assure you you're safe with me."

"I doubt she'd consider that assurance comforting, coming from you."

Smiling, he drew his hand back to rest on the back of the sofa again. "Probably not, but in time I'll prove I'm trustworthy."

"Speaking of time..." She glanced at her wristwatch and rose. "I better get back to the shop. I've been away too long as it is."

He stood and followed her to the door. "I hope

you don't mind, but I nosed around some in the garage this morning. Looks like you have all the tools I'll need to get started on the car."

She paused in the open doorway. "They were my brother's. When I had his car towed over here, I had them bring his tools, too."

With her back to him, he couldn't see her expression, but he was sure he caught a hint of sadness in her voice.

"The two of you…" he began hesitantly. "Were you close?"

She stood there a long moment, then heaved a sigh and started down the stairs. "Yeah, we were."

Two

Having lived in other areas of the world for the last several years, Sam had forgotten how hot Texas summers could get. In a matter of hours, the temperature in the garage rose from a slow simmer to a rolling boil, leaving him drenched in sweat and struggling for every breath.

After two days of sweltering in the garage, he decided a change of venue was necessary if he hoped to make any progress on the car. He scoped out possible locations, then raised the garage door and pushed the Mustang out onto the driveway. With the sun beating down on him like a blowtorch, he pushed and strained some more until he'd maneuvered the car beneath the shade of the breezeway.

Deciding that the new location was a bit more bearable, he fetched tools from the garage, then lay down on the creeper and pushed himself beneath the car to examine the underside.

After a careful inspection, he decided, considering its age, the undercarriage wasn't in too bad a shape. Not that it was going to be easy to repair the damage that thousands of miles and years of neglect had inflicted. He tapped a wrench against a brace and was rewarded with a shower of powdery rust. No, he thought, dragging a hand across his eyes to clear them, this wasn't going to be easy.

He used his boot heel to push the creeper along, following the line of the exhaust pipe to the rear of the car, and noted that rust corroded the entire system from the connection at the engine all the way to the rear bumper. Pulling a pencil stub and scrap of paper from his jeans pocket, he scribbled *muffler* and *tailpipe* on the growing list of parts he would need.

He was wheeling himself from beneath the car when he heard the scrape of footsteps on the drive. Hauling himself to his feet, he glanced in that direction and saw Craig heading up the drive.

Smiling a welcome, he pulled a rag from his

back pocket to wipe his hands. "Hey, Craig! How's it going?"

Craig shrugged but didn't slow down. "All right, I guess."

Sam gestured toward the car. "You're just in time to help remove the exhaust pipe."

"Got homework," Craig mumbled and passed him by.

Sam watched him in silence, surprised by the kid's refusal, as he specifically remembered Leah telling him the kid wanted to help with the restoration.

Shaking his head, he hunkered down in front of the rolling tool cart and selected a couple of wrenches from one of the drawers, then stretched out on the creeper again and wheeled himself beneath the car.

He wasn't going to push, he told himself. If the kid wanted to help, he'd let him.

And if he didn't...well, Sam would figure out a way to rope him into getting involved.

Leah braked to a stop on the drive, her eyes widening in dismay at the mess that blocked the breezeway and her normal path to the garage. In the middle of the destruction sat the Mustang, its hood up and its doors propped wide, looking like a bird preparing for flight. Tools of every description were scattered over the drive and along the car's fenders. A muffler and a twisted tailpipe lay in the flower bed that ran along the side of the house, crushing the blooms of her geraniums.

Incensed, she leaped from her car and marched to the partially dismantled Mustang and the man whose head was hidden beneath the hood.

"What on earth do you think you're doing?" she demanded angrily.

Sam drew his head from beneath the hood only far enough to look at her. "Working on the car. What does it look like I'm doing?"

"Destroying my yard, that's what!" She flung out an arm. "Just look at this mess! You've turned my driveway into a junkyard!"

"What the hell did you expect?" he asked impatiently. "A car has to be dismantled before it can be restored."

Pulling a rag from his hip pocket, he straightened, dragging it down his face and chest. Her jaw dropped when she saw that he wasn't wearing a shirt. Glancing quickly around to see if any of the neighbors were watching, she grabbed him by the elbow and hustled him into the backyard. "You can't parade around half-dressed," she whispered angrily. "What will my neighbors think?"

He jerked his arm from her grasp. "I don't give a tinker's damn what your neighbors think. It's hot as hell out here. Wearing a shirt makes it that much hotter."

Flattening her lips, she folded her arms across her breasts. "I suppose I should be glad you didn't take off your pants."

He reached for the first button on his jeans. "Now that you mention it—"

She slapped his hand. "Don't you dare!"

In the blink of an eye she found her hand in his grasp and her body thrust up against his, his face inches from her own.

"I've never struck a woman in my life," he informed her coldly, "but slap at me again, and I might consider it."

She gulped. "I—I just wanted to stop you from taking off your jeans."

His scowl deepened. "Believe it or not, I have a few scruples, one of which is not bearing my ass in public. So there's no need for you to worry that pretty little head of yours that I'll strip naked and flash your snooty neighbors.

"And as far as the mess on your driveway goes," he continued, "it's too damn hot to work in the garage. I pushed the car out here, where I could get some air. But if having all this *junk,* as you call it, scattered around upsets your anal-retentive person-ality, you didn't have to jump me about it. All you had to do was ask and I'd have moved it to the back and out of sight."

He released her and took a step back. "Now," he

said, and used the rag to wipe his hands, "is there anything else bothering you?"

She gulped again. Swallowed. "N-no."

"Good." He stuffed the rag back into his hip pocket. "So? How was your day?"

Thrown off balance by his quick mood change, it took her a moment to find her voice. "B-busy."

"Yeah, mine, too." He picked up the wrench he'd set aside and returned it to the tool cart. "You ought to do something about that tension in your shoulders. It's bad for your health."

She started to roll her shoulders, then squared them instead. "I had a stressful day."

"I take it Mrs. Snotgrass dropped by."

She blinked, surprised that he'd remembered her client's name. "*Snod*grass," she corrected. "And yes, she was in the shop this afternoon."

He rolled the tool cart closer to the car. "I noticed there's a spa attached to your pool. You ought to put it to use. Let it work out some of the kinks in your shoulders."

"I'll keep that in mind."

"If it's all right with you, I might use it later." He dropped a wrench into the drawer, then flexed his arm. "I used muscles today I haven't used in a while."

She stared in fascination at the play of sinew beneath his sweat-slickened skin. "F-fine with me."

"Appreciate it." He stooped and picked up a

pair of pliers, tossed them into an open drawer. "Craig's home."

At the mention of her nephew, she glanced toward the house, then back at Sam and frowned. "Why isn't he helping you?"

"Said he had homework."

Her scowl deepened. "He pulls that card when he doesn't want to do something."

He glanced over his shoulder. "I thought you said he wanted to help with the car?"

"He does—did." She lifted her hands, then dropped them helplessly to her sides. "I don't know what he wants anymore. The last couple of weeks he's withdrawn more and more into himself, refuses to talk me. I was hoping that restoring the car would pull him out of whatever funk he's in. Breathe some life back into him."

"Where's his mother? Why doesn't she do something to help him?"

She shook her head sadly at the mention of her sister-in-law. "Patrice is buried so deep in her own grief half the time she's not even aware Craig's around."

He frowned thoughtfully as he wiped the grease from a wrench. "I could have a go at him if you want. See if I can get him back on track." He tossed the wrench into a drawer, bumped it shut with his knee. "He might respond to a man quicker than he would a woman."

She looked at him in puzzlement, surprised by his offer. "Why would you want to do that? You don't even know Craig. "

He shrugged. "Losing a dad can screw with a kid's head. Having a man to talk to, hang out with, might help him open up, share what's on his mind."

She opened a hand in invitation. "If you think you can help him, be my guest."

"You may not like my methods. If you don't, you have to promise not to interfere."

She'd done her own research on the subject of troubled teens and was familiar with some of the commonly used methods—tough love, wilderness survival training, behavior modification—and the names alone were enough to terrify her. "He won't be in any danger, will he?" she asked uneasily.

He gave her a droll look. "I wasn't planning on torturing the kid."

She didn't find his assurance all that comforting, considering his earlier rough treatment of her. But she feared if something wasn't done soon, she was going to lose Craig, either to drugs…or, worse, to suicide. Chilled by the thought, she drew in a steadying breath. "Just the same, I don't want him hurt."

He stripped off the pad he'd used to protect his

stomach while working on the engine and turned away. "Too late. He's already hurt."

The sunroom at the rear of Leah's house was her favorite room in the house. Shortly after moving in, she'd painted the walls a soft buttery yellow and the ceiling with a mural of a cloud-filled sky. She'd chosen wicker to fill the space and positioned the chairs in front of the casement windows to capture the best views of her pool and landscaped backyard.

In the daytime sunlight flooded the room, creating a sunny and cheery nook in which to relax. At night it was no less restful, with lamplight washing the room with a soft golden glow.

But on this particular night the sunroom failed to work its magic charm for Leah.

Seated in a wicker chair, her feet propped on the matching ottoman, her thoughts were anything but restful as she stared at the apartment over the garage, considering the man inside.

She didn't know what to make of Sam Forrester. He both baffled and intrigued her. She didn't particularly care for the rough way he'd treated her earlier when she'd confronted him about the mess he'd made of her yard. But, in retrospect, she supposed she'd had it coming. She *had* slapped at him, as he'd accused her of doing.

Yet, in spite of now knowing that he could become physical when provoked, she wasn't afraid of him. That knowledge was simply something she'd keep in mind the next time she decided to go toe-to-toe with him.

But she was still a little miffed about the "anal-retentive" comment.

She wasn't obsessive, she told herself. She simply appreciated order. She supposed growing up in a home in which disorder reigned might have influenced her desire for neatness. But she certainly didn't consider that a personality fault. To her it was a virtue, a method of survival.

She frowned thoughtfully as she considered again his offer to serve as a mentor of sorts for her nephew. A man who was willing to befriend a troubled teenager couldn't be all bad, she told herself. But what she couldn't figure out was why he would want to do something like that. He didn't know Craig, had no ties to him. Why would he care one way or the other what happened to him?

As she continued to stare, the door to the apartment opened, and her thoughts shattered as Sam stepped out. She gaped when she saw that he was wearing swim trunks and carried a towel draped over his shoulder. Sliding farther down in her chair, she watched him cross to the spa. The lights in the backyard were off, but the lights in the pool and spa were on, offering enough illumination for her to see his movements…as well as his physique.

A slow shiver chased down her spine as she remembered being held against that body that afternoon. The damp heat that had seeped through her blouse, the muscled wall of chest crushed against her breasts. She shivered again at the memory as he tossed the towel onto a chair and sat down on the spa's stone edge. He dipped his fingers into the water, testing the temperature, then glanced toward the house.

She froze, realizing that with the lamp on she was clearly visible. A smile spread across his face as he spotted her, and he motioned for her to join him. She considered ignoring the invitation, planning to tell him, if questioned later, that she had dozed off in the chair and hadn't seen him.

He robbed her of that excuse by rising and striding toward the house. Prepared to send him on his way, she met him at the French door that opened to the outside.

He greeted her with a friendly smile. "Come on out and join me. The water's just right."

It was an effort, but she managed to keep her gaze fixed on his face and not let it slip to the magnificent view of his chest. "Thanks, but I was just about to head upstairs for the night."

"It's too early to go to bed," he chided. "Besides, you'll sleep better after relaxing in the spa for a while."

"No, really, I…"

He leveled a finger at her nose. "You have exactly five minutes to change into a swimsuit," he warned. "Then I'm coming after you."

Before she could refuse again, he turned and walked away. Frowning, she closed the door. She considered locking it but knew that would be a waste of time, since she'd given him a key to her house in order for him to have access to the kitchen and laundry room.

Surely he wouldn't make good his threat, she told herself.

"Four minutes, thirty seconds," he called loudly.

Convinced that he would, she ran for the stairs and raced up to change into her swimsuit.

Breathless and with only seconds to spare, she hurried outside to find Sam already sitting in the spa. Chest-deep in the bubbling water, his arms spread along the spa's stone edge, he watched her approach.

Feeling uncomfortably conspicuous, she unwrapped the towel she'd cinched at her waist and carefully folded it before placing it on the chair with his.

As she turned for the spa, she saw the amusement on his face and stopped. "What?"

He tipped his head toward the towel. "Are you sure you got all the wrinkles out? You might have missed one or two."

She jutted her chin, remembering his anal-retentive comment. "Just because I'm careful with my things doesn't make me anal."

"Uh-huh. Whatever you say." Water sluiced down his body as he rose and offered her a hand. "You're going to thank me for this later," he assured her as he helped her into the water.

"I wouldn't hold my breath," she muttered and snatched her hand from his. She sank onto the circular bench opposite him. Jets churned the warm water around her, making her skin tingle and the underwater lights dance beneath the surface.

With a contented sigh he dipped his head back and closed his eyes. "Heaven, huh?"

"It does feel good," she said, willing to concede only that much.

"Nothing eases sore muscles faster than a good soak in a spa. Other than a full-fledged massage," he amended, then lifted his head to peer at her through one eye. "I don't suppose you'd be willing to give me one?"

The smile she offered him was saccharine-sweet. "You're right. I wouldn't."

"I'd return the favor."

She shook her head, then couldn't help but laugh when he slid beneath the water, his face a mask of dejection.

Moments later he reemerged, slicking his hair back from his face.

She lifted a brow. "Kind of shallow for swimming, don't you think?"

He blinked the water from his eyes. "Wasn't trying to swim. I was checking out your legs."

She snatched her knees up and hugged them against her breasts. "If I'd known you'd invited me out here to ogle me, I would've stayed inside."

His smile smug, he reared back, splaying his arms along the spa's stone edge again. "Honey, me ogling you is the least of your worries."

She tried to frown but couldn't help but laugh. Pushing out a hand, she shot a spray of water at him. "You're incorrigible."

"No," he corrected, dragging a hand down his face. "I'm just a man who recognizes a pretty woman when he sees one."

"Much more of your bull, and I'll need boots."

He shot her a wink. "No bull, ma'am. Just fact."

Deciding it best to ignore him, she slid farther down the wall of the tub and propped her feet against the bench opposite her, wanting to take advantage of the spa's therapeutic effects. The new position aimed jets of water at her upper back and shoulders, pulsing away at the tension knotted there. She would have purred her pleasure, but she refused to give Sam the opportunity to say I told you so.

"Tell me about your family," he said after a moment.

She opened her eyes wide enough to narrow them at him. "Why?"

"It might give me some insight into what's troubling Craig."

At the mention of her nephew she sat up, frowning thoughtfully as she swept her hair up to knot it on top of her head. "We don't have much family left. You already know about my father and brother. My mother died about five years ago, which just leaves Craig, Patrice and me."

"How did your mother die?"

"The official ruling was suicide, but I prefer to believe she grieved herself to death."

"Over the loss of your father?"

Uncomfortable with the subject, she plucked a leaf from the bubbling water, trying to think how best to answer.

He lifted a brow at the action.

"That's not being anal," she informed him and dropped the leaf over the side of the tub. "It would end up in the filter anyway, which I have to clean out. I was just saving myself some time."

"Uh-huh."

Flattening her lips, she directed the conversation back to his question. "And yes, my mother never got over losing my father. She never gave up hope, either. She always believed he'd come home some day."

"Was Craig close to her?"

She shook her head. "No. Mom was so consumed with finding my dad she didn't have time for much else."

"She searched for him?"

"She didn't go to Vietnam, if that's what you mean. But she spent hours and hours combing through reports about POWs and MIAs, hoping to find some mention or reference of my dad." Knowing what most people thought of her mother's obsession, she grimaced. "You probably think she was crazy."

"Not in the least. A woman who loved her husband as deeply as your mother obviously did deserves my admiration, not my scorn."

Though surprised by his response, she didn't pursue it, as she preferred not to talk about her parents. "Tell me about your family," she said instead.

"Not much to tell. I'm an only child. My parents divorced when I was fifteen. Dad moved to Atlanta, remarried and has three kids."

She gave him a chiding look. "And you said you didn't have siblings."

"Since I've never been allowed to see or talk to them, I don't consider them siblings."

"You've never even *seen* them?" she asked incredulously.

"Nope. My stepmother's rule. She likes to pretend I don't exist, that my dad's life began when he married her."

"And he puts up with that?"

"Not entirely. He and I get together a couple of times a year. At a neutral location," he added. "Never at their home."

Stunned, she sank back against the tile wall. "What a bitch."

"You won't get an argument out of me."

"What about your mother?" she asked after a moment. "Where is she?"

"In Seattle. Moved there after I graduated from high school. According to her, that was as far away from Dad as she could get without falling into the ocean."

She winced. "I take it their divorce was unpleasant."

"Their *marriage* was unpleasant."

"Fifteen," she said, thinking out loud. "That's a difficult age to have your parents divorce. It must have been hard on you."

"No worse than living with them while they were married."

She gave him a doubtful look. "Was it really that bad? I mean, I never lived with both my parents. Not that I remember, anyway. But I'd think there has to be something positive to be gained from having lived as a family, even if it was only for a short time."

He shook his head. "Can't prove it by me. My parents fought like cats and dogs. Rather than be caught in the crossfire, I stayed away from home as much as possible."

"But you said you and your father rebuilt cars together," she said in confusion. "Surely that would require you spending time together."

"We did. But only at his shop. That was the one place he could escape Mom."

She studied him curiously, intrigued by this part of his life he was sharing. "How did you react to their divorce?"

"Went a little wild. Was in trouble more often than not."

"What kind of trouble?"

"You name it, I did it at one time or another." He shook his head. "There was a guy I ran with. Ty Bodean. He was rotten to the core, though I was too blind to see at the time. The two of us pretty much terrorized the town. It's a wonder somebody didn't kill us just to put us out of our misery."

As she listened, she found it easy to believe that he was once a bad boy. "You seem to have turned out all right."

"Thanks to Ty's half brother. He was always riding us about Ty's and my behavior and how we were going to screw up our lives if we didn't straighten up. Ty mostly tuned him out, but he never gave up on him. Or me, for that matter.

"The night we graduated from high school, Ty

and I thought it would be fun to shoot the windows out of some of the stores downtown. Cops caught us and hauled us to jail. Ty called his half brother and he came and bailed us out. Ty thought he would just take us home, give us the standard lecture and that would be the end of it. Instead he drove us to the prison in McAllister and had the warden give us the grand tour. When we were done, he sat us both down and told us that he hoped we liked what we had seen because that was going to be our home if we didn't change our ways.

"Ty laughed off the warning, but I sure as hell didn't. Seeing the inside of that prison shook me clean to the bone. I guess his half brother realized there was hope for me yet, because he started spending time with me, talking to me about things. More by his example than anything else, I began to see what a lowlife I had become and decided to clean up my act." He opened his hands. "So here I am, a reformed rake."

She released a long breath, having been caught up by his story. "Wow. You're lucky he cared enough to take you under his wing."

"Nobody knows that better than me. Fact is, I owe him my life."

She looked at him curiously. "That's why you offered to help Craig, isn't it? Because of what your friend's half-brother did for you?"

He shrugged. "Partly." Smiling, he scooted around on the bench and draped an arm along the edge of the tub behind her. "But mostly I did it because the kid's got a good-looking aunt."

With him so close, she could see nothing but his face. The chiseled line of cheekbone, smoky blue eyes, the sensual curve of his lips. Sure that he was about to kiss her, she nervously wet her lips. "I thought you said you were a *reformed* rake."

His lips curved higher, revealing the most adorable dimples.

"Even a reformed rake slips now and again." Cupping a hand at her cheek, he touched his lips to hers, withdrew with a low hum of pleasure, then returned for a second taste.

"Sweet," he murmured, tracing his tongue along her lower lip. Angling his body more fully toward hers, he pushed his fingers through her hair and took the kiss deeper, holding her face to his.

God help me, she thought weakly. Though every nerve in her body demanded she respond, intellectually she knew what a mistake that would be. Sam worked for her, and any kind of intimacy, no matter how innocent, could jeopardize their business relationship.

If that wasn't reason enough for her to put an end to this foolishness, he was a virtual stranger. She didn't know him. Not in the sense a woman needed to know a man before making out in a hot tub with him. More importantly, she didn't trust men. After the hell Louis had put her through, she had learned to keep her guard up when dealing with the male species.

In spite of all the reasons pointing her away from Sam, she found herself melting against him until every thought leaked from her mind save one. Him. The pleasure evoked by his lips. The strength in the hands that held her to him. The knee wedged firmly against her thigh. The tickle of stubble that rasped her chin and upper lip.

Much too soon, he dragged his mouth from hers. Disappointed that he'd ended the kiss, she forced open her eyes and found his gaze on her.

He stroked a thumb along her cheekbone, his smile slow, sexy. "Even better than I'd imagined."

It took her a moment to find her voice. "W-what?"

"Kissing you." He slid his hands down her back and looped them low at her waist. "And, believe me, what I'd imagined was already topping the charts."

Both pleased and embarrassed, she dropped her gaze, unsure what to say.

He saved her a reply by rising and taking her hand. "We better head in."

He climbed from the spa, then turned and helped her out. Plucking her towel from the chair, he draped it over her shoulders, then used its ends as a rope and tugged her to him for one last kiss.

Drawing back he smiled down at her. "Good night, Leah."

Finding it difficult to tear her gaze from his, she murmured, "'Night, Sam," then spun and hurried for the house before she did something really stupid.

Like drag him upstairs and chain him to her bed.

Three

Sam had known a lot of women in his life, but not a one of them had ever dominated his thoughts the way Leah did. He seldom thought of her without sex slipping into his mind, too. Legs that seemed to stretch forever. A firm, taut body. Lips ripe for kissing. Breasts begging to be touched.

"Thinking with your Johnson," he muttered under his breath as he strained to remove the frozen spark plugs from the Mustang's engine. And when a man let his Johnson do his thinking, he was asking for trouble. What he needed to do was focus on his real reason for being here: getting the information for Mack. He'd been a guest in her apartment for over a week and wasn't one whit closer to finding out what he needed to know.

The spark plug gave and the loss of pressure had him pitching forward. Heaving a weary sigh, he ducked from beneath the hood and dragged an arm across the sweat that dripped into his eyes. He cut a wistful glance at the pool, thinking a swim would feel really good about now. His gaze slid to the spa, and an image of Leah rose in his mind, her damp hair twisted up on top of her head, her breasts pushing at the scrap of fabric that covered them. With a groan, he dropped the wrench and headed for the house, hoping a cold drink of water would cool his thoughts.

At the back door he toed off his boots, knowing Leah would pitch a walleyed fit if he tracked grease onto her pristine floors. Once inside, he poured himself a glass of cold water from the container in the fridge, tipped the glass back and emptied it in three long gulps.

His thirst quenched for the moment, he back-handed the moisture from his mouth, propped his hips against the edge of the cabinet and looked around. As usual, the kitchen was neat as a pin, with not so much as a dish towel out of place.

It was also eerily quiet, as was the rest of the house. Not surprising, since Leah was at work and Craig at school.

Slowly becoming aware of a loud, rhythmic ticking sound in the silence, curious, he walked through the house, tracing it to the entry hall, where a stately grandfather clock stood like a sentry against one wall. Obviously an antique, the heavily carved piece consisted of two sections, the uppermost framing the face of the clock. In the glass-encased lower portion a brass pendulum slowly swung from side to side.

Satisfied that he'd identified the ticking sound and that the house wasn't about to blow up, he headed back to the kitchen. As he passed through the den, he slowed, his gaze drawn to the wall of bookshelves on his right. Wondering what kind of literature appealed to a woman like Leah, he moved to stand before the unit and scanned the books' spines. Gardening, psychology, interior design, biographies and a couple of paperback mystery novels. Amused by the wide range of subject matter, he started to turn away but stopped when he spotted a photo album lying on the bottom shelf.

Judging by its worn cover, he assumed it was from her youth, possibly even dating before her birth. He was tempted to pick it up and look through it, hoping to find information about her dad—specifically the piece of paper Mack had requested he locate. But snooping through her things would violate the trust Leah had placed in him when she'd given him the key to her house.

He vacillated a moment while his conscience and his curiosity duked it out.

With a resigned sigh, he turned his back on the tempting album and headed for the kitchen, his conscience, as well as his integrity, still intact.

Just as he stepped outside to resume his work on the Mustang, Leah's SUV turned onto the drive. Relieved that he hadn't given in to the temptation to snoop, he watched her leap from the vehicle and run for the house. When she dashed past him, without so much as a how-do-you-do, he grabbed her arm. "Hey. Where's the fire?"

She tugged free. "Haven't got time to explain," she said breathlessly as she yanked open the kitchen door. "I'm in panic mode."

Panic mode? Shaking his head, he watched her disappear inside the house, thinking the woman lived in that state.

But she had seemed a little more stressed than usual, he thought with a frown. Could something have happened? Maybe to Craig?

Determined to find out what was up, he reached for the door and was nearly bowled over when she came flying back out.

"Wait a minute," he said as she rushed past him. "What's going on?"

She called over her shoulder, "Later. Gotta go."

Sure that concern for her nephew was the only

thing that would cause her this level of distress, he plucked his T-shirt from the roof of the Mustang and ran after her, sliding into the passenger seat just as she pulled the gearshift into reverse.

"What do you think you're doing?" she cried. "I need to go!"

"Then go. I'm not stopping you."

She set her jaw. "I have exactly four hours to set up for a party. Would you please just get out? I'm already late."

"Don't get all huffy with me. If you're late, it's your fault, not mine."

"It isn't my fault! I only got the call ten minutes ago! Now will you *please* get out?"

"Not until you tell me what's going on."

She pressed a hand to her forehead and inhaled a deep breath as if struggling for patience. "The job's for the city. I bid on it months ago, but the contract was awarded to another company. They bailed at the last minute, and now the city has asked me to step in." She looked at him with pleading eyes. "This is important. Really important. If I do a good job, it'll mean more business for me in the future. So, please, get out so I can go."

He clicked his seat belt into place. "You probably could use some help."

She clamped down on her jaw. "Fine," she said, grinding out the words, and reversed into the street.

"But if you get bored, don't even think about asking me to bring you home, because I won't."

She stomped on the brake to shift into drive.

He braced a hand against the dash to keep from being thrown forward. "Oh, I doubt I'll get bored," he replied mildly. "Not with you behind the wheel."

With nothing left for him to do, Sam moved to the far end of the country club's ballroom and waited while Leah double-checked each table one last time. He shook his head as he watched her turn a centerpiece a millimeter to the left. The woman got way too caught up in details.

He still couldn't believe the warehouse she'd taken him to collect the equipment and supplies she'd needed. On the outside the building had looked like most of the others in the complex. It was the interior where the differences lay.

Row after row of shelving filled the cavernous space, each loaded with neatly stacked boxes and crates. Hanging from a clipboard at the beginning of each row, a laminated inventory listed all the items found on that row—in alphabetical order, no less. If that wasn't enough to prove her anal tendencies, a card was attached to each container, with a detailed description of its contents.

In spite of her obsessiveness for organization, he had to admit the woman knew what she was doing when it came to decorating for an event. To satisfy her client's request for a patriotic theme, she had designed centerpieces using white hydrangeas, blue delphiniums and red geraniums. She had come up with a pretty clever way of incorporating fireworks into the scheme, as well, by filling thin silver tubes with sprays of red, white and blue star garlands cut into varying lengths and placing them strategically among the flowers in the centerpiece. When the votive candles scattered around the tables were lit, the multicolored foil stars shimmered and sparkled like fireworks exploding on the Fourth of July.

Sam had helped create the faux fireworks, but he'd spent the majority of his time setting up tables and chairs and draping the tables with—get this— *three* tablecloths, arranged by size, starting with the largest and ending with the smallest, which Leah had informed him was called a topper. She'd had specific instructions for placing the cloths, and if he failed to spread one exactly as instructed, she'd stop whatever she was doing, march over and adjust the cloth herself.

He'd finally managed to escape her evil eye when Kate, her assistant, had asked him to help her put the fireworks together. Cute girl, he reflected, and *very* protective of her boss. When Leah had first introduced them, Kate had been polite enough. But during the early part of the afternoon he had caught her watching him suspiciously on several occasions. He supposed working with her on the fireworks had dispelled whatever doubts she had about him, because by the time she left she was laughing and joking with him as if they were old friends.

Reminded that only he and Leah remained, he glanced at his watch and decided it was time to put an end to her *anal*-yzing.

Crossing the room, he caught her elbow and gave it a tug. "Come on. I'll buy you dinner."

She tugged right back. "Not yet. I still have six more tables to check."

"They're fine," he assured her and all but dragged her from the room.

Though he succeeded in getting her to her SUV, he could tell her mind was still inside the ballroom and the decorations she'd set up. This became even more evident when she didn't kick up a fuss when he bundled her into the passenger seat and took the wheel himself.

"You don't think the centerpieces are too busy?" she asked uncertainly as he started the engine.

"No. They're fine."

She reached for the door handle. "Maybe I should remove the sparklers. Simple is sometimes best."

He grabbed her arm before she could climb out. "The sparklers or fireworks or whatever the heck you call them are sensational. In the morning you'll have guests lined up at your door wanting you to plan their next party."

His assurance was almost a direct quote from a comment Kate had made to him earlier, but since he shared her opinion, he didn't feel badly about offering it to Leah now.

She looked at him hopefully. "You really think so?"

"Wouldn't have said it if I didn't." He put the vehicle in gear before she could attempt to hop out again. "Do you stress about all the events you plan as much as you have over this one?"

"No—yes." She heaved a sigh. "I give my best to all my clients, but this job is really important."

He turned onto the main road, leaving the country club behind. "What's so special about this one? I'd think, if anything, you wouldn't care as much, since the bid was originally given to someone else."

"It should've been mine from the beginning."

He cut a glance her way at the bitterness he detected in her tone. "Why wasn't it?"

"My ex serves on the city council."

Louis Banks. He remembered reading about her ex-husband's business and civic activities during the search he'd done on the Internet.

"One man has that much power?" he asked doubtfully.

"The family does. The Banks family is what's

known as 'old Tyler.' They've lived here for generations and, as a result, have clout out the wazoo.
Four years ago I controlled eighty percent of the
event-planning business in this area. Within a month
of our divorce my business dropped twenty-five
percent. By the end of the year it hit forty."

He stole a glance at her. "Is it still going down?"

"No." She quickly rapped her knuckles against
the dash. "Knock on wood. I've clawed and scraped
my way back up. I haven't reached my former
numbers, but I'm getting there. That's why this job
is so important. It's my chance to get my foot back
in the door with the city."

He scowled at the road ahead. "Screw 'em."

She turned her head to peer at him. "Excuse me?"

He tossed up a hand. "If they'd let a guy with his
jockstrap in a twist influence their decisions, you
don't need their business."

Sputtering a laugh, she turned to face the front
again. "Don't I wish."

He spotted a restaurant ahead and slowed,
thinking food would get her mind off the party, as
well as her ex. "How about Italian?"

Wrinkling her nose, she shook her head. "I'm
really not in the mood to deal with a crowd. How
about I make something for us at home?"

He sped up. "I have a better idea. Let's order
pizza in."

* * *

Sam topped off the wine in Leah's glass, then glanced at her empty plate. "Another slice of pizza?"

She sank back in her chair, holding her hands over her stomach. "No. I'm stuffed."

He set the wine bottle down, plucked a slice from the box and sank his teeth into the cheesy wedge as he settled back. Feeling her gaze, he glanced her way and found her smiling at him.

"Thanks."

He licked sauce from the corner of his mouth. "I should be the one thanking you for turning me on to Mario's. They throw a mean pizza."

She laughed softly. "I didn't mean buying my dinner, although I do appreciate it. You were a tremendous help today. I don't know what Kate and I would have done without you."

"You'd have managed." He picked up his wineglass to wash down the pizza. "Do you and Kate usually set up everything yourself? Handling those tables was no easy job."

"I usually hire temps to take care of whatever heavy lifting is necessary. Unfortunately, due to the short notice we received, no one was available."

"Then I'm glad I insisted on going along." Smiling, he tapped his glass to hers. "Here's to a successful event."

"Amen to that." She took a sip of her wine, then tipped her head back with a sigh and closed her eyes.

"Tired?" he asked.

She opened her eyes to smile at him. "Exhausted. But way too wired to sleep."

"Same here." He glanced around, then gestured at the lounge chairs beside the pool. "Why don't we sit out there, where we can be more comfortable?"

She scraped back her chair. "Good idea."

He let her take the lead, then followed. On impulse, instead of sitting next to her, he moved to stand behind her chair and dropped his hands over her shoulders.

She struggled to sit up. "What are you doing?"

He drew her back against the chair. "Relax," he soothed as he pressed his thumbs into her tensed muscles. "I'm going to give you a massage."

Her shoulders remained rigid beneath his hands—whether from wariness or stress, he wasn't sure. But after a few minutes the tendons began to soften beneath his fingers' urging.

He leaned to peer over her head and saw that her face was lax, her eyes closed. Biting back a smile, he pushed his thumbs up the gentle curve of her neck, then down, letting them slide beneath the neckline of her shirt. Keeping one hand cupped on her shoulder, he pushed the thumb of the other along her shoulder blade, lengthening the muscle. Though innocent, the action dragged her shirt and bra strap to the edge of her shoulder.

The exposed skin was satin-smooth and tinted a soft golden-brown. Noticing that there wasn't a tan line, he wondered if she sunbathed topless. Curious, he continued the massage, easing her shirt and bra strap farther down her arm to reveal more of her chest, planning to search for a tan line.

He heard her low moan, felt a tightening of response in his groin, but managed to keep his fingers moving, continuing the massage, while he peeked over her head to see if he'd mistaken the sound.

Oh, man, he thought, stifling a groan as his gaze settled on the soft swell of her breasts and the shadowed valley between. And no tan line, which meant either she was blessed with olive skin tones or she sunbathed topless.

Deciding that her level of arousal was a hell of a lot more important than determining genes versus sun-kissed skin, he brought his hands back to her neck, then smoothed them down her front. She moaned again, and this time there was no mistaking the sound for anything but arousal.

Leaning over, he covered her mouth with his and captured the sound. Though he'd expected her to come up, kicking and clawing, her lips remained soft beneath his, pliant, accepting.

With him all but standing on his head, blood rushed to his head, pulsed in his ears. Knowing he couldn't maintain this position for long, he eased around to her side while managing to keep his mouth on hers. Since she still didn't offer an objection, he opened the top two buttons of her shirt. He felt the rush of her breath against his lips, the tremble that shook her...but detected nothing that indicated refusal or indignation. Taking her silence as assent, he cupped his hands over her breasts and drew back to meet her gaze. "Feeling more relaxed now?"

Eyes wide, she gulped. "Th-that was smooth, Forrester."

"Think so?" Grinning, he gave her breasts a playful squeeze, then caught her hand, pulled her up. "Let's go skinny-dipping." He grabbed the bottom of his T-shirt, ripped it over his head and reached for the snap of his jeans.

She lunged forward and clamped her hand over his. "I'm not going skinny-dipping with you."

"Why not?"

"Because—because public nudity is against the law."

Hiding a smile, he dropped his gaze to her chest and dragged a finger along her shoulder. "No tan lines," he said, then lifted his gaze to hers in challenge. "You must not be too particular about breaking the law." With a shrug, he hooked his thumbs in the waist of his jeans. "But if it'll make you feel better, we'll leave our underwear on."

Not giving her time to argue, he stripped off his jeans, kicked them aside, then crossed to the edge of the pool and dipped a foot into the water. "The temperature is just right," he called to her.

Without waiting to see if she'd follow his lead, he sprang to his toes and dived in.

Leah stared at the ever-widening ring that marked the spot where Sam had disappeared into the pool. She shouldn't do this, she told herself. She should go inside and leave him to skinny-dip alone, if that's what he wanted to do. Just because he'd turned her into a puddle of quivering need with his dang seductive massage didn't mean she had to lose her senses completely.

But, oh, God, how she wanted to, she thought, gulping. It had been so long since she'd done anything wild, so totally uninhibited. And it seemed like forever since she'd felt anything close to desire.

As she continued to waver uncertainly, he surfaced on the far side of the pool, scraping his hair back from his face. Treading water, he called to her, "What are you waiting for? Come on in. The water's great."

She shouldn't, she told herself. This was insane, crazy. He was a flirt, a sex maniac.

Oh, God, she thought again and rose, stripping

off her blouse and shoving down her shorts. Bare but for her flesh-colored bra and panties, she moved to the edge of the pool, drew in a steadying breath, then dived in.

Seconds later she burst from the water, her mouth open and gasping. "You liar!" she cried. "This water is freezing!"

He swam a few strokes to meet her. "Probably seems that way since you were so hot when you got in."

She flattened her lips, wanting to hang on to her anger with him, then sputtered a laugh. "You are hopeless."

"Incorrigible, hopeless," he said, reciting the adjectives she'd used to describe him. "It's a wonder my head doesn't swell with all the compliments you shower me with."

Rolling her eyes, she struck off for the shallower end of the pool. Sam followed, matching her stroke for stroke. When they reached the end, she climbed from the water and flopped down on the highest step, while he hauled himself up to sit beside her.

Gathering her hair between her hands, she twisted it into a long rope and squeezed, noticing that Sam watched the water drip onto her chest. Seemingly fascinated, he reached to trail his finger along the path of one droplet as it trickled down. When his finger dipped between her breasts, she sucked in a shocked breath.

He lifted his eyes to hers, and she gulped at the heat that darkened his blue eyes.

Hooking a finger in the front closure of her bra, he hauled her to him.

"Enough foreplay," he murmured and nipped at her lips. "It's time we got down to business."

"Sam…" she began weakly.

He dipped his head to nuzzle her neck and cupped her breast. "That's my name."

"I don't think—" He squeezed, kneading her flesh, and she dropped her head back with a groan. "Oh, Sam."

Hiding a smile, he kissed his way up her neck to her mouth. "I like the way you turn my name into two syllables instead of just the one." He rolled her nipple between two fingers. "Really turns me on."

"And *that*," she said with a shiver, "turns me on."

"Then let's kick up the speed a bit." He flicked open the front closure of her bra, freeing her breasts, then used his mouth to force her back against the edge of the pool.

She gasped at the contact, then knotted her fingers in his hair and clung as he suckled greedily. She didn't even consider asking him to stop. She needed this, him. Deserved it after four long years of celibacy.

He shifted, drawing her body to position between his thighs, then focused his attention on her breasts again.

In the distance, music played softly from the outdoor speakers hidden beneath the eaves of the house. A blues number, the whine of the sax sexy and low. The only other sound in the night came from the water's rhythmic lapping against the sides of the pool. Combined, they provided the perfect accompaniment for a slow seduction.

But Leah wasn't sure she could endure slow. It had been too long since she'd been with a man, and this one was unbelievably skilled with his mouth, his hands.

Anxious to touch him, too, she closed her fingers around his sex and was stunned to find him already rock-hard beneath his boxers. She stroked her fingers down his length, up, but soon became frustrated by the fabric that kept her from touching him fully and slipped her fingers inside the fly.

He flinched at the contact, then groaned and dropped his forehead to hers. "Leah?"

She gulped, barely able to breathe. "What?"

"Are you on the pill?"

Thrown off by the question, she drew back slowly to peer at him. "Well...no."

His shoulders sagged. "Damn. I was afraid you were going to say that." Heaving a sigh, he flopped down on the step next to her and dropped his head to his hands. "And to think I was once a Boy Scout," he said miserably.

She sat up slowly, drawing the cups of her bra together and fastening them into place while trying to reconcile her mind, as well as her throbbing body, that her celibacy wasn't going to end that night. "What does being a Boy Scout have to do with anything?"

"'Be prepared.' It's the motto Boy Scouts live by."

She rolled her lips inward, trying her best not to laugh.

He glanced her way and bumped his shoulder against hers. "Cut it out. This isn't funny."

"No," she agreed, then doubled over, laughing. "It's hysterical!"

Leah entered the last figure into her calculator, then hit the total button. After typing the amount into the appropriate column on the spreadsheet, she hit save, then sank back in her chair with a sigh of relief, the dreaded paperwork done for the day.

She should've finished earlier—and would have if she'd been able to keep her mind on her work and off Sam. She chuckled, remembering his disappointed expression when he'd admitted to his failure to live up to the Boy Scouts motto of Be Prepared. He could be so darn cute at times. At others, totally irresistible.

He had his faults, she reminded herself and straightened to tuck the invoices she'd recorded back into the file. He was stubborn, cocky and more than a little overbearing.

He was also kind and thoughtful and unbelievably sexy.

Kate stuck her head into her office. "Last customer just left."

Leah shot to her feet. "Quick. Put the Closed sign in the window before anyone else can get inside."

Tapping a finger to her temple in a salute, Kate disappeared from sight.

Leah quickly shut down her computer, snagged her purse from beneath her desk, then headed out, slowing only long enough to switch off her office light.

"How about a glass of wine?" Kate suggested. "My treat."

Leah hesitated a moment. She knew it was ridiculous, but she wanted to go home and see Sam.

But then she remembered that this was Kate's husband Frank's, night to play softball with the guys, which meant Kate would be alone. "Sounds good," she said, forcing a smile. "But I'm buying. You deserve a reward for the extra hours you put in this week."

"Won't get an argument out of me," Kate replied and led the way to the front door. "Let's try out that new bar on the corner. I hear they serve nachos during happy hour. I'm starving."

"Fine with me." Leah locked the door, then walked with Kate the short half block to the bar.

Once inside, she hesitated, daunted by the number of people already crowded into the room. She glanced back toward the doorway. "Maybe we should try someplace else," she suggested hopefully.

Kate looped her arm through Leah's. "No way," she said as she dragged her into the melee. "I skipped lunch, remember? Another second without sustenance and I'll faint dead away." Spotting a couple leaving, Kate tugged Leah in that direction and pushed her into the booth they'd occupied before someone else could claim it.

"Chardonnay okay with you?" she asked.

Leah flapped a hand as she pulled a credit card from her purse to give to Kate. "Whatever you're drinking is fine with me. Tell the bartender to open a tab." While Kate went to the bar to order their drinks, Leah pulled out her cell phone and punched in her home number, wanting to let Craig know that she would be late. After four rings, the answering machine clicked on. Frowning, she disconnected the call.

Kate returned, setting a glass of wine in front of Leah. "Problem?"

Leah slid the phone back into her purse. "I called the house, but Craig didn't answer."

Shrugging, Kate took a sip of her drink. "Maybe Patrice picked him up early for a change."

Leah gave her a pointed look.

"Okay," Kate conceded reluctantly. "So the woman isn't a contender for Mother of the Year."

"That's putting it mildly," Leah said drily, then winced. "Maybe I should go home and check on him. Just to be safe."

Kate narrowed an eye. "You're not going anywhere. Craig is old enough to look after himself. Besides, Sam's there, isn't he?"

"Probably."

"So if the house caught fire or something equally bad had happened, Sam would call you, right?"

"I suppose."

"Then there's no reason for you to worry." Kate lifted her glass in a toast and smiled. "Here's to another successful event staged by the highly acclaimed Stylized Events."

Reminded of the complimentary mention her business had received in the morning newspaper, Leah tapped her glass against Kate's and added, "Which wouldn't have been possible without the help of my talented assistant."

Kate took a sip of her wine. "Not that I don't adore praise, but Sam deserves a chunk of the credit. I swear, that man's got muscles on top of muscles. Did you see the way he was tossing those tables around? As if they were made of paper instead of two tons of metal and wood."

"He was definitely a lifesaver," Leah agreed.

"And he even helped make the sparklers. Frank would cut off his right arm before he'd touch anything crafty like that. 'Girl stuff,' he calls it." She huffed. "He acts like any activity that doesn't end in the word *ball* will emasculate him."

Leah chuckled, always entertained by Kate's exaggerated stories about her husband Frank. "I have to admit, Sam surprised me with his willingness to tackle whatever we put in front of him."

"And he's such a hottie, too. Have you checked out his butt? The man's got a body to die for."

Leah took a sip of her wine to avoid Kate's gaze. "He's okay, I guess."

Kate choked a breath. "Are you blind? He's drop-dead gorgeous!"

When Leah said nothing, Kate narrowed her eyes. "Oh, I get it," she said slowly. "You've got the hots for him and don't want to admit it."

Leah dropped her mouth open, then quickly looked around to make sure no one had overheard. "I do not," she whispered angrily. "And would you please lower your voice. I'd prefer my personal life remain private."

Kate hooted a laugh. "So there is something going on between you two." She braced her arms on the table and leaned forward expectantly. "Spill. I want all the details."

Leah drew back and took a nervous sip of her wine. "There's nothing to tell."

As stubborn as a bulldog once she sank her teeth into something, Kate leaned closer. "I bet he's a good kisser, isn't he?"

Leah felt a blush creep up her neck. "If you like your job, you'll drop this subject, and I mean *now.*"

"Come on, Leah," she begged. "Give an old married a woman a thrill."

"Three years of marriage doesn't qualify as 'old.'"

"It does when you're married to ESPN. Come on, share. Wet? Dry? French?"

Leah rolled her eyes. "You're sick. Really sick."

"I'll bet he Frenches."

Leah dropped her forehead to the table with a moan.

"Uh-oh," Kate murmured. "Trouble at six o'clock."

Leah jerked up her head, knowing by Kate's tone what she meant by *trouble.*

"Well, look who's here," a male voice said from behind her.

Leah set her jaw, then turned to greet her ex. "Why, Louis," she said, her smile as fake as his. "What a surprise seeing you here. Cheryl must have lengthened your leash. I don't believe I've ever seen you stray this far without her."

His eyes darkened at the sugarcoated barb, but he managed to keep his smile in place. "As a matter of fact, she'll be joining me soon."

Since she'd rather choke to death than breathe the

same air as her ex and the woman he'd had an affair with through most of their married life, she glanced at her wristwatch.

"Would you look at the time?" she said in dismay and gathered her purse. "Sorry to rush off," she said as she rose and brushed past Louis, "but I need to get home and check on Craig."

"Please tell me you're not still playing nurse-maid to that dysfunctional family of yours?"

The cruel remark struck her back like a knife, dragging her to a stop. Hauling in a deep breath, she forced herself on, telling herself it didn't matter. Louis's opinion was no longer important to her. She wasn't married to him any longer. And she certainly wasn't in love with him.

Sometimes she wondered if she ever was.

Four

That night, Leah lay in her bed, unable to sleep. Craig hadn't been home when she'd arrived, which alone would have been enough to keep her awake worrying about his safety, his whereabouts. The fact that Sam wasn't home, either, only increased her concerns.

She'd finally broken down and called her sister-in-law and was relieved when she'd overheard Craig talking to someone in the background. She had wanted to question Patrice about Craig's activities that afternoon, but she'd feared she would only upset her sister-in-law if she did. The woman was already teetering on the edge of emotional instability, and Leah wasn't about to take a chance on knocking her over the edge into a complete breakdown.

Knowing that Craig was safe should have relieved her enough to allow her to sleep. But her mind refused to shut down, building every possible scenario to explain Craig's break from their agreed routine.

Hoping a glass of warm milk would settle her nerves, she climbed from bed and tugged on her robe as she traipsed down the stairs. She had just pulled the milk from the refrigerator when she heard a noise behind her. Sure that it had come from the laundry room, she set the milk down and tiptoed toward the closed door. Easing it open, she peeked inside.

And found Sam sitting on the floor, his back propped against the dryer, reading a magazine.

She pushed the door wider. "What on earth are you doing?"

He looked up from the magazine, then laid it aside, his expression sheepish. "Sorry. I was trying to be quiet."

Distracted by his bare chest and the faded sweat-pants that rode low on his hips, it took a moment for what he'd said to register. She shook her head. "You didn't wake me. I came downstairs to get a glass of milk."

"Trouble sleeping?"

She dragged a hand over her hair, assuming her

wild hairstyle was what had given her away. Reluctant to share her concerns, especially after Louis's catty remark about her dysfunctional family, she said hesitantly, "Sort of," then decided she had to know. "Did you see Craig this afternoon?"

"Yeah. Not for long, though. He didn't get here until just before his mom came to pick him up. Why? Is there a problem?"

She paced the width of the laundry room and back, worrying her thumbnail. "I don't know. Kate invited me to have a glass of wine after work. I tried to call from the bar to tell Craig that I was going to be late, but I got the answering machine."

"He didn't get the message. I can vouch for him on that one, because he never went inside. Barely made it up the drive, before his mom showed up."

"Did he say where he'd been?"

He shook his head. "No. But, to be honest, we didn't talk. Wasn't time."

She wrung her hands. "I knew I shouldn't have gone with Kate. I should've come straight home like I always do."

He caught her hand and pulled her down to sit on the floor with him in front of the dryer. "Now don't go beating yourself up over this," he scolded gently. "You're entitled to a life, too."

She hugged her knees to her chest. "But he's my

responsibility. If something had happened to him or he'd gotten into some kind of trouble, I'd never forgive myself."

"And you being home is going to prevent either of those things from happening?"

"Yes," she said defiantly.

"Come on, Leah. Even if you had been home, you couldn't have done anything. He wasn't *here* for you to protect."

She dropped her chin to her knees in dejection, knowing what he said was probably true.

He draped an arm around her shoulders and hauled her back to hug against his side. "Raising kids is hell, isn't it?"

"You have no idea," she said miserably. She hesitated a moment, then decided he might as well know it all. "Craig's been running around with a different crowd lately. Some real losers, if you ask me. I haven't actually caught him at it, but I'm afraid he might be experimenting with drugs."

"Peer pressure is tough these days. A lot worse than when we were kids." He stretched out his legs and settled her more comfortably at his side. "But I wouldn't give up on Craig just yet. He seems like a good kid."

"He is...or was."

"Focus on *is*," he ordered firmly, then gave her an encouraging smile. "He'll come around. You'll see. Heck, look at me. I got into more trouble than ten kids put together and I turned out all right."

In spite of her concern for her nephew, she bit back a smile. "In your opinion, maybe."

He drew back, feigning hurt. "You don't think I'm a nice guy?"

She lifted a shoulder. "You're okay, I guess."

"Just okay?" He heaved an exaggerated sigh. "Man, you really know how to hurt a guy."

She bumped her shoulder against his chest. "As if I could hurt that overinflated ego of yours."

Chuckling, he hugged her to his side. "So tell me did you and Kate have a good time?"

She shrugged again. "At first."

"Don't tell me you girls had a tiff?"

"No. Nothing like that. Louis showed up. My ex." Her anger returned as she remembered his parting remark. "He really knows what buttons to push to set me off. I can't believe I ever thought myself in love with him. He's heartless, cruel and would lie when the truth would serve him better."

"Sounds like a real charming fellow."

"Oh, he can be charming, all right," she said drily. "Don't doubt that for a minute. The problem is, it's usually when he wants something or after he's done something wrong and he's trying to weasel his way back into your good graces." She pressed her fingers to her temples and shook her head. "I don't want to talk about him. When I so much as *think* his name, I wind up with a headache."

"All right by me," he said agreeably. He waited a beat, then said, "I went shopping today."

She swept at a piece of lint that clung to her robe. "I wondered where you were when I got home. What did you buy? More car parts?"

"That, too."

She glanced his way, wondering why he was being so evasive. "Am I supposed to guess?"

"That might be fun."

Hiding a smile, she gave him a slow look up and down. "Well, it certainly wasn't clothes."

"I'll give you a hint. Drugstore."

She stared, her smile fading as she realized what he'd bought. "Oh," she said, unable to think of a response.

He beamed a proud smile. "Giant economy-size package. Nearly gave the little white-haired lady at the checkout a heart attack."

She laughed, imagining him plopping his purchase down on the counter in front of some sweet old lady. "You probably did."

When he said nothing more, only looked at her expectantly, she lowered her gaze and plucked at the ends of her robe's sash. "This is awkward."

"Second thoughts?"

She shook her head. "No. It's just that before it

was…spontaneous. This seems so—I don't know—premeditated."

"*Premeditated* is a word reserved for courtrooms and murder trials."

"You know what I mean."

"Yeah," he said, and heaved a disappointed sigh. "I guess I do." He forced a smile and hugged her to his side. "There's nothing that says we have to use them tonight."

Unsure if she was relieved or disappointed that he'd accepted her reluctance so easily, she pushed slowly to her feet. "I guess I better get back to bed. It's late."

"Yeah, it is." He picked up the magazine he'd been reading and began to flip pages. "'Night, Leah."

Unsure why she suddenly had the wildest urge to snatch the magazine from his hand and bop him over the head with it, she mumbled a halfhearted "'Night, Sam" and turned for her room.

Leah couldn't blame her sleeplessness on worries over Craig any longer. Now it was Sam who was keeping her awake.

She flopped to her side and punched her pillow beneath her check, silently cursing him for telling her about the stupid condoms. If he'd kept quiet about his purchase, she wouldn't be thinking about him right now. Or sex, either, for that matter.

She'd be asleep and not twisting and turning in frustration.

She heard a rustle of movement at the door and lifted her head. With the blinds shut tight to block the moonlight, the room was pitch-black, making it impossible for her to see so much as her hand in front of her face. She squinted hard, and her breath froze in her lungs when she saw a shadowed form moving across the room. She considered screaming, but before she could shape the sound, the sheet lifted and the shadow slipped into her bed. Though she still couldn't see, there was no mistaking the feel of the body that cuddled up against hers.

"Sam?" she whispered in disbelief.

His lips spread across hers in a smile. "Is this spontaneous enough for you?"

She wanted to laugh at his outrageousness, weep at his thoughtfulness in providing her the spontaneity she'd said was missing, but shivered instead as he slid his hands beneath the hem of her silk teddy.

Wrapping her arms around his neck, she said, "Perfect."

He stroked his hands slowly up and down her back as they kissed, and she shivered again as nerves danced to life along her spine.

Needing a connection, an anchor, she twined her legs with his and was shocked when her toes met bare skin. "You're naked," she said, wondering if he'd traipsed through her house in that state.

Smiling, he bumped his nose against hers. "You will be, too, in a minute."

Smoothing his hands up her back, he dragged her teddy up and over her head, dropped it over the side of the bed. He settled his hands at her waist. "Halfway there," he teased.

Laughing, she lifted her hips, making it easier for him to peel off her tap pants, then snuggled close, weaving her legs through his again. "You're full of surprises tonight, Forrester."

"I may have one or two more up my sleeve." Lying opposite her, he cupped his hand around her breast. "If I remember correctly, your breasts are a turn-on for you."

He flicked a thumb over her nipple, and a low guttural moan slipped past her lips.

"Yeah," he murmured and dipped his head to catch the nipple between his teeth. Tugged. "That's the sound I remember."

Desire shot through her, piercing her belly, and spread to a deep, aching throb between her legs. "Oh, Sam," she groaned.

He opened his mouth over her breast and sucked her in. Weakened by the sensations that whipped through her, she filled her fingers with his hair and clung. "Oh, Sam."

He lifted his head and pressed his mouth to hers. "There you go again. Stretching my name into two syllables instead of one." He hitched himself higher on the bed. "Feel that?" he asked as he rocked his hips against hers. "That's what hearing you do that does to me."

Satin and steel. Those were the only two words she could think of to describe the feel of his erection rubbing against her groin. But then he slipped a hand between her legs and she lost all ability to think.

"You're hot," he whispered as he pushed a knuckle along her fold. "And wet."

She clamped her knees together, all but coming apart at his fingers' teasing. "Sam—" She swallowed, her mouth dry as dust, then wet her lips, prepared to beg if necessary.

He saved her that humiliation by sliding a hand down her thigh and drawing her leg up and over his. Anticipation quivered beneath her skin as he pushed his hips against hers, forcing himself between her legs. Every nerve in her body seemed centered on that one spot, tingling and burning with expectancy, with need. Closing her eyes, she arched her hips, and the tip of his shaft nudged her opening.

The pressure was so erotic, so unbelievably pleasurable that she arched again, a silent plea for more. "Sam," she whispered, barely recognizing her voice for the huskiness in it. "I want you. Now."

"Wait a sec."

She nearly screamed in frustration when he moved away and stretched to pluck something from the nightstand.

She heard the crinkle of foil and knew he was opening the condom package and rolling the protection into place.

"Okay," he said on a sigh and dragged her leg back over his. "Where were we?" Before she could tell him, he pressed his lips to hers and pushed inside, stealing her breath.

Jerking her mouth from his, she dropped her head back on a low moan as her body pulsed around him, then softened to accommodate him.

He moved his hips against hers, his shaft spearing deeper and deeper inside her with each slow thrust. Instinctively she followed his movements, meeting the rhythm he set and demanding a faster pace of her own.

Pressure built inside her, a smothering heat that slicked her skin, stripped much-needed oxygen from the air. She wanted to scream her frustration, beg for this moment to go on and on, weep at the glorious feel of him filling her so completely.

His breathing ragged, he closed a hand around her breast. She heard the low growl that built from deep inside him, felt the quiver of his legs against hers, the tension that strained his body, and gave herself up to the explosion of sensation that rocked through her body. Desperate to squeeze every nuance of pleasure from the experience, she grasped his buttocks in her hands and held him to her, letting him send her higher, higher still.

Like a leaf drifting in the wind, she floated slowly down, melting against him. She inhaled one deep, cleansing breath, then opened her eyes to find his gaze on hers. Awed by his rugged handsomeness as much as by what she'd just experienced, she touched a finger to his cheek to make sure she hadn't been dreaming. "Wow," she said, releasing the breath on a shuddery sigh.

Smiling, he brought her hand to his lips. "Yeah. Wow."

She snuggled close. "Tell me—do Boy Scouts have a badge for something like this?"

Chuckling, he shook his head. "I don't think so."

Pursing her lips in a sympathetic pout, she tucked her head in the curve of his shoulder. "That's too bad. You definitely would've earned yours."

Leah awakened slowly, vaguely aware of a slight soreness between her legs. Remembering the cause for the discomfort, she smiled and reached a hand out in search of Sam.

When her fingers met only cool sheets, she lifted

her head and looked around. Finding herself alone, she dropped her head back to her pillow, telling herself it was best he'd left without waking her, saving them both the dreaded morning-after awkwardness.

In spite of her reassurance, tears of disappointment filled her eyes.

Refusing to give in to them, she threw back the covers and climbed from the bed. Just as she started down the stairs, she caught a whiff of what smelled like coffee brewing. Quickening her step, she hurried down the stairs and into the kitchen, where she found Sam standing before the stove.

"You're still here," she said in surprise.

He glanced over his shoulder, a brow lifted in question. "Was I supposed to leave?"

"No. No. It's just that…well, when I woke up and you weren't in bed, I assumed you'd gone back to the apartment."

Shaking his head, he turned his attention back to the stove. "It's that internal alarm clock of mine. It's set for five, and I've never figured out how to shut the dang thing off."

Relieved to know it wasn't regrets that had made him leave her, she crossed to see what he was cooking. "Pancakes?" she asked in surprise.

"Yep. Hungry?"

"Starving."

He shifted the spatula to his opposite hand and

slid his arm around her waist. "Me, too. Guess we worked up a pretty good appetite last night, huh?"

Reminded of her almost insatiable desire for him, she blushed to the roots of her hair. "Yeah, I guess we did."

He dipped his head to nuzzle her ear. "I believe I could go another round or two without dying of hunger. How about you?"

She drew back to look at him, sure that he was teasing. When she saw the heat in his eyes, she melted against his chest with a smile. "I'm willing to chance it if you are."

Later that morning, Sam paused beneath the automotive store's awning to put on his sunglasses, thinking what a wild night of sex could do for a man's energy level. With only a couple of hours' sleep the night before, he felt as if he could wrestle a grizzly to the ground and make him cry uncle.

Chuckling, he stepped out onto the sidewalk but stopped again when a car full of teenagers pulled up at the red light, rap music blasting so loud the bass made his teeth ache.

"They'll be deaf before they hit thirty," he grumbled, then frowned when he saw a cigarette being passed around. "If they live that long."

With a woeful shake of his head, he started for the parking lot where he'd left his truck but stopped short and slowly turned back around, sure that he'd recognized one of the boys in the backseat.

"Craig?" he said, praying he was wrong.

Setting his jaw, he strode to the car and yanked open the rear door.

"Hey!" Craig cried and grabbed for the handle.

Sam stepped into the opening and bodily dragged the boy from the car.

"What do you think you're doing?" Craig cried, trying to wrench free. "Get your hands off me."

"Leave him alone," the driver of the car yelled.

Sam burned the driver with a look. "If you know what's good for you, you'll get the hell out of here before I call the cops and report you for truancy."

The kid must have believed him, because he peeled out before the other passenger in the backseat had time to shut the door.

Sam turned his anger on Craig. Seeing the cigarette that dangled from the boy's fingers, he snatched it from him and threw it down on the sidewalk. "Don't you know these things will kill you?" he said as he ground the cigarette out beneath his boot.

"Gonna die someday," Craig said arrogantly. "One way's as good as any other."

"If you believe that, you're dumber than you look."

"Are you calling me dumb?"

"I said you *look* dumb." Sam pointed a stiff finger at the crushed cigarette. "Especially when you're holding one of those." He narrowed an eye at Craig. "Aren't you supposed to be in school?"

Craig ducked his head, shrugged. "So I cut a few classes. Big deal."

"You're going to think big deal when your aunt finds out."

Craig snapped up his head, his eyes filled with dread. "You're gonna tell her?"

"Nope," Sam informed him. "You are." Taking the boy by the arm, he hustled him toward the truck. "But first you and I are going to pay a visit to your school principal."

Lying beneath the Mustang, Sam turned the wrench, tightening the last bolt on the new muffler he'd installed. Beyond him, the whirr of the lawn mower's engine assured him that Craig hadn't gone AWOL again.

The trip to the school had been an eye-opener for Sam. He still couldn't believe the punishment for skipping school these days was a few lousy hours of detention. The one and only time he had cut school, he'd gotten three licks for every class he'd missed. Three *hard* licks delivered by the baseball coach, who had spent some time in the minor leagues and had the swing to prove it. Sam hadn't been able to sit down for a week.

With a rueful shake of his head, he gave the

tailpipe a tug, testing its stability, then pushed his boot heel against the drive and rolled the creeper from beneath the car. Standing, he dragged a rag from his back pocket and wiped his hands as he watched Craig make another sweep around the backyard. The lawn-mowing duty had been Sam's idea, one he figured would keep the kid busy and out of trouble until Leah got home from work.

And judging by the deep grooves that creased the boy's forehead, it appeared Craig wasn't looking forward to his aunt's arrival.

With a glance at his wristwatch, Sam decided to call it a day and began picking up his tools. Though it would have been a lot easier to leave everything out, he'd made a few concessions in his work habits in order to pacify Leah's concerns about him turning her home into a junkyard. The first order of business had been constructing a canopy over the car to shade it— and him—during the hottest portion of the day. Second on his list had been the placement of a tarpaulin beneath the car to protect the driveway from any oil and fluid spills. The last concession he'd come up with—actually a time-saver for him—was storing the most frequently used tools in the car's trunk.

And he hadn't made those concessions because he'd slept with Leah, he assured himself. It had simply taken him a while to figure out a compromise that would satisfy them both.

After depositing in the Mustang's trunk the tools he'd used that day, he stepped out into the yard to survey the work area he'd created. All in all, it wasn't too bad a setup, he decided. Leah would probably still consider it an eyesore, but she'd just have to deal. He'd done all he intended to do to appease what he considered her anal need for perfection.

Hearing a car door slam, he glanced over his shoulder and watched as Leah climbed from her SUV. He felt the stirring of desire in his groin and grinned, thinking of the night ahead.

She strode beneath the breezeway, her gaze fixed on the canopy. "Wow. Somebody's been busy."

Though he was a little disappointed she found the canopy more interesting than him, he turned to admire his handiwork. "You didn't want me working on the car out front, and I couldn't take the heat in the garage." He lifted a hand, indicating the canopy. "This is the compromise I came up with."

She walked around the perimeter of the structure, studying it closely. "You put this up by yourself?"

"Craig helped. He held the canvas in position while I secured it to the poles."

She looked at him in surprise. "*Craig* helped?"

"Yep." He nodded toward the backyard, where Craig was working. "He's mowing the yard, too."

She turned to peer at her nephew. "I can't believe this. I've asked him a zillion times to mow the yard and he always has an excuse." She glanced at Sam. "How in the world did you get him to do it?"

He buffed his nails on his chest and preened. "Oh, I have my ways."

"Well, don't be selfish. Share them with me. Nothing I've tried has ever worked."

Craig mowed the last strip and turned the mower toward the garage. When he spotted Leah standing with Sam, he stumbled a step, gulped, then pushed on, keeping his head down to avoid her gaze.

"Hi, Aunt Leah," he mumbled.

Smiling, she ruffled his hair. "Hi, yourself. And thanks for mowing the yard. I really appreciate it."

He lifted a shoulder. "No big deal."

"I'll put that away for you," Sam offered and took the mower from Craig. "You go on into the house with your aunt. I'm sure y'all have things to talk about."

His shoulders drooping, Craig nodded and turned for the house.

Leah looked at Sam in confusion. "What was that all about?"

"You'll find out soon enough."

Leah tried her best to keep her anger in check as she listened to Craig's explanation. When he finished, she sat in silence for a long moment, unsure what to say for fear whatever she said would distance her nephew even further.

"Does your mother know about this?" she asked.

"No. Just you. And Sam."

She curled her hand into a fist in her lap, curbing the desire to comb his hair back from his eyes so she could see his face.

"You said that Sam took you to see the principal."

"Yeah," he muttered sourly. "I got slammed with two weeks of detention."

A mild punishment, in her estimation, but she wasn't about to share her opinion with Craig.

"When do you begin serving them?"

"Monday. Seven-thirty to eight-thirty every day for two whole weeks."

She firmed her lips at his resentful tone. "Ten hours spent studying certainly won't hurt your grades any."

He tucked his chin closer to his chest at the mention of his downward-spiraling grades.

A horn beeped outside, and Leah glanced toward the front of the house, knowing it was Patrice. She turned to face Craig again. "Are you going to tell your mom about this?"

He lifted a shoulder, dropped it. "She's so wigged-out all the time, she probably wouldn't even hear me if I did."

Leah made a decision that she hoped wouldn't come back to haunt her. Reaching across the table, she covered her nephew's hand with her own. "Let's just keep this between us for now."

"Whatever."

The horn beeped again and Craig dragged himself to his feet. "I better go." He hitched his backpack over his shoulder and turned to leave.

In the doorway he hesitated a moment, and she held her breath, praying that he'd say *I'm sorry* or something that would indicate he regretted what he'd done. But he stepped outside, letting the door close behind him, without uttering a word.

Leah watched him leave, her heart breaking. He looked so much like Kevin had at that age. Legs too long for his body. Hair long and shaggy. Eyes that harbored a sadness that nothing could reach. Like his father, Craig had no mother to turn to for comfort and reassurance. In her own way, Patrice was as oblivious to her son's needs as Leah and Kevin's mother had been to theirs.

Tears filled her throat and she dropped her forehead to her folded arms, willing them back. Crying wouldn't bring Kevin back or absolve her fears for Craig. She'd shed enough over the years to know they were nothing but a waste of time.

"Leah?"

She lifted her head and found Sam standing in the doorway. She quickly scraped her hands across her cheeks and rose, not wanting him to see that she'd been crying. "Craig told me what happened this morning."

His expression somber, he stepped inside. "I was hoping he would."

She had the most irresistible urge to bury her face against his chest and sob. To keep herself from giving into it, she turned for the refrigerator. "I appreciate what you did for him. Taking him back to school and making him tell the principal what he'd done."

"Facing the music is always hard. Figured he might need a little encouragement."

She pulled a pitcher of lemonade from the refrigerator, her smile wistful as she closed the door. "Encouragement is something he's short on right now."

"He has you," he reminded her.

Shaking her head, she took two glasses from the cabinet. "I'm not enough. I can't reach him any more. He needs is his father." Feeling the tears rising again, she firmed her lips and focused her attention on filling the glasses. Turning, she forced a smile and offered one to Sam. "How about some lemonade?"

He accepted the glass. "Thanks."

She gestured toward the sunroom. "Let's sit out there."

She led the way, with Sam following, and settled in a wicker chair.

He took the chair next to hers.

"Craig tells me that you and the principal have an agreement to keep Patrice on a need-to-know basis only."

She nodded. "Patrice is...fragile. I handle whatever problems arise at school to save her the additional stress."

"Do you mind if I ask you a question?"

She stole a glance his way. "That depends on the question."

"Why do you avoid talking about your brother?"

Blanching, she looked away, not wanting to share her reasons. "I'd think that would be obvious."

"If you mean grief, that I can understand. It's hard losing someone you love. But I think it's more than just grief."

Pursing her lips, she swept a drop of condensation impatiently from her glass. "You can think whatever you like."

"Leah?"

When she refused to look at him, he laid a hand over hers.

"Leah, look at me."

Though she'd have preferred to look anywhere other than at him, she met his gaze. The compassion she found in his eyes nearly brought her to her knees.

"You're mad, aren't you?" he said quietly.

She felt the sting of tears and blinked them back. "Why would I be mad at you?" she asked, purposely misunderstanding his question.

"Not me. Your brother."

The tears surged higher, a wall of emotion that

blocked any hope she might have had of denying his assumption a second time.

Before she realized his intention, he had tugged her from her chair and onto his lap.

"Ah, Leah," he said miserably. He tucked her head beneath his chin and pressed a kiss on top of her head. "I'm not Craig or Patrice. You don't have to keep up a brave front for me. I won't think any less of you for admitting that you're angry with Kevin for dying."

She gulped but couldn't hold back the emotion that choked her. She turned her face against his neck. "He didn't have to die," she sobbed miserably. "He could've stayed home with his family. With me."

He stroked a hand over her hair. "Soldiers aren't given a choice," he reminded her. "They go where they're sent, where their country needs them."

She shook her head. "He never should have enlisted. He was barely eighteen. Too young to know what he was doing or what he wanted to do with his life. He only did it because of Mom."

"Your mother asked him to enlist?" he asked in confusion.

"No. He did it to get her attention. Maybe to spite her. I don't know." She squeezed her eyes shut, remembering the hours she'd spent pleading with him not to join the Army. "I begged him not to do it, told him that it wouldn't make any difference, that Mom was never going to change no matter what either of us did. But he wouldn't listen. It was like he needed to prove something. Or maybe get even with her for ignoring him."

Hitching a breath, she pressed a hand against her lips and shook her head. "I don't know. But no matter how much I screamed and begged, I couldn't get through to him. And Mom—she was oblivious. Didn't say a word to him. Just kept on with her stupid research, as if Kevin wasn't making the biggest mistake of his life."

"I take it you've always been the one in charge, looking out for your mother and brother."

She swiped at her cheeks. "Somebody had to, and Mom couldn't or wouldn't."

"And now you're looking out for Craig and Patrice."

She lifted her head, shot a hand beneath her nose. "I have to. Kevin's not here to take care of them."

"And who takes care of Leah?" he asked softly.

She stared, then turned her face away, unable to meet his gaze.

He placed a hand on her cheek and turned her face back to his. "Who?" he prodded.

She stared, her lip quivering, thinking of all the times she'd wanted someone to lean on, someone to help carry the burden for a while. She'd hoped, prayed, that Louis would be that someone. Instead he'd ridiculed her concern for her family, refused to spend any holidays in their company and done everything he could to distance her from them.

Jutting her chin, she shoved his hand away. "I don't need anyone to take care of me. I can take care of myself."

"Everybody needs somebody."

She pushed from his lap. "Well, I don't. And if you think my sleeping with you gives you the right to interfere in my life, you're wrong."

Five

Sam stood with a shoulder braced against the doorjamb of the apartment, his arms folded across his chest, looking up at the night sky. To say he was frustrated would be the understatement of the year. He'd thought he'd be sharing Leah's bed again tonight, but the conversation they'd had in the sunroom had nixed any chance of that happening.

But sex wasn't the cause of his frustration. Not solely, anyway. He was worried about Leah. He was afraid if somebody didn't do something, and soon, she was going to crumple beneath the weight of the family responsibilities she carried. Granted, her sense of duty to Craig and Patrice was admirable, but Sam was a firm believer in the teach-a-person-to-fish approach to dealing with problems. In his opinion, as long as Leah continued to take care of Craig and Patrice, they would never step up to the plate and assume responsibility for their own emotional and physical needs. They'd continue to drain Leah until she had nothing left to give them.

He wanted to help her. If nothing else, to offer her some much-needed support. But every time he tried, the damn fool woman stiff-armed him, insisting she could take care of herself, just as she had that afternoon.

He supposed he could understand her obstinance. She'd been taking care of herself and those around her so long it had probably become a habit, one she couldn't break.

But he was convinced there was something more behind her stubborn refusal to accept help from anyone…and he had a sneaky suspicion it stemmed from her mother's suicide. He remembered when she'd told him about her mother's obsession with finding her father, Leah saying he probably thought her mother was crazy, the same as everyone else in town. Reason enough for her to refuse offers of help from outsiders, as she wouldn't want to subject her family to more public scorn.

But it wasn't reason enough to refuse Sam's.

In his mind, her refusal represented a lack of trust. And that irritated the hell out of him, as trust was a trait he valued and strived hard to earn.

He'd never given her any reason to distrust him, he told himself. He had a key to her house, yet he'd never once taken advantage of that privilege. He bought his own groceries and what other necessities he needed and was careful to always replace what items of hers he used. He even helped out around the house, emptying the dishwasher when it needed it, sweeping the kitchen floor the few times he'd tracked dirt inside. And he'd started cleaning the pool, figuring it was the least he could do, since she allowed him to use it. He even helped her keep an eye on Craig.

You didn't tell her you were in the Army.

He flinched at his conscience's prodding, then squared his shoulders. And for good reason, he thought defensively. Leah blamed the Army for the loss of her father and brother. She'd made it clear from the get-go that she wanted nothing to do with anyone associated with the military. If he'd told her he currently served with Special Forces, he would've lost any chance he had of getting the information he'd promised Mack.

Leading her to believe you were a mechanic who'd come to apply for the job of restoring the car is the same as lying, which is reason enough to earn her distrust.

It's not the same, he argued stubbornly. He'd never out-and-out lied to her.

He just hadn't given her the whole truth.

He rolled his shoulders, trying to shake free from the guilt his conscience was piling on him, but it stuck like glue, refusing to budge.

With a resigned sigh, he glanced toward Leah's darkened bedroom window and wondered if she was having trouble sleeping, too. He could imagine her there, tossing and turning, worrying about Craig, grieving for her brother. He wanted to go to her, share her burden, offer what comfort he could, but knew he'd only alienate her more if he did.

Maybe he ought to come clean, he told himself. Tell her the truth about who he was and why he was at her house. She'd be madder than a hornet, there was no question about that. But surely after she'd cooled down she'd understand, perhaps even admire his determination to honor his promise to Mack, sympathize with his need to provide his friend's wife with another piece of the puzzle to her father's life. Once she realized the honorableness of his mission, she'd give him the piece of paper he wanted and he could be on his way, putting her and her family's problems behind him.

His gaze fixed on her window, he realized that leaving was no longer an option. He couldn't walk away from Leah when he knew how badly she needed help. Not only in restoring her brother's car but with her nephew, too. The boy was headed for trouble, a place Sam was all too familiar with. What the kid needed was guidance, a firm hand, the influence only a man could provide a young, impressionable boy quickly approaching adulthood.

And Leah needed Sam. She'd never admit it, might not even be aware of the lack in her life. But he was. She was haunted by her father's and brother's deaths, possibly even her mother's, and had devoted her life to protecting her nephew and sister-in-law from any more hurt.

She deserved a life of her own, one free of obligation and responsibility to others. But she'd never know any true peace, any happiness, until she stopped avoiding her past and dealt with it once and for all.

And when she did that, she was going to need someone to lean on, someone to comfort her, lend her strength.

And Sam intended to be that someone.

The overhead light snapped on, yanking Leah bolt upright in bed.

Sam stood in the doorway, his hand on the switch.

"What are you doing?" she cried.

He flipped off the light and started across the room. "Seeing if you were awake."

He stopped beside the bed, and though it was

dark, his movements were clear enough for her to know he was stripping off his sweatpants.

"Just because I slept with you once," she said angrily, "doesn't give you the right to march into my bedroom anytime you want."

"I'm not here for sex."

She blinked, taken aback, then set her jaw. "Then why are you here?"

He lifted the sheet and slid into bed beside her. "Couldn't sleep. You really should get a new mattress for the apartment."

"There's nothing wrong with that mattress!" she cried indignantly.

"For Fred Flintstone, maybe. It's like lying on a slab of stone."

"You never complained before."

He tugged her down to lie beside him and settled his head next to hers on the pillow. "Wasn't aware of the difference until I slept in yours."

"Sam," she warned when he hooked an arm over her waist and cuddled close.

"Shh." He closed his eyes. "You need to get some sleep. We both do."

Leah wanted to argue, but he began to stroke his hand up and down her back, distracting her. She waited, convinced that any second he'd give up the ruse and attempt to seduce her and she could kick him out of her room for the liar he was.

But with each slow glide of his hand more and more of the tension melted from her back and her eyelids grew heavy. Heavier still.

She slept, lulled by the rhythmic sound of Sam's breathing.

Leah opened her eyes, startled awake by the sound of a car on the drive. It took her a moment to associate the unusual warmth at her back and the weight that pinned her legs with Sam. She started to close her eyes and snuggle back against the warmth but flipped them wide when she heard a car door open and slam.

Throwing back the covers, she ran to the window and lifted a slat to peek through the blinds.

"Oh, no!" Whirling, she cried, "You've got to get out of here!"

Sam pulled the pillow over his head. "It's Saturday," he mumbled. "Come back to bed."

She snatched the pillow from his head. "Patrice just dropped Craig off. You've got to get out of here."

He blinked up at her, his hair tousled from sleep. "Why?"

"He can't find us in bed together! What would he think?"

"That we were tired?" he asked hopefully.

She flattened her lips. "Sa-am…"

He knew by the warning she placed in the two-syllable pronunciation of his name that she wasn't making the distinction because she was aroused. He also knew he wasn't getting any more sleep.

"Okay, okay," he grumbled as he rolled from the bed. He scooped his sweatpants from the floor and tugged them on as he headed for the door. "I'll go downstairs and intercept him."

"Dressed like that?" she cried. "You can't! He'll know the minute he sees you that you spent the night." She worried her thumbnail, trying to think of a plausible explanation. "Tell him I saw a mouse. Yeah, a mouse," she said, liking the idea. "And I called you to come and catch it for me."

He looked down his nose at her. "Do you really think he's going to fall for a cock-and-bull story like that?"

She gave him a push. "He will if you make it sound convincing."

Shaking his head, he jogged down the stairs, leaving her to dress. When he entered the kitchen, Craig was pouring cereal into a bowl.

"Hey, Craig," he said. "I didn't know you were coming over today."

Craig looked up. He glanced in the direction Sam had appeared, then back at Sam. "What are you doing here?" he asked suspiciously.

Rolling his eyes, Sam crossed to the refrigerator and pulled out a jug of orange juice. "Your aunt saw a mouse. Called me, all hysterical, begging me to come and catch it for her."

Craig's expression remained dubious. "So where's the mouse?"

Sam snorted as he poured orange juice into a glass. "You ever known a person who caught a mouse with his bare hands?"

Craig smothered a laugh. "No."

"Me either," Sam replied and took a swig of juice. Backhanding the moisture from his mouth, he dragged out a chair and swung it around, straddling it as he sat opposite Craig at the table. "Women. Nothing but a bunch of sissies. Guess this means I'll be making a run to the store for a mousetrap."

"Yeah. Looks like it."

"Want to go with me?"

"I guess."

Leah breezed into the kitchen wearing an over-bright smile and a T-shirt turned wrong-side out. "Morning, Craig. I suppose Sam told you about the mouse?"

He glanced up, then ducked his head and scooped up a spoonful of cereal. "Yeah. He told me."

Sam ducked his head, too, deciding it might not be the best time to tell Leah about her wardrobe blunder.

Oblivious to their amusement—or her state of dress—Leah pulled a bowl from the cabinet. "I didn't know you were planning on coming over today," she said to Craig.

"Wasn't. Mom's having one of her…spells."

Leah's face crumpled. "Oh, honey," she said sympathetically and draped an arm around her nephew's shoulders. "I'm so sorry."

Craig shrugged. "No big deal. I'll just hang out here till she settles down."

Nodding, Leah seated herself at the table and reached for the cereal box. "Maybe you and Sam can work on the car," she suggested hopefully.

Craig peeked at Sam from beneath his mass of bangs. "Maybe," he said, hiding a smile. "But we gotta buy a mousetrap, first. Right, Sam?"

Craig stood beside Sam, holding the wing nut, while Sam fitted the cover back over the carburetor.

"You spent the night with Aunt Leah, didn't you?"

The question came out of nowhere and had Sam fumbling the cover. He straightened slowly and pulled off his ball cap to drag an arm across the sweat on his brow. "Yeah, I did," he admitted reluctantly.

"So why did y'all make up that crazy story about the mouse?"

Sam puffed his cheeks and blew out a breath, knowing he was treading on thin ice. Slinging an arm around Craig's shoulders, he guided him toward a bench beneath a tree. "Because your aunt didn't want to give you the wrong impression."

Craig flopped down on the bench and peered up at Sam. "What? That she sleeps around?"

Since Sam couldn't see Craig's eyes, he didn't know whether the kid was being serious or a wiseass. Frustrated, he shot a hand through the boy's hair and slapped his ball cap over the top of his head.

Craig threw up his hands. "Hey!" he cried, trying to duck. "What are you doing?"

Sam tugged the cap down, pinning the boy's hair beneath it, then stooped and put his face level with Craig's. "Getting your hair out of your eyes," he informed him. "That's what. When I talk to a person, I want to see his eyes."

Craig spun the cap around, placing the bill in the back. "What's the big deal about seeing a person's eyes?" he grumbled.

Sam dropped down on the bench beside him with a sigh. "Because eyes don't lie. If you want to know what a person is thinking, you've got to be able to look them square in the eyes."

"That's bull."

"Think so?" Sam challenged. He turned his back to Craig. "I've never been in jail in my life," he said, then faced Craig again, careful to keep his expression blank. "Was I lying or telling the truth?"

Frowning, Craig studied him closely for a moment. "The truth."

Sam fixed his gaze on Craig's. "Keep your eyes on mine and let's try that again. By the time I was eighteen I'd been thrown in jail a minimum of six times." He sank back and braced his spine on the trunk of the tree. "So? Truth or lie?"

Craig's eyes rounded. "Holy smoke. You've really been in jail that many times?"

"Yeah," Sam admitted reluctantly, then gave Craig a stern look. "And I didn't use that example because I'm proud of my past. It was only to make a point." He jerked up his chin, indicating the cap. "People who keep their eyes hidden are hiding something else, too—usually the truth. If you want a person to believe you, you've got to look him straight in the eye."

Craig tugged the cap off, combed his hair back over his forehead and pulled the cap over his head again. "Even more reason to keep my hair in my eyes. Nobody'll ever know when I'm lying."

"Oh, they'll find out eventually," Sam informed him. "A man's lies catch up with him sooner or later. But you're missing the point. You can't trust what a man tells you unless you can look him square in the eye." He waited a beat, then said, "And your aunt does *not* sleep around."

Grimacing, Craig dragged off the cap and shoved his hair beneath it again. "I know that."

"Well, I want to make damn sure you do. Your aunt's a nice woman. A lady. And I won't have you thinking or saying bad things about her."

Craig cast him a sideways look. "You like her?"

Though he wasn't ready to share his newly discovered feelings for Leah just yet, Sam kept his gaze fixed on Craig's, knowing—after the lecture he'd just delivered—to look away would be a mistake. "Yeah, I do. You got a problem with that?"

Craig shrugged. "That's cool with me. Aunt Leah hasn't had a boyfriend since she divorced Louis the Loser."

Sam choked a laugh. "Louis the Loser?"

Craig scowled. "That's her ex. I never liked him. Nobody did."

"Your Aunt Leah must have. She married him."

His scowl deepened. "She might've married him, but I don't think she liked him all that much."

Sam knew it was wrong to press the kid for details, but he wasn't about to let an opportunity like this pass. "If she didn't like him, why'd she marry him?"

Craig bent over and picked up a twig from the ground. "I heard my dad tell my mom she married him for his money."

Sam had a hard time swallowing that line of reasoning. Leah didn't seem the type who'd trade her freedom and her heart for a bank account, no matter how many zeros followed the dollar sign. "Do you think that's why she did it?"

His gaze on the twig he spun between his fingers, Craig shook his head. "Nah. Aunt Leah's no gold digger."

"Then why do you think she married the guy?"

Craig lifted his head and looked at Sam. "Because she wanted somebody to love and thought he'd love her back."

There was no questioning the sincerity in the boy's eyes. "And he didn't?"

Scowling, Craig reared back and threw the twig as far as he could. "Louis the Loser loves one person. Himself. Aunt Leah was nothing but a game to him. She's pretty, smart, built her business up all by herself. Every single guy in town was chasing her, so Louis did a snow job on her. Bought her presents all the time, took her nice places, acted like she was the only woman in the whole universe. Made her feel special. Loved."

"I take it once they were married he quit treating her that way."

Craig snorted. "He was screwing around on her the day they got back from their honeymoon."

Sam gave him a doubtful look. "You don't know that for sure."

"Yeah, I do." Craig rose and started for the car. "Aunt Leah knew it, too," he called over his shoulder. "She caught him coming out of a motel room with some woman. Cried for days."

Sam couldn't shake free of the image Craig had planted in his mind of Leah crying for days after catching her husband in a compromising position.

If what Craig had said was true, then Leah must have loved Louis despite her nephew's insistence that she hadn't liked the man. Why else would she have cried when she'd caught him cheating on her?

Didn't matter, Sam told himself as he dragged the skimmer over the pool's surface. Whether Leah loved Louis or not, that was all in the past. It was the now that concerned him. Specifically Leah's now.

He'd learned some other things from Craig—turned out the kid was a real Chatty Cathy once a person got him talking. Through carefully phrased probing, Sam had discovered that the boy knew almost nothing about his grandfather. According to Craig, his grandfather's name was taboo with everyone except his grandmother, and she was so "weirded out," as Craig had described her, that he'd learned not to mention his grandfather's name in front of her, either.

Another item of interest he'd gleaned from the kid was the fact that Leah and her brother had grown up in near poverty. Amazing, considering her current digs and her obsession for neatness and order.

Or maybe that explained why she was the way she was, he realized slowly.

Growing thoughtful, he dragged the net across the pool's surface, scooping up leaves. When he added to the equation the fact that Leah was raised by a present-in-body-only mother, it made sense that she would strive to make up for all that was lacking in her youth.

It also explained how she'd developed her mother-hen tendency toward her family.

As the oldest, she more than likely would have assumed the responsibilities her mother shirked, including watching out for her little brother, a responsibility she'd carried with her into adulthood. And when "little brother" died, leaving a widow and orphaned son behind, she'd spread her mother-hen wings a little wider and drawn his family close, assuming the role of their protector.

Oh, yeah, he thought in satisfaction as he dumped the waterlogged leaves into the trash can. He had figured out the whys and why-fors behind Ms. Leah Kittrell's personality quirks.

Now he just had to figure out how to put the information to use to free her from her past.

The most likely place to start seemed to be with her father, since her father's classification as MIA seemed to be the point when the family began to fall apart. If he could somehow manage to dispel the mystery surrounding her father's death, he could give Leah the closure she needed, which would allow her to begin healing other areas of her life.

And he knew just the man to call to assist him in uncovering the information he'd need to give her that closure.

Pulling out his cell phone, he punched in a number, then waited through two rings.

"Hey, Jack," he said to the man who answered. "It's Sam. How're you doing?"

He laughed at Jack's sarcastic response, then said, "Listen, buddy. I need a favor. I have a friend whose father was listed as MIA in Vietnam. Jessie Kittrell, from Texas. I need you to find out what you can about him. Where he was last seen, any intelligence that mentions him or other soldiers from his unit, who were listed as MIA at the same time—that kind of thing."

Scrunching up his nose, he scratched his head as he listened to Jack's grumbled complaints. "Yeah, I know it's not much to go on, but that's all I've got."

He listened again, then grinned. "I knew I could count on you, buddy. I owe you one."

Pleased to have made a step in the right direction, he slipped his cell phone back into its holster at his waist and picked up the pool net again.

"You don't have to do that."

He jumped at the sound of Leah's voice, then

turned, praying she hadn't overheard his conversation. "Only fair. I use it as much as you." Noticing that she was wearing a business suit, he looked at her in puzzlement. "It's Saturday. Why are you dressed for work?"

"I have a committee meeting." She stepped out onto the patio. "I wanted to thank you before I left."

"You don't owe me any thanks. Like I said, it's only fair since I use the pool, too."

She shook her head. "No, I meant for spending the day with Craig. He needed the distraction. When Patrice gets likes this, it upsets him."

He nodded soberly. "Yeah, I imagine it does."

She dropped her chin, as if she had something else to say but was having a hard time getting the words out.

"About last night…" she began.

"What about it?" he prodded.

She lifted her head and met his gaze. "I'm sorry for the things I said. I don't want you to think I don't appreciate your kindness to me. It's just that…" She drew in a deep breath. "I don't like people telling me how to handle my family."

"That wasn't my intent. I just wanted to help is all. It seems you're carrying an awful heavy load."

"They're my family. All I've got. I'd do anything for them."

"Yeah. I imagine you would."

She hesitated a moment. "I want to thank you for sleeping with me, too." She dropped her chin, a blush staining her cheeks. "I know how stupid that sounds. How childish. But it was comforting to know that you were there, that I wasn't alone."

"Leah—" he began.

She looked at her watch. "I really need to go. I'm already late."

"Is it a dinner meeting?" he asked.

She shook her head. "Strictly business."

"How about I cook tonight? Something on the grill."

Her eyes brightened. "Are you serious?"

"As a heart attack."

A slow smile spread across her face. "Well, yeah. That would be great. I should be through by seven-thirty, eight at the latest."

"Come home hungry."

Steaks flame-broiled over mesquite wood. A bottle of Chianti wine. A table set for two beneath a moonlit sky. Roses scenting the night air.

Sam had planned the evening down the last detail, wanting to give Leah a relaxing, stress-free evening…or was he trying to prove to her that he could be as charming as her ex?

Grimacing, he lowered the lid over the grill, silently cursing Craig for telling him about Louis the Loser and the damn snow job he'd done on Leah to persuade her to marry him.

This wasn't a competition, he told himself. He wasn't trying to outromance Louis the Loser. And he wasn't interested in marriage. He just wanted to give Leah something she seldom, if ever, enjoyed. A night free from worry, even those associated with preparing a meal.

"Wow."

He turned, and his heart shifted in his chest when he saw Leah poised on the steps of the house. She still wore her business suit but had removed the jacket. But she could've had on worn-out sweats and looked just as beautiful to Sam. A woman couldn't hide that kind of beauty even if she'd tried.

She started toward him but stopped to examine the table he'd set and lifted a brow. "China?"

"Only the best for the owner of Stylized Events."

"You didn't have to go to so much trouble," she scolded as she crossed to him. She rose to her toes and placed a kiss on his cheek. "But it's lovely." She braced a hand against his chest and looked around. "Everything is."

He lifted the dome on the grill to check the steaks. "Ten minutes," he reported and closed the lid. "How about a glass of wine?"

"I wouldn't turn one down."

He poured two glasses, passed her one. "How was your meeting?"

"Boring."

He hid a smile behind the rim of his glass as he watched her rearrange the silverware beside the plates. "I guess I must've missed the etiquette class on proper table settings."

She snatched her hand behind her back. "Sorry," she said, wincing. "Habit."

He chuckled as he pulled out a chair for her. "Considering your line of business, I'd imagine it's more than habit."

She looked up at him over her shoulder as she sat down. "I hate to sound ungrateful, but—" she spread her hands "—what's all this about?"

He seated himself across the table from her. "No reason. Just thought you could stand some spoiling."

She picked up the rose he'd placed across her plate and lifted it to her nose. She closed her eyes as she inhaled its fragrance, then smiled and tucked it behind her ear. "I definitely rate this as spoiling. I can't remember the last time anyone went to this much trouble for me."

He lifted his glass. "Even more reason for you to enjoy it."

Bracing her arms against the table, she leaned to study him from across the table. "I can't figure you out. One minute I want to strangle you and the next

I want to bottle you so that every woman can enjoy your sweetness."

"Sweet? Me?" Laughing, he shook his head. "I've been called a lot of things in my lifetime, but 'sweet' was never one of them."

"But you are," she insisted. "And thoughtful and kind and generous, too."

His smile soft, he braced his arms on the table, mimicking her posture. "You just described yourself."

She stared, then pushed out a hand, laughing. "See? I'm trying to pay you a compliment and you won't accept it."

"Right back at you."

Holding up her hands, she sank back in her chair. "Okay, I give up. You're incorrigible and impossible."

He smiled proudly. "Now you're talking." He glanced at his watch and pushed from his chair. "Steaks should be about ready. Hungry?"

"Starved. What can I do to help?"

"I made salad. It's in the refrigerator, if you don't mind getting it."

She scraped back her chair. "Anything else?"

He shook his head as he lifted the lid. "I've got everything else right here on the grill."

"Sam?"

He glanced over his shoulder. "Yeah?"

"You really are sweet."

* * *

Sweet.

Sam glanced back at the bed where Leah slept and shook his head. She wouldn't think he was so sweet if she knew the truth about him.

Heaving a sigh, he turned to stare out the window again. Telling a couple of half-truths shouldn't bother a man who lived a life of subterfuge and espionage, but the duplicity surrounding his relationship with Leah was beginning to wear on his nerves.

He knew he couldn't keep up the charade much longer. Not when he'd grown to care for her. He stopped, considering the thought, then slowly relaxed. It was true—he did care for her, was possibly even falling in love with her.

He frowned again. But that in itself made it even more important for him to tell her who he was and what he was doing at her house. He'd planned to come clean earlier, after dinner, but the timing just hadn't seemed right. She had been so pleased with the dinner he'd cooked for her, so happy and relaxed, he'd hated to ruin it all just to free himself of guilt.

"Sam?"

He whipped his head around to find Leah propped on an elbow, her forehead pleated in concern.

"Are you okay?" she asked.

Smiling softly, he returned to the bed. "I'm fine."

He hooked an arm over her waist and settled his head on the pillow opposite hers. "Couldn't sleep. Probably ate too much."

Her smile sleepy, she nuzzled her cheek against his chest. "I'd have thought we worked off that meal."

Chuckling at the reminder of the amount of time they'd spent at sexual aerobics, he pressed his lips against her hair. "We gave it our best shot, that's for damn sure."

She placed a hand over his heart and closed her eyes. "Go to sleep," she murmured. "Morning will be here soon."

The tenderness of her touch seemed to burn through his chest and wrap around his heart. Closing his eyes against the ache that swelled there, he buried his nose in her hair and drank in her scent.

And wondered if she'd still be willing to share her bed with him once he told her the truth.

Six

Sam strained to fit the new battery beneath the Mustang's hood. After only three weeks of mildly intense labor he was close to getting this little baby running.

"Hey, Sam!"

He glanced up and had to do a double take to make sure it was Craig who was jogging up the drive.

He gave the battery a last shove, clicking it into position on its frame, then hitched his hands on his hips. "Well, look at you. What happened? Get your head caught in a fan?"

Breathless from running, Craig dumped his backpack on the drive. "Got a haircut."

Sam circled him, admiring the shorter style. "Damn if you aren't pretty. Who'd have guessed there was a face under all that hair?"

Blushing, Craig ducked his head. "Cut it out. It's just a haircut."

Chuckling, Sam scrubbed his knuckles over Craig's head. "This calls for a celebration. Shakes on me."

Craig's face lit up. "Cool! Can I drive?"

Sam crossed to his truck and opened the passenger door. "Do you have a license?"

"Come on, Sam. You know I don't."

"Guess that means I'll be doing the driving."

Grimacing, Craig climbed into the cab.

"How am I ever going to learn to drive," he complained as Sam slid behind the wheel, "when nobody'll ever let me?"

"There's a time and place for everything," Sam informed him as he started the engine. "And city streets aren't the place for driving lessons." He put the truck into gear. "That's what country roads were made for. Know any?"

Craig's eyes widened. "Does that mean you'll teach me?"

"If you know a remote road we can use."

"Out by the lake. There's millions out there and people hardly ever use 'em."

"The lake it is, then," Sam said, then glanced at Craig. "Unless you still want that shake."

"Heck no! I want to *drive!*"

With Craig serving as his navigational director, Sam located a remote country road perfect for giving a teenager his first turn behind the wheel.

After pulling onto the shoulder and switching off the ignition, he said to Craig, "Okay. So tell me how much experience you've had at driving."

Craig scrunched up his nose. "Not much. Aunt Leah has let me drive her SUV a couple of times."

"Then you know the basics. Accelerator, brake, that kind of thing?"

"Yeah." Craig studied the controls on the dash behind the steering wheel. "Everything looks pretty much the same as on Aunt Leah's."

Sam opened his door. "Then let's get this show on the road."

While he rounded the hood, Craig climbed over the console and dropped down behind the wheel. By the time Sam settled into the passenger seat, Craig had touched and tested every dial on the dash, including the radio.

Grimacing, Sam turned down the volume. "You'll need to adjust the seat," he instructed. "Controls are on the left-hand side. Push the longest to move the seat forward or back. The shortest up or down to adjust the seat's height."

"Right." His forehead pleated in concentration, Craig pressed a button. The seat moved forward a couple of inches, then stopped, and the motor began to grind.

He yanked his hand off the button and looked at Sam in alarm. "Did I do something wrong?"

Amused by the kid's fear, he shook his head. "Probably something caught on the glide blocking it and keeping the seat from moving. Reach underneath and see if you feel anything."

Craig groped a minute, then shook his head. "Can't reach that far."

"Then you're going to have to get out and look."

Craig opened the door, hopped down, then bent over and peered beneath the seat.

"I see something," he said and stuck his arm under the seat, straining to reach it. "Got it!" he exclaimed and pulled out a metal box.

Sam swallowed a groan when he saw the olive-green box, with *Property of Sam Forrester, U.S. Army, Special Forces* emblazoned across the lid.

"What's this?" Craig asked in puzzlement.

Sam stretched across the seat and snatched the box from the boy's hand. "Just some old papers," he said vaguely and stuffed the box under the passenger seat and out of sight.

Frowning, Craig climbed back into the truck and shut the door.

Sam pasted on a smile. "Okay, hot rod. Give her a whirl."

Craig turned the key, starting the engine. He started to pull down the gearshift, but dropped his hand and turned to look at Sam. "You're in the Army, aren't you?"

Sam silently cursed his own stupidity for not remembering that he'd stuck the box with his paperwork beneath the seat. "Yeah," he admitted reluctantly.

"Does Aunt Leah know?"

He shook his head. "I thought it best not to mention it, considering how she feels about the military."

"She's going to be majorly P.O.'d when she finds out."

Sam heaved a sigh. "Yeah, I know." He hesitated a moment, then said, "Listen, Craig. I'd appreciate it if you wouldn't say anything about this. I'd prefer to tell her myself."

"Why'd you lie to her in the first place?"

"I didn't lie," Sam said defensively. When Craig merely looked at him, he scowled. "I didn't lie," he said stubbornly. "I just didn't tell her the whole truth."

"Which is…?" Craig prodded.

Sam gave him a long look, knowing he was going to have to tell the kid the whole story. How could he do any less when he'd been preaching truth and honesty to the kid?

"I'm not a mechanic," he admitted. "At least not professionally. I'm a lieutenant in the United States Army, currently assigned to Special Forces."

Craig's eyes rounded. "You're a Green Beret?"

"Yeah, I am." He peered at Craig closely. "Do you have a problem with that?"

"Heck, no. Green Berets are awesome. They're like superninjas. They can do anything."

Chuckling, Sam shook his head. "Not quite everything."

"Aunt Leah's gonna blow a gasket, though. She hates the Army."

"Yeah, I know," Sam said miserably.

"So when are you going to tell her?"

Sam turned his face to the passenger window. "Soon," he promised. "Just waiting on the right time."

"I'll go with you to tell her if you want."

Sam glanced at the kid, surprised by the offer. "You'd do that?"

Craig shrugged. "Only fair. You went to the principal's office with me."

Leah grabbed Craig's face and held it between her hands. "Just look at you! You cut off all your hair!"

Scowling, he wriggled free. "Yeah. Mom took me to the barbershop yesterday. Guess what?" he said, his face brightening.

"What?"

"I drove Sam's truck."

"You *what?*" she cried, then looked at Sam for confirmation.

He shrugged. "Country road. No traffic. It was safe."

"And I didn't wreck it or anything," Craig said proudly.

Leah sputtered a laugh. "Well, thank heaven for that."

He turned to Sam, his face flushed with excitement. "How long before you think the Mustang's ready to drive?"

"Couple of days. By the weekend at the latest."

Leah's stomach knotted, realizing what that meant. Once the Mustang was finished, there would be no reason for Sam to stay.

Numbed by the thought, she turned away. "I don't know that you're ready for the Mustang just yet," she said to Craig.

"Sure I am! Tell her, Sam. I drove really good, didn't I?"

Chuckling, Sam ruffled Craig's hair. "Yeah, you did good."

"What'd I tell you?" Craig said to Leah. "And if I can handle Sam's big truck, the Mustang oughta be a piece of cake."

"We'll see," she said vaguely.

The familiar beep-beep of Patrice's car horn

sounded from outside. "There's your mom," she said to Craig. "Hurry and get your things."

Craig scooped his backpack from the kitchen table and raced for the door. "Wait till I tell her I drove Sam's truck. She's gonna flip out for sure!"

The back door slammed behind Craig, leaving Leah and Sam alone in the kitchen.

Though Leah wanted to put her head down and weep at the thought of Sam leaving, she pasted on a cheerful smile. "Well, you certainly made his day."

Sam lifted a shoulder. "He deserved a treat for cutting off that mop of hair."

"Were you behind that, too?"

He shrugged again. "I might've planted the seed."

"You've been a tremendous influence on him. I don't know how to thank you for all you've done."

"No thanks needed. He's a good kid."

Afraid if she didn't do something she would drop to her knees and beg him to stay, she opened the dishwasher door and began unloading the clean dishes. "Did you see his face when he left? I haven't seen him that excited or happy in ages."

"Doesn't take much to make a kid happy."

She stretched to place a stack of plates in the cupboard. "He used to be such a happy guy. Laughing all the time. I'd forgotten what it was like to see him smile."

"Leah—"

Something in his voice told her she didn't want to hear what he had to say, and she cut him off. "I can't believe you're almost finished with the Mustang."

"Still needs to be painted. You'll have to find someone local to do that for you. Leah, I need to—"

She closed the dishwasher door and turned for the refrigerator. "I'll bet your hungry. I know I am. I think there's some salad left from last night. I could toss in some grilled chicken and maybe some feta cheese—"

He caught her arm and turned her around, forcing her to meet his gaze. "Leah," he said firmly. "We need to talk."

His expression was so somber, his tone so serious, she wanted to clap her hands over her ears to keep from hearing whatever it was he wanted to say.

Instead she sat down at the table. "If it's about you leaving…" she began, hoping that broaching the subject herself would take some of the sting out of him saying it.

He shook his head and took the seat opposite hers. "No. It isn't that."

She looked at him in puzzlement. "Is something wrong?"

"Would you do me a favor?" He stretched out a hand. "Would you hold my hand?"

She laughed nervously. "Sam, you're scaring me. What's this all about?"

"Just hold my hand. Please."

Gulping, she placed her hand over his palm.

He curved his fingers around hers, gripped them tightly. "I haven't been totally honest with you."

Stunned, she tried to pull her hand free, but he tightened his grip, refusing to let her go.

"Please, hear me out."

She jutted her chin, knowing she had no other choice. "All right."

"I'm not a mechanic."

She stared, then laughed. "Don't be ridiculous. Of course you're a mechanic! I've seen you work on the car."

"You don't have to be a mechanic to know how to fix a car."

Her smile slowly faded and she searched his face, waiting for him to laugh, to tell her he was pulling her leg, that this was all some huge joke. But his expression remained somber, his blue eyes steady on hers.

"But...why?" she asked. "Why would you lie?"

He lowered his gaze and stroked a thumb across the back of her hand. "Because I knew you'd send me packing if you knew who I really am."

Her eyes widened in alarm. "You're not Sam Forrester?"

His lips curved in a wan smile. "Sam I am. It's the rest I kept from you."

Her mind whirled with questions, a thousand possibilities, but she couldn't bring herself to voice a single one.

"If you'll remember, I told you I had taken a sabbatical, to consider a career change."

"Is that what this is about?" she asked hopefully. "You've decided what you want to do?"

He shook his head. "To be honest, I've been so caught up in your life I haven't given much thought to my own."

Guilt stabbed at her. "I'm sorry. I didn't mean to drag you into my family's problems."

"I'm not sorry. In fact, I've enjoyed being here with you. Getting to know you and Craig. The thing is, Leah, I don't want to leave."

Her eyes widened in surprise.

He grasped her hand between both of his. "I told you I was from Lampasas, and that's true...to an extent. Lampasas is where I grew up, but I don't have a home there." He snorted a wry breath. "Hell, I don't have a home at all, which is one of the reasons I took the sabbatical."

His expression softened and he gave her hand a squeeze.

"Then I met you. I know we haven't known each other all that long, but I've grown to...care for you and I'd like the chance to play that out, see where it leads."

Leah swallowed hard, unsure how much of her own feelings to reveal. "I'd like that, too."

He lowered his gaze to their joined hands, tapped his thumb against hers. "There's just one problem. More than one, really."

"If it's because I'm so obsessive about everything—" she said quickly, fearing that was the reason behind his reluctance to make a commitment.

He shook his head. "No. I can live with your analyzing." He lifted his head and met her gaze. "I've looked death in the face more times than I care to think about, but I've never been as scared as I am right now."

Aware of the tremble in his hands, the uncertainty that shadowed his eyes, she didn't doubt for a second that what he said was true. "I don't understand. What is there to be scared of?"

"Losing you."

"Oh, Sam," she said, her heart melting. "Why would you think you could lose me?"

"Because I'm a soldier."

She froze, praying that she had misunderstood. "Did you say…soldier?"

At his nod, she shot to her feet, this time succeeding in pulling her hand from his. "No," she said, backing away. "No. No. No."

He stood and reached for her. "Leah."

She jerked away. "No! I won't go through this again. I can't."

"Leah, please."

"No!" she cried. "I lost my father and brother. I won't go through that again. I can't. The waiting, the worrying. Fearing that every time the doorbell rings it's a chaplain coming to deliver bad news." She shook her head. "I can't do that. I won't. Not even for you."

Sam stuffed his spare boots into the duffel, zipped the bag closed, then reared back and hurled the duffel against the door. He was mad. Good and damn mad. And, as the old saying went, he was getting the hell out of Dodge.

He'd known going in what Leah's reaction would be when he told her what he did for a living…but knowing how she'd react and living the experience were two entirely different matters.

She had hurt him, dammit. For the first time in his life he'd offered a woman his heart, and she'd drop-kicked it back into his face.

And all because he was a soldier, a man who loved his country, was willing to fight for it, lay down his life in the name of freedom.

Well, to hell with her, he told himself as he stormed to the bathroom to collect his shaving kit. If she wanted to live the rest of her days in fear of what *might* happen, so be it. He wasn't going to sit around crying in his beer over a woman who'd allow a tragic past to twist her up so much emotionally she was afraid to live.

To hell with her, he thought again. There were other fish in the sea. Leah Kittrell wasn't the only single woman left in the world.

Groaning, he sagged down on the bed and dropped his face to his hands. Who was he trying to kid? he asked himself miserably. She may not be the only woman left in the world, but she was the only one who mattered to him.

With a sigh, he dragged his hands down his face and braced his arms on his thighs, trying to think what to do. Attempting to talk to her again would be a waste of time. No amount of reasoning was going to change her feelings about the military. She'd spent too many years building her wall of resentment for him to have a hope of knocking it down in the time he had left.

Four days and he had to report back to headquarters. And he had only a day, two at the most, of work left to do on the car. Not enough time to undo all the damage losing her family had done to her.

But he could keep his end of their agreement, he told himself. He'd finish the car, thus fulfilling her brother's promise to Craig.

Rising, he crossed to his duffel and picked it up.

But in return, Leah was going to help him fulfill a promise.

The one he'd made to Mack.

* * *

The sun was barely up when Sam lifted the hood of the Mustang and began work on the engine. He'd been at it for nearly two hours when he heard the kitchen door open and knew it was Leah leaving for work.

He'd thought she would ignore him, climb into her SUV and drive away without acknowledging his presence.

Instead she marched straight toward him.

"You don't need to concern yourself with the car any longer," she said coolly. "I'll find someone else to finish the job."

If she'd slapped him, she couldn't have hurt him any more.

He straightened to face her. "You said you wanted to fulfill your brother's promise to restore the Mustang for Craig and hired me for the job. I finish what I start. And I intend to see that your brother's promise is met."

She opened her mouth, then closed it with a click of teeth and spun away.

Sam grabbed her arm and spun her back around. "You never asked me why I came here."

She snatched free, her eyes snapping with anger. "And listen to another lie? Sorry. I've heard all the lies I want to hear from you."

He bit down on his temper, determined to tell her

whether she wanted to hear it or not. "I came at the request of a friend. His wife's father served with yours in Vietnam."

She jerked up her chin. "I don't care why you came. Your leaving is all that interests me."

"Then I can put your mind at rest. I'll be pulling out as soon as I finish the car. But I'm taking something with me, when I go."

She eyed him suspiciously. "W-what?"

"I promised Mack I'd get the information he wanted. His wife has a torn piece of paper her father sent her mother while he was in Vietnam. Addy thinks your father might have sent your mother a similar piece."

She sucked in a shocked breath at the mention of Addy's name. "Addy McGruder?"

"Yeah, the lady you refused to talk to on the phone, the one whose letters you never answered. Unlike you, she cares about her father and wants to resolve the mystery surrounding his life."

She flinched at the accusation, then jutted her chin. "I was two years old when my father was in Vietnam, too young to read whatever letters he sent my mother."

"That may be, but your mother read them. Probably kept them, too. Addy says the pieces of paper, when combined, might have some value. She doesn't care about the money. She only wants to add another piece to the puzzle in hopes of discovering what it was her father went to such lengths to see that she received."

She hesitated a moment, and he was sure that she was going to agree to give him the information he needed.

Instead she turned for her car.

"Tell your friend I'm sorry," she called over her shoulder, "but I can't help her."

He swore under his breath at her stubbornness, then shouted, "Can't or won't?"

She stumbled a step, then squared her shoulders and strode on.

Sam's cell phone rang. Since his hands were full, pouring oil into the crankcase, he said to Craig, "Get that, would you?"

"Sure."

Craig plucked the cell phone from the holder at Sam's waist and punched the connect button. "Sam's personal secretary," he wisecracked.

Chuckling, Sam shook his head while Craig listened to the caller's response.

Craig snatched the phone from his ear and shoved it at Sam. "It's some mean-sounding dude," he whispered. "Says it's a matter of national security."

Sam dropped the oil stick and swore when it dropped down into the engine.

"I'll get it," Craig offered and bumped the phone against Sam's arm. "You better see what he wants."

Mindful of the oil that slicked his hands, Sam gingerly lifted the phone to hold between his shoulder and ear while he pulled a rag from his back pocket. "Forrester," he said curtly, then chuckled when he recognized Jack's voice.

"Your timing sucks," he said to his friend. "I'm hip-deep in a Mustang's engine."

He listened a moment, then caught the phone and held it closer to his ear, his amusement fading. "Say that again."

He listened intently while Jack repeated his findings. "Are they sending in a team?" he asked.

"What do you mean, 'That's the good part'?" he said, in response to Jack's reply.

He sank weakly against the Mustang, bracing his hips against the grill. "Yeah," he said drily after Jack explained. "That's ironic, all right. Guess I better call headquarters and find out when I'm scheduled to leave."

"Yeah, me, too," he said to Jack's wish that he could go along for the ride. "But desk jockeys aren't allowed in the field, remember?"

Smiling, he nodded. "Yeah, yeah. I've heard that story before."

He listened again, then shook his head. "No, I haven't made a decision yet." He glanced down as

Craig scooted from beneath the Mustang, the oil stick in hand. Noticing the stricken look on the boy's face, he said to Jack, "Listen. I gotta go. Appreciate your help, buddy. Next time I'm in D.C. I'll buy you a beer."

He disconnected the call and pushed the phone back into the holster at his waist, then extended a hand and pulled Craig to his feet.

His eyes fixed on Sam's, Craig asked hesitantly, "You're leaving?"

Sam dropped his chin to his chest. "Yeah. Looks that way."

"But what about the car? You haven't got it running yet."

Sam heard the panic in the kid's voice and knew it was more than the car he was worried about. He slung an arm around the boy's shoulder. "It will be by morning. You can bank on that."

Sam figured it was an indication of a masochistic side of his personality he wasn't aware of, but he felt it only right that he should let Leah know that he was leaving in the morning.

Since he no longer considered it appropriate to use the key she had given him, he knocked on the kitchen door, then waited for her response.

He didn't have to wait long.

"What do you want?" she asked curtly through the small crack she'd made in the opening.

He stuck his hands in his pockets to keep himself from shoving the door wide and shaking some sense into her. "Just wanted to let you know I'll be leaving in the morning. I'll strip the bed and do the laundry before I go. The keys to the apartment and the house will be on the kitchen table."

There was a long stretch of silence in which Sam held his breath, silently praying that it was a sign that she regretted the things she'd said, might even be about to beg him to stay.

His hopes were dashed when she said, "Fine," and closed the door in his face.

Leah knelt before her bedroom window, her gaze on the canopy below. Sam had hung lights on each of the poles supporting the covering, directing their beams on the Mustang. Though it was dark, the lights gave Leah a clear view of the canopy and the immediate area around it. But the canopy's canvas blocked her view of Sam.

She glanced at the illuminated dial of her wrist-watch and saw that it was three in the morning. She turned her gaze back to the window, unable to believe he was still outside working. She supposed when he'd told her he finished what he started, that, at least, hadn't been a lie.

She felt the swell of tears and bit her lip, willing them back. A soldier, she thought, balling her hand into a fist against the sill. Of all the men in the world to choose from, why did she have to fall in love with a soldier?

She heard the whine of an engine cranking and held her breath, waiting for it to catch. The sound stopped, started again. Stopped, started again. When it caught, the powerful roar of the engine filled the night, then settled to a low hum.

She smiled through her tears, remembering that sound and the long nights Kevin had spent as a teenager doing exactly what Sam was doing now. Revving the engine, letting it idle to listen to the purr, revving it again. *Boys and their toys,* she had teased Kevin.

But Kevin had been determined to make the car run again. It was if he'd believed that in doing so he could bring their father back to life, too.

Sighing, she propped her chin on her arms on the windowsill. Their mother wasn't the only one who'd never given up hope on their father returning home. That same hope had burned in Kevin, too.

Seven

When Leah returned home from work, her gaze settled on the two keys sitting on the center of the table. He was gone. Sam had really left her.

Feeling the swell of tears, she set her jaw and turned away, dropping her briefcase over the top of the keys to block them from sight. "Craig?" she called. "Where are you?"

"In here," he yelled.

Prepared to deliver a lecture if he was watching television without having completed his homework assignments, she strode to the den.

She found him sitting on the floor in front of the

bookcases. "What are you doing?" she asked in puzzlement as she squatted down beside him.

He lifted an opened book from his lap. Her stomach knotted when she saw that he was holding the family photo album.

"Look at this," he said and plopped the book on his lap again to point. "It's a picture of Dad standing beside the Mustang."

She gulped but eased closer. She remembered when the picture was taken. It was the day Kevin had registered the Mustang and received the new set of license plates making the vehicle legal to drive. He'd spent months working on the car, putting it back in running condition and doing the repairs required to pass state inspection. His pride was obvious in the swell of his chest, the smile on his face. He'd been seventeen at the time and obsessed by the memory of a father he'd never known.

She sank down beside Craig and draped an arm along his shoulders. "You look like him," she said softly.

He turned his head to peer at her. "You think so?"

Smiling, she brushed back his much shorter bangs from his forehead. "Yes, I do. Sometimes when I look at you, it's like seeing him at your age."

A slow smile spread across his face. "Really? Cool." He dropped his gaze to study the picture again. "See that?" he asked, pointing to a dent on the Mustang's rear panel. "That's not there anymore. Sam took it out. Used this giant suction cup. Said if it had been any deeper, a body shop would've had to do the work because it would require filling and sanding."

She gulped back emotion at the mention of Sam. "Yes, I would imagine it would."

He turned to peer at her. "He's gone, you know."

She swallowed hard. "Yeah, I know."

"He left me a note."

Pain pierced her heart at the thoughtfulness in the gesture. She wanted to ask what Sam had written in the note, if he had mentioned her, but said instead, "That's nice."

"He's going to Vietnam."

Stunned, for a moment she could only stare. "How do you know where he is going?"

"Sam told me. And get this—he's on a secret mission to recover MIAs."

She closed her eyes, afraid if she didn't she would shatter into a thousand pieces.

"He's hoping he'll find my grandfather."

She flipped open her eyes. "Your grandfather is *dead*," she said furiously.

He drew back, with a frown. "I know that. But his body was never found. That's why he doesn't have a grave like Grandma's."

She surged to her feet. "He doesn't have a grave

because your grandmother refused to accept the fact that he was dead!"

"Why are you yelling at me?" he shouted back at her. "I didn't do anything."

She dug her fingernails into her palms, fighting for calm, knowing Craig didn't deserve her anger. "I'm sorry. I didn't mean to yell."

Scowling, he slammed the book shut and shoved it back onto the shelf. "Sam was right," he grumbled as he pushed to his feet.

When he would've brushed past her, she caught his arm, stopping him. "Right about what?"

He snatched his arm free. "You're mad at everybody for dying. My dad, your dad, Grandma. You're mad at 'em all."

Leah couldn't sleep that night. She kept thinking about what Craig had said.

You're mad at everybody for dying. My dad, your dad, Grandma. You're mad at 'em all.

She wanted to deny his statement. In fact, she had spent the last six hours attempting to do just that, if only to convince herself.

But she couldn't deny it any longer. She *was* mad. At her father, her mother, her brother. Each of their deaths—in her mind, at least—had been sense-less, avoidable. If her father hadn't joined the Army, he wouldn't have been killed. If her mother had accepted her father's death, she never would have committed suicide. And if her mother had focused on meeting Kevin's needs rather than infecting her son with her own obsession, Kevin wouldn't have joined the Army and been killed in Iraq.

Whether their deaths had been avoidable or not, they were gone, and being angry with them for dying wasn't going to bring them back. She knew that…or at least she did intellectually. It was her heart she couldn't convince.

She heaved a sigh, thinking of all the years she had spent resenting her mother for clinging to the hope that her husband would come home someday. She had considered her mother's obsession foolish, misguided, an emotional sickness that kept her, as well as the rest of their family, from living a normal life.

In retrospect, Leah could see that her anger wasn't all that different from her mother's obsession. By clinging to it, she had allowed it to control her life, her actions…and, it seemed, destroy her future.

She turned her face to the pillow, ashamed of the way she'd treated Sam. She'd said such horrible things to him, insulted his choice of career, something he obviously felt strongly about. Worse, she had let him leave without telling him she cared for him, too, that, like him, she wanted a chance to let their relationship play out, see where it took them.

And all because he was a soldier.

With a groan, she rolled to her back and pressed the heels of her hands against her eyes as her mind circled back to the source of the problem: Sam's chosen career.

It didn't matter how much she cared for him. She couldn't live the life of a soldier's wife. The fear, the worry, the loneliness. She hated the military. It was the military that had destroyed her family, cutting huge chunks out of her heart, her life.

No, she'd been right in letting Sam leave without sharing her feelings with him or asking him to stay. If she had, she would've only been postponing the inevitable. She could never become seriously involved with a soldier and she certainly could never marry one. How could she when she knew that would mean living her life in fear of having what was left of her heart ripped from her chest?

She rolled from the bed. But she could do something for him, she told herself as she tugged on her robe. She could return at least a part of the kindness he'd shown her. She could help him keep his promise to Mack.

She didn't know if the piece of paper he'd mentioned existed, but she knew where to look.

Leah stood in the doorway of the attic, staring at the tower of mismatched boxes that lined one wall. The sight alone was enough to make her skin crawl, as they represented her mother's obsession. Crammed inside the boxes was every document, report or newspaper clipping printed about the POWs and MIAs from the Vietnam war. Pictures and souvenirs her father had sent home. The hundreds of letters he'd written to her mother.

After her mother's death, she'd intended to throw the entire mess away, had even carried one load to the curb for the garbage service to pick up. But when she'd returned with the second, she'd discovered she couldn't do it, couldn't throw her mother's dreams away. So she'd loaded up the boxes and brought them to her home to store in her attic.

And there they'd remained, undisturbed for the past six years.

She had never opened the boxes, never had a desire to explore their contents. She knew what was inside. Throughout her life she had watched her mother build her stash, filling box after box with her dreams, her hopes. Sometimes she'd find her mother sifting through the contents, tears streaming down her face; at others she'd be digging through them with a frenetic frenzy, as if the key to locating her husband was buried inside and she had only to find it.

Taking a bracing breath, Leah forced herself to approach the wall of boxes and scanned the scrawled words on their fronts until she found the one marked *Letters*. She carried the box to the center of the room and knelt down, placing it on the floor in front of her and folding back the flaps.

She balled her hand into a fist to still her fingers' trembling, then reached inside and pulled out a handful of envelopes. Giving in to her need for order, she sat down and, using her lap for a desk, began to sort them by the postal dates stamped on the front. She tensed when her own name seemed to leap at her from the front of an envelope. Unlike the other letters, where the addresses were written in cursive, this one was penned in a first-grader's print, each letter standing alone. She blinked back tears, knowing that he'd written it that way especially for her.

Anxious to read what he'd written, she dashed the tears away and pulled out the single page tucked inside.

Hi, pumpkin!
How's my little girl doing today? Daddy sure misses you. I hope you're taking good care of Mommy. I really liked the picture you drew of her. Her belly is really getting big! I'll bet you grow up to be an artist someday.

Mommy tells me you don't want a little sister, only a little brother. Well, I hate to tell you this, pumpkin, but you don't get to choose. God decides whether our baby will be a boy or a girl. Since He knows best, we'll love whatever He sends us. Right?

Every night before I go to sleep I pull out the picture of you and Mommy I carry in my pocket and tell you good night. Do you hear me when I say it? I hear you saying it back to me. And when I put the picture against my cheek I can feel your sweet good-night kisses.

I bet you've grown a foot since I saw you last. Tell Mommy to put a rock on your head so that you won't grow any more, okay?

You be a good girl and take care of Mommy for me. I miss you, baby, and I can't wait to see you again.

Love,
Daddy

Choked by tears, Leah stared at the words he'd written, sensing his loneliness, overwhelmed by the love that all but poured from the page. Pressing the letter against her heart, she closed her eyes, trying to draw an image of him in her mind. She had no memories to pull from, only the photographs her mother had kept scattered around their home. She was too young to recall the things he'd mentioned in the letter—kissing him good-night, him calling her "pumpkin." But it was obvious that he'd remembered and had treasured those memories while he'd been away, in order to keep her close to his heart.

Guilt seized her, a shame that sliced to the marrow of her bones. He'd clung to her memory while she'd done everything humanly possible to block his.

Not any longer, she told herself and scooped up the letters, stuffed them back into the box. Lifting it, she stood and stumbled her way downstairs, then returned for the box of pictures and souvenirs.

Her movements were frantic as she pulled item after item from the boxes, determined to get to know the man she'd spent a lifetime shunning.

"Aunt Leah?"

She jumped at the sound of Craig's voice, then called, "In here!" and went back to her sorting.

"Are you sick or something?"

She glanced up and saw the concern in his eyes. "No, sweetheart. I'm fine. Why?"

"It's almost noon and you've still got on your pajamas."

She looked down and sputtered a laugh, not realizing until that moment that she'd never bothered to get dressed. From the moment she'd hauled the last box to her den she had thought of nothing else but the box's contents.

She cleared a spot on the carpet. "Come and help me."

He dropped down beside her. "What are you doing?"

"Getting to know my father."

He looked at her warily. "Are you sure you're not sick?"

Laughing, she gave him a hug. "No. I'm perfectly fine. In fact, I've never felt better."

"If you say so," he said doubtfully.

She picked up a pile of letters and dumped them in his lap. "We're on a treasure hunt," she told him and picked up another stack for herself to examine.

"Treasure?"

"Yes. A torn piece of paper. I don't know what it looks like or what it is exactly, but I know it's got to be here somewhere."

"A torn piece of paper," he repeated doubtfully.

"Yes. Sam told me about it. That's why he came here. To find it."

He picked up an envelope from those scattered on his lap. "Is the piece of paper a clue or something he needs to find the MIAs in Vietnam?"

Busy shaking the pages of the letter she held, she shook her head. "No. This is something that my dad sent home to my mother while he was in Vietnam. Sam says it may be valuable."

"Is that why he wants it? Because it's worth money?"

She tossed aside the letter and picked up another.

"No. It's actually a friend of his who wants it. Or rather, his friend's wife. Her father served in the same unit as my dad. She has a piece of paper, too. It's like a puzzle we have to put together."

"Cool!"

Obviously excited at the prospect of finding treasure, he shook out the envelope's contents, examined the pages, tossed them aside, grabbed another.

Leah picked up a letter but frowned when she noticed that the handwriting on the front was different from the others. Curious, she pulled out the letter enclosed and began to scan. She'd read only two lines when she flung out a hand and grabbed Craig's arm. "Listen to this," she said in disbelief, then read,

"Dear Helen,
We've never met, but I would imagine your husband has mentioned me a time or two. My name is Larry Blair—or Pops, as the guys in our unit call me. T.J. made me promise that I'd write to you if anything should happen to him. It grieves me that I have to keep that promise now, but I can't let T.J. down. I gave him my word.

The day before T.J. was shot, we lost a guy in our unit. Buddy Crandall. We were caught in a battle we couldn't win and had

decided to make a run for it. Several of our men went down prior to the decision being made. We managed to drag two of them out with us, but we couldn't get to Buddy. We knew he was dead and there was nothing we could do for him, but it broke our hearts to leave a friend behind. T.J. took it particularly hard.

The next morning, when the chopper came to retrieve the bodies, T.J.'s thoughts were on Buddy's family. He knew, we all did, that since Buddy's body wasn't recovered, he would be listed as Missing in Action rather than as Killed in Action. That bothered T.J., as he was worried about Buddy's family and how not having him to bury would affect them. It was then that T.J. made me promise to write this letter should the same thing happen to him.

I saw T.J. go down. You don't need to know the details of how he died. I can spare you that much pain. But please know that he fought bravely to the bitter end. And know, too, that if it had been within our power, we would have brought T.J. back with us. He'd have done the same for any one of the rest of us, and we would've done it for him if it had been possible. No soldier ever wants to leave a friend on the field.

*Along with this letter, I send you my heart-
felt sympathy, as well as that of the rest of our
unit. T.J. was a good man, a good friend and
was never shy about telling us how much he
loved his family.*
Sincerely,
Larry Blair"

Leah sat in silence, staring down at the handwrit-
ten words, unable to believe her mother had continued to hope her husband would come after having
read Larry Blair's letter.

"I don't get it."

Having forgotten about Craig, Leah reached to
squeeze his hand. "What, sweetheart?"

"Why would Grandma keep telling everybody
he was going to come home when the letter proves
he was dead?"

She gulped back tears and shook her head.
"Hope. She loved him too much to give up believing he'd come home someday."

"That's just stupid," Craig muttered and picked
up another envelope to examine.

They worked together for almost an hour before
Craig let out a whoop.

"I found it!" he cried.

Leah dropped the letter she was reading and
stared. "Are you sure?"

"It has to be." He examined the piece of paper closely. "There's words on it, but they don't make any sense."

He pushed the paper at Leah. "See if you can figure it out."

Afraid it would crumble if handled overmuch, Leah laid the scrap of paper on the floor in front of her. "Doesn't make sense to me either," she murmured as she studied the partial words fragmented by the tears. Frowning, she turned the piece of paper over. "But that's my father's signature."

She popped to her feet. "Call your mother. Tell her that you're going on a little trip with me."

He jumped up, too, to run after her. "Where are we going?"

"To fulfill a promise Sam made to his friend."

Leah smiled as she watched Craig play with the baby. Stretched out on his stomach on the floor, he lay head-to-head with the infant, spinning dials and punching buttons on a learning toy to make the baby laugh.

"Careful, Craig," she warned as he tried to persuade the baby to push one of the buttons. "Remember, he's just a baby."

She started to rise to intervene, and Mack placed a hand on her arm, stopping her. "Leave 'em be. They're doing fine."

PEGGY MORELAND

"Are you sure?" she asked doubtfully. "Craig's never been around a baby before."

"They aren't as fragile as they look."

A shrill squeal had Leah whipping her head back to the two, her heart in her throat.

Mack chuckled. "That's Johnny Mack's newest form of expression. Means he's having a good time."

Leah sank back weakly against the sofa. "If you say so."

"Craig's good with babies. Most boys his age would be bored to death by now."

She smiled sadly as she watched Craig dab a cloth at the drool on the infant's chin. "He always wanted a brother or sister."

"Sam told me about your brother. I'm sorry for your loss."

Her heart twisted at the mention of Sam, then twisted again at the thought of Kevin. "Thank you. Losing him was hard on us all. Especially Craig."

Mack turned his gaze to study Craig. "He seems to be doing okay. Kids are tough. Resilient. He'll come out of this okay."

She glanced his way. "You sound so sure."

He smiled and patted her knee. "The voice of experience."

She stared, remembering the stories Sam had told her about his wild friend and the half brother who was responsible for turning Sam's life around. "You're Ty's half brother?"

He lifted a brow. "You know Ty?"

She shook her head. "No. Sam told me about him. How you were always bailing the two of them out of trouble."

"Still am. Or was," he amended.

Understanding the defeat she heard in his voice, she laid a hand over his. "You may have failed with Ty, but you certainly made an impression on Sam. He credits you with saving his life."

He smiled fondly. "Sam was a good kid. A little wild, but he had a good heart. His parents are to blame for the problems he had. They were so busy fighting they forgot they had a son to raise."

Leah glanced at Craig, knowing that her nephew suffered similarly. His mother was so consumed with her own grief she never recognized that her son was grieving, too, and needed her comfort. As a result, he'd looked for attention elsewhere and found it with a group of thugs.

But she'd seen a change in him recently, she reminded herself. He laughed more, showed more enthusiasm for life, stayed closer to home rather than hanging out with his friends. "Thanks to Sam," she murmured, knowing it was Sam who was responsible for the difference.

"Excuse me?"

She glanced at Mack and dropped her gaze, embarrassed that she'd spoken her thoughts out loud. "Sorry. I was thinking about Sam, the difference he's made in Craig's life." She looked up at Mack. "It's because of you. What you did for Sam, Sam did for Craig."

"What goes around, comes around," Mack stated prophetically, then smiled. "Sam was always hanging around our house. He was like a brother to me. I worried about him." He shook his head sadly. "In fact, I still do."

Her stomach knotted, remembering where Sam was, what he was doing. The danger he might be in. "I wish he hadn't gone."

He gave her knee a reassuring pat. "He'll be all right. Sam knows how to take care of himself." He shook his head. "But I wasn't talking about his profession. Sam's struggling with a decision right now. Trying to decide whether to take a desk job or remain in the field. It's a tough one for a man like him to make. He's not one to sit on his hands. When he sees a problem, he'd rather be in on the action to resolve it than sitting in a meeting discussing it."

"Then why is he considering changing?" Leah asked in confusion.

"Sam could probably explain that best." He opened his hands. "I've never had any military experience, so I don't know that I completely understand it myself. But from what Sam has told me, it seems if a man remains in the field too long, he begins to lose his edge, take unnecessary chances. It becomes a game to him, one in which he's constantly raising the stakes in order to achieve the same adrenalin high."

Leah stared, wondering if that was why Kevin had volunteered for duty in Iraq. He'd enlisted in the service shortly after his eighteenth birthday and had remained in the Army until his death. His assignments had taken him all over the world. Korea. The Philippines. Japan.

Had he grown bored? she wondered. Was that why he'd requested a tour in Iraq? Was it the danger he'd sought and not the need to prove something, as she'd always believed?

She gulped, unsure of the answer.

"But I think there's more bothering Sam than just a career decision," Mack went on to say. "I believe he's questioning his life right now. His lack of roots. Lack of family. He's thirty-four years old, an age when most men have settled down with a wife, a home and one-point-five children.

"He's had an exciting life, traveled the world. But I think he's beginning to realize there's something missing, something only a family can provide."

He tipped his head to peer down at Leah. "I thought he'd found that with you. From the things he told me, I was sure that he'd finally found the woman who made him want to settle down, quit thumbing his nose at danger. Was I wrong?"

She dropped her gaze. "I care for Sam. I do. But I'm not cut out to be a soldier's wife. I couldn't stand living with the fear that he might not come home someday. I've lost two people I love to the service. I won't lose any more."

"Where did they go?"

She looked up at him in confusion. "My father and brother?"

"No, your feelings for Sam. Did he take them with him when he left? Did you flush them down the toilet? Throw them in the trash?"

She drew back with a frown, wondering if he'd lost his mind. "Of course not. I still care for him."

"Then what does it matter if he's with you or halfway around the world? If you love him, you'll feel the loss either way."

Eight

After completing his ten-day mission in Vietnam, Sam flew directly to Washington, D.C., where he was to meet with his commander and file his report. If he'd had his way, the plane would've flown directly to Texas. Specifically Tyler, Texas. The pilot wouldn't even have had to worry about landing. Sam would've jumped to save himself the time a landing would've required.

Soon enough, he promised himself and forced himself to concentrate on the report he was giving.

"Four bodies recovered, possibly more," he told his commander. "The lab guys can verify the

number and provide names, depending on the avail-
ability of dental records and possibly DNA."

"So our contact was correct in telling us we'd
find bodies in that location."

"Yes, sir," Sam confirmed. He folded his beret
and laid it across his thigh. "The local officials were
cooperative. Not helpful," he clarified. "But they
didn't attempt to obstruct our examination of the
area in question."

The commander nodded solemnly. "The best
we can expect under the circumstances." He
frowned, considering. "Any chance more bodies
were buried there?"

"In that particular location?"

The commander nodded.

"I suppose it's possible, but our search was
methodic and the equipment we used was the best
technology has to offer. I don't see how we
could've missed finding anything more than what
we brought home."

The commander gave his chin a decisive nod.
"Your opinion is good enough for me. Your record
speaks for itself. You're thorough and have the reputation of sticking with a task to its end. Which
brings up another subject." Rearing back in his
chair, the commander templed his fingers before his
chest and studied Sam over their tips. "Your reen-
listment. Have you made your decision concerning
your assignment?"

"Yes, sir, I have."

When Sam offered nothing more, the commander said impatiently, "Well? Do you plan to share your decision or keep it to yourself?"

"I've put in sixteen years, sir, and I think it's time I returned to civilian life."

"I'm sorry to hear that," the commander said with regret. "Our country needs good men like you."

"Thank you, sir. I've enjoyed my time in the service, and I'm grateful for the knowledge and experience I've gained. Hopefully I'll be able to find a way to continue to serve my country as a civilian."

"I'm sure you will. If I can be of assistance in helping you find your calling, let me know."

"Thank you, sir."

The commander stood, signaling the end of the meeting. "So where are you headed now?"

Sam stood, too. "Home, sir. To Texas." He hesitated a moment, knowing the favor he was about to ask broke protocol and probably every other military regulation.

"Something on your mind, Forrester?" the commander asked.

Sam nodded slowly. "Yes, sir, there is. One of the sets of dog tags found belonged to the father of a friend of mine. I'd appreciate it if you would allow me to personally deliver them to her and give her the news that her father's body was recovered."

The commander squared his shoulders. "You know as well as I do that information is considered classified until the bodies have been positively ID'd."

"Yes, sir, I do. But this family's suffering exceeds those normally associated with an MIA. They need closure, and I would like to be the one to give it to them."

"I'm sorry, Forrester, but I can't allow that. Everything that was collected during the exhumation was shipped directly to the lab for identification."

Sam ducked his head. "Uh, not everything, sir. I have the dog tags that were collected. Each set was bagged on-site and properly marked with location and placed in my pack for safekeeping."

"Your orders were to collect all items found during the exhumation and escort them home in the container provided."

Sam felt a trickle of sweat work its way down his spine, knowing what he'd done had defied a direct order and could result in a reprimand...or worse, if the commander chose to pursue it.

"Yes, sir. I'm aware of that. But considering the sensitive nature of our findings and the hostility that still surrounds our presence in some areas of Vietnam, I thought it best to keep the tags on my person."

Scowling, the commander rounded his desk and

walked with Sam to the door. "Those tags are the property of the United States Army and fall under its jurisdiction. I order you to turn them over to proper authorities ASAP."

All hope of presenting Leah with the closure she needed drained from Sam. "Yes, sir. I'll take care of it as soon I leave this office."

The commander stopped at the doorway and shot Sam a sideways glance. "You said four bodies were found?"

"As best as we could determine. Possibly more."

"And how many sets of tags were recovered?"

"Three."

"Were the tags positioned in such a way that you were able to determine which body each belonged to?"

"Yes, sir. Without question. We digitally recorded each find before moving so much as a grain of sand."

"So if a set of tags were to disappear or become lost, it wouldn't effect the results of your mission or lessen the chances of identifying the bodies?"

A smile began to spread across Sam's face as he realized what the commander was trying to tell him. "No, sir. Not at all."

Leah had thought she would feel better after giving a copy of the torn piece of paper to Addy

McGruder—Mack's wife—thus fulfilling Sam's promise to his friend…as well as the request he'd made of Leah. But, if anything, her trip to Lampasas had left her feeling more miserable and confused than ever.

It wasn't that she hadn't liked Sam's friends. She'd enjoyed visiting with the McGruders, and Craig had had a ball playing with their baby, which had been an unexpected bonus for him.

The cause of her discontent was something Mack had said, a question he'd posed while Addy had been preparing their dinner.

Then what does it matter if he's with you or halfway around the world? If you love him, you'll feel the loss either way.

She had wanted to rail at him, tell him that it *did* matter, that he had no right to make such a statement when he'd never suffered as she had.

Thankfully she had bitten her tongue and kept her opinion to herself, which had turned out to be a good thing, as she'd learned later from Addy that Mack had lost his first wife and his son in a car wreck.

Knowing Mack had suffered similarly hadn't diminished her own grief, but it had made her think.

She loved Sam. She didn't doubt her feelings for him for a minute. And she missed him. Oh, God, how she missed him. But as hard as she had tried, she couldn't think of a way for them to be together and both of them be happy.

No closer to a resolution than she had been two weeks earlier, when she'd made the trip to Lampasas, she opened another one of the boxes she'd hauled down from the attic. She'd decided to go through each and every one, catalog its contents and repackage it in something more substantial than the ragged boxes her mother had kept the material in.

She shook her head sadly at her mother's harum-scarum filing system. After days of attempting to find some method to her mother's madness, she'd finally given up and decided to develop her own. She glanced around the room at the reams of paper stacked on every available surface and sputtered a laugh. Of course, she'd destroyed her den in the process. It seemed Leah, the queen of organization, had finally toppled from her thrown.

Hearing the kitchen door open, she picked up a stack of papers and carried them to the pile marked *MIA Reports, 1986–1989,* knowing it was Craig coming to help her.

"In here, Craig," she called, then added, "And bring me a soda, will you? I'm dying of thirst."

She thumbed through the documents, scanning the dates on each, then braced a knee against the stack to support it, while she wedged the papers she held into the proper order.

"Would you settle for a lemonade?"

She whirled, and the stack toppled over, papers sliding to cover the floor. Sam stood less than ten feet away, a glass of lemonade in his hand. Decked out in his dress uniform, he looked handsome, regal…intimidating.

She wanted to tell him she was sorry, that she loved him, but all that came out was a breathy, "Sam."

He held up the glass. "Sorry. No soda. Only lemonade."

She searched his face for any sign of emotion. That he'd missed her. That he loved her. But his expression remained unreadable, his eyes a cool sky-blue.

Gulping, she said, "Lemonade's fine."

He crossed to hand her the glass. She took it and had to grip it between both hands, she was shaking so much.

"When did you—"

"How are—"

They both stopped and he opened a hand. "Ladies first."

"When did you get back?"

"Yesterday." He glanced at his watch. "Or rather, today." At her confused look, he explained. "The time difference. Vietnam's a day ahead of us."

"Oh."

"How are you?"

She forced a smile. "Fine." She glanced around the room. "Busy, as you can tell by the mess."

He crossed to a chair and picked up a document from the stack piled on it. "What's all this?"

"My mother's obsession." When he glanced back at her in question, she shrugged and lifted a hand, indicating all the stacks that filled the room. "These are all the documents, reports and newspapers clippings about MIAs that she saved over the years."

He tossed the document back onto the stack. "What are you doing with it?"

"Sorting, cataloging." She laughed self-consciously. "Being my anal self."

He gave her a chiding look at the anal comment. "I meant, why is it here?"

She drew in a shuddery breath and looked around, thinking of all the discoveries she'd made since opening that first box, how the things she'd found inside had changed her.

"It was all stored in the attic. When I was looking for the piece of paper for Addy, I decided to bring it down and try to put it in some type of order."

"Did you find it?"

"Yes...or rather, Craig did. We took it to her. Craig and I. She was thrilled to have it, but I don't think it was much help."

"You went to Lampasas?" he asked in surprise.

Tears surged and she could only nod.

"But…why? When I asked you to give it to me, you refused. What changed your mind?"

She dropped her gaze and pushed a finger through the condensation on the glass. "I don't know. A lot of things, I guess. Mostly I wanted to do it for you."

"Ah, Leah."

She lifted her head, tears brimming in her eyes. "I'm so sorry, Sam. I know you must hate me for all the awful things I said."

He crossed to take the glass from her and set it aside, so that he could gather her hands in his. He gave them a squeeze. "Not a chance. I couldn't hate you if I tried."

The tears pushed higher. "You were nothing but kind to me, and the one thing you asked of me, I refused."

"It doesn't matter. Not anymore."

She tugged a hand free to drag an arm across her eyes. "I don't know how you can say that after all the mean things I said."

"It's easy to forgive someone you love."

She froze, then slowly lowered her arm to look at him. "You love me?"

Smiling, he nodded. "More than life itself." He reached into his pocket. "I have something for you."

She blinked to clear her eyes and shot them wide when he held up a chain with dog tags dangling at its end. She shifted her gaze to his. "My father's?"

He nodded, then opened her hand and let the chain snake down to pool on her palm. "I found it, along with his remains, outside the village where he was killed." He closed her fingers around the tags. "He's not missing anymore, Leah. Your father's finally coming home."

"Oh, Sam," she said tearfully and threw her arms around his neck. "Thank you. Thank you so much."

He held her tight and pressed his lips against her hair. "I wanted to give you closure, Leah. Your whole family. I just wish your mother could be here to welcome him home and give him the burial he deserves."

She shook her head. "They're together. I know they are. She loved him so much. That's why she took her life. She couldn't stand living without him any longer."

He pushed her to arm's length, his forehead pleated in a frown. "You sound like you've forgiven her, like you're not mad anymore."

She sniffed, shook her head. "Losing my dad destroyed her. Searching for him gave her something to live for. Hope, I guess. She did the best she could for Kevin and me. I realize that now. In her place, I don't know that I could've done any better. Sam—" She stopped and caught his hand, drew him to the sofa, needing its stability beneath her before she told him the rest.

When confronted with the stacks of papers that covered the sofa's cushions, she hesitated a moment, then raked them onto the floor and plopped down.

Sam stared at her in disbelief. "Did I see what I thought I just saw?"

She looked up at him in confusion. "What?"

"Did Leah Kittrell just make a *mess?*"

Pursing her lips, she tugged him down beside her. "Don't be a smart aleck. We need to talk."

"I believe I said those same words before I left for Vietnam."

"Yes, you did. But I wasn't ready to discuss it then. I am now."

He settled back. "Okay. Shoot."

She bit her lower lip, trying to think how best to tell him what she wanted to say. "We love each other," she began carefully.

"I can verify the *W* in that we."

She gave him an exasperated look, then continued. "And when two people love each other, they need to be together."

He draped an arm around her shoulders. "I couldn't agree more."

She drew back, finding it hard to concentrate with him so close. "Your job takes you all over the world, and mine is here in Tyler. I have my family. Responsibilities. I have Craig to think about it. He needs me."

"Yes, he does."

"But I want to be with you."

"And that's a bad thing?"

"No," she said in frustration. "But I can't be with you and here with my family at the same time. I told you that I hated the military, that I couldn't live my life in fear of losing you."

"And that's still true?"

She released a shuddery breath. "Yes. Sort of. But I think I can deal with it better now."

"What brought about the change?"

"Mack."

"Mack?" he repeated.

"Yes. He said something that started me thinking. He said that if I loved you, it wouldn't matter where you were. I'd feel the loss either way."

His smile soft, he swept her hair back from her face. "I always knew that man was a genius."

"You're missing the point," she said, her frustration returning.

"And that would be…?"

"That I love you and want to be with you."

He leaned to press his lips to hers. "Not a problem."

She nearly wept at the feel of his lips on hers but flattened a hand against his chest and pushed him back, refusing to let him distract her until they'd reached an agreement of some kind. "It *is* a problem," she insisted. "I can't be in two places at once."

"You don't have to be."

She filled her hands with her hair. "Sam!" she cried in frustration. "How can we fix this if you won't even admit that we have a problem?"

"Because we don't."

When she glowered at him, he only smiled.

"I resigned from the Army."

For a moment she could only stare. Then she shook her head. "No. I won't let you do that. You love the Army, your job. I won't allow you to sacrifice your happiness for mine."

"Don't you get it? Being here with you, with Craig—that's what important to me. That's what makes me happy." He cupped a hand at her face, holding her gaze to his. "I had a good run, Leah. Sixteen years. But now I want to come home. Start a family. With you, Leah."

She searched his face, afraid to believe what he was telling her, grasp what he was offering her. "Sam, are you sure?"

"As a heart attack."

With a squeal of delight, she threw her arms around his neck and hugged him tight. "Oh, Sam. I want that, too."

She kissed him, holding nothing back, desperate to show him how much she loved him, how much she needed him, what a wonderful life they would have together.

Her heart full to near bursting, she drew back to look at him…and frowned as a thought occurred to her. "But what will you do? For a job, I mean."

He teased her with a smile. "What? Afraid you'll have to support us?"

Pursing her lips, she gave his chest a push. "No. But I know you. You wouldn't be satisfied sitting around doing nothing."

"You're right. I wouldn't. I've been playing with some ideas."

"Like what?"

He pointed a stern finger at her nose. "If I tell you, you have to promise not to go ballistic on me. What I'm considering is perfectly safe."

"I'm not going to go ballistic," she said impatiently. "For heaven's sake, just tell me!"

"I'd like to work with families of POWs and MIAs to help them locate their husbands, sons and brothers."

She pressed her hand over her heart, knowing how much those families needed the closure Sam had given her. "Oh, Sam. That's wonderful."

"I've got skills to offer. Contacts, too. But I wouldn't charge for my services. Only what expenses are incurred. I've set enough back over the years that my savings will take care of our living expenses. We won't be rich by any stretch of the imagination, but we won't starve, either."

"Oh, Sam," she said tearfully. "I don't care about

being rich. All I want is for us to be together. Happy. The rest will take care of itself."

He framed her face between his hands. "Marry me, Leah. Nothing would make me happier than having you as my wife, the mother of my children."

Laughing through her tears, she wrapped her arms around him and held him tight. "Yes, yes, a thousand times yes!"

* * * * *

Look for more of Peggy Moreland's latest mini-series coming to you in Desire in 2008.

BEDDED *THEN* WED

by
Heidi Betts

Dear Reader,

There's just something about a cowboy, isn't there? As many of you probably know, I began my publishing career writing Western historical romances, each one exploring a different aspect of that great American icon – the man who wears faded jeans, dusty boots and a well-worn stetson to perfection. But even though I have since made the transition to the contemporary time period, I'd always hoped for the chance to bring those elements with me into the modern world.

Which is why I'm so excited to share with you *Bedded* Then *Wed*, my first Mills & Boon® Desire™ book with a cowboy hero. Mitch Ramsey is definitely the strong, silent type, but I think Emma Davis is just the woman to tame him. I hope you'll agree!

And if you have a moment, please drop by my website at www.HeidiBetts.com, where you can read about current and forthcoming releases, enter contests, chat with other readers on the message board and even blog with me. I'll look forward to seeing you there.

Happy reading!

Heidi Betts

HEIDI BETTS

An avid romance reader since junior school, Heidi
knew early on that she wanted to write these
wonderful stories of love and adventure. It wasn't
until her freshman year of college, however, when
she spent the entire night reading a romance
instead of studying for finals, that she decided to
take the road less travelled and follow her dream. In
addition to reading, writing and romance, she is the
founder of her local Romance Writers of America
organisation and has a tendency to take injured and
homeless animals of every species into her central
Pennsylvania home.

Heidi loves to hear from readers. You can write to
her at PO Box 99, Kylertown, PA 16847, USA (an
SAE with return postage is appreciated but not
necessary), or e-mail heidi@heidibetts.com. And
be sure to visit www.heidibetts.com for news and
information about forthcoming books.

In loving memory of my cousin,
Kathy (Stock) Mulder. A beautiful, caring soul,
taken from us much too soon.

And always, for Daddy.

One

The last, slow strains of an old Tammy Wynette song spilled from a small portable radio set up on the steps of the park's gazebo to replace the more elaborate sound system that had been used earlier that evening, and Emma Davis covered her mouth to hide another yawn.

Lord, she was exhausted. She'd spent all yesterday cooking and baking for today's Fourth of July shindig, then most of the morning helping to decorate the town square.

The Gabriel's Crossing holiday celebrations were legendary, and she was more than happy to lend a hand wherever she could. But now, at eleven o'clock at night, she was just plain exhausted. She wanted nothing more than to go home, fall into bed, and sleep for a week...or at least until noon the next day.

Unfortunately, it didn't look like she would get to do any of those things for quite some time yet.

She cast a glance over her shoulder, to where her father and three of his cronies sat at a worn card table, playing what had to be their two-dozenth hand of poker. Unlike Emma—and everyone else, who had pretty much collected their things and headed home hours ago—her father didn't seem anywhere near ready to leave.

With a soft groan, she lowered her head to where her arms rested atop the rough planks of the picnic table and closed her eyes. If she couldn't get to her own bed, then she would sleep right here. At this point, she wasn't particular.

"Need a ride home?"

The low, gravelly voice penetrated her tired brain and she lifted her head to stare up at her neighbor and one of her closest friends since childhood.

Closest friend and secret crush…or at least he had been in high school.

Oh, who was she kidding? Just looking at Mitch Ramsey, with his black-as-sin hair and gray, penetrating eyes, was enough to send the blood pumping through her veins.

A moment ago she'd been so tired she could barely put a single thought together, now she felt wide awake and ready to do the two-step…as long as Mitch was two-stepping right along with her.

When she didn't answer right away, Mitch tapped his beat-up Stetson against the side of his muscular thigh and offered her a kind smile. "Your father seems to be pretty involved in his card game, but you look about ready to drop. Why don't you let me take you home, and he can come along whenever he's ready."

My hero, she thought, and could have sworn her heart skipped a beat.

It had always been that way with Mitch…he smiled and

her belly flip-flopped. He drawled her name, and she felt it all the way down to her toes.

This wasn't the first time he'd come to her rescue, either. Mitch was a gentleman right down to his born-and-bred Texas roots.

"That would be great, thank you." She pushed herself up from the bench seat of the picnic table and brushed her hands on the legs of her jeans. "Let me just go tell Pop I'm leaving."

Mitch gave a small nod, staying where he was while she wandered over to the group of poker buddies.

"Hey, Pop," she said, curling her hands over her father's shoulders and leaning in to kiss his bearded cheek.

Wyatt Davis gave a chuckle, laid out his cards, and said, "Read 'em and weep, boys." His full house clearly beat his friends' hands, and he wasted no time dragging his winnings toward him across the table.

Once he had all the chips in front of him, he turned his head and tipped his face up to Emma. "Hey, there, baby girl. How are you doing?"

"I'm tired and ready to go home." Before his mustachi-oed mouth could turn down in a frown, she added, "Mitch has offered to take me so you can stick around and play cards as long as you like."

Wyatt glanced past her to where Mitch was standing, fitting his hat on his dark head. "That's awfully nice of him. You sure you don't mind?"

She smiled and gave his shoulders a squeeze. "Of course not. You have fun. No more drinking, though, or we'll have to find someone to drive *you* home, too."

Her father grinned and pointed to the brown bottle to his right. "Don't worry about me, pumpkin, I'll be nursing this one the rest of the night."

"All right." She leaned over and kissed the top of his

head. "See you in the morning. Win big. Bye, guys," she said, waving to her father's friends as she made her way back to Mitch.

"Ready to go?"

She nodded, grabbing her purse from the picnic table and following Mitch to his dark blue truck, shining near-black in the moonlight. He held the door open while she climbed in, then slammed it behind her and walked around to the driver's side. After he'd gotten in behind the wheel and started the engine, he adjusted the air-conditioning to cool the inside of the cab and turned on the radio so that a familiar country tune played in the background.

"Thanks again for this," Emma murmured softly when she realized he didn't intend to carry on a conversation. "I had visions of spending the night curled up on that picnic table. If I'd known Pop planned to stick around playing cards all night, I'd have suggested we take separate cars."

"No problem. I was headed in your direction, anyway." He graced her with a quick grin that creased the corners of his mouth.

"Yeah. If I'd thought of that, I probably would have asked you for a ride hours ago."

Mitch's ranch, the Circle R, bordered her father's property. There were plenty of acres in between, but for all intents and purposes, they were next-door neighbors.

"So, what were you doing hanging around the celebration this late? I'd have expected you to hightail it out of there at the first opportunity."

Mitch was a hometown favorite and more than willing to help out any time Gabriel's Crossing needed him, but ever since his divorce from Suzanne four years earlier, he'd become quiet and withdrawn. He spent most of his time alone on his ranch, going into town only when he needed supplies, or for an event like tonight's—the town's annual Independence Day celebration. But even then, he usually only made a brief appearance before disappearing again, back to the Circle R.

"Chase took Mom home after the fireworks, but since he was in charge of the sound system he needed someone to stick around and dismantle everything." He hitched a thumb over his shoulder, indicating the equipment piled into the truck bed. "I'll have to drop that stuff off in the morning."

"Why didn't you take your mother home?" she pressed, knowing that would have been Mitch's choice over staying to the very end of the town-wide party.

Even from where she was sitting, on the opposite side of the bench seat, she could see the wry twist of his lips.

"Because my family thinks I'm becoming a hermit and need to get out more. And that if I stuck around long enough tonight, I might have met a nice girl and gotten married again."

His tone told her how enamored he was of that idea, but she couldn't help the tiny flicker of awareness that bloomed to life inside her.

She opened her mouth to speak, then had to clear her throat before she thought the words would come out as more than a squeak. "Did you? Meet a nice girl, I mean."

"No," he answered without reservation, and with the slightest hint of an edge to his voice. "But then, I wasn't looking for one."

The flicker in her belly sputtered and died. She shouldn't be surprised. It was no secret that Suzanne's infidelities and the divorce had hit him hard. He'd never been the most outgoing guy to begin with, but after the divorce he'd become noticeably more sullen. Nothing anyone said or did seemed to shake his sour mood.

And he had never looked at her as anything other than a neighbor and friend—no matter how much she might wish he would.

Not that she'd ever done anything about it. She could have flirted a little, or come right out and told him she had the hots for him. Instead, she'd kept her feelings to herself while pining after him from afar.

She was such a coward. Maybe if she hadn't been, he wouldn't have married Suzanne in the first place and wouldn't be so miserable now.

Swallowing uncomfortably, she rubbed her palms along the tops of her jean-clad legs and breathed a sigh of relief when she realized they were nearing her house. Getting home would mean an end to the awkward silence filling the cab.

Mitch pulled up in front of the pale yellow, ranch-style house and cut the engine.

"You want me to walk you to the door?"

Considering the walk would take all of about two seconds and ten steps, it was a gracious but unnecessary offer.

"Thanks, but I need to check the livestock one last time before I go to bed, anyway."

She released the latch on her seatbelt and opened the passenger side door. When she turned from closing it, she was surprised to find Mitch moving toward her in that long, lanky stride of his.

"What are you doing?" she asked, her mind drawing a complete blank as to why he'd bothered to get out of the truck at all.

"Helping you with the livestock."

"That's all right, I can handle it." It might not be her favorite pastime, but she'd grown up pitching hay, mucking stalls and grooming horses, and—along with several ranch hands—still helped her father on a daily basis. Checking water buckets and tossing out a little extra grain by herself would be child's play.

"I know you can," he told her, catching an arm around her shoulders. "But things will go faster and you'll be able to get to bed quicker if we both do the work."

She couldn't argue with his logic, so she said nothing as they made their way across the grass-sprigged dirt yard to the big gray barn.

One half of the large double doors was propped open. They walked inside, and Emma flipped a switch to her left to turn on the lights. The uncovered bulbs dangling high above their heads weren't very bright but illuminated enough of the building so that they could see what they were doing.

Mitch had spent so much time at the Double D as a child that he knew where everything was. The horses nickered at the interruption to their rest, and Mitch patted more than one equine nose as they passed.

While she shook a bit of fresh hay into each horse's feed trough and checked to make sure they had clean water, Mitch hauled a bale outside. She knew he would carry the hay out a ways into the field, then spread it on the ground for the cattle to find during the night.

They finished at nearly the same time. She was wiping her hands on the seat of her jeans when he strolled back in, the leftover baling twine clutched in one hand. He hung the strings on a nail sticking out of a nearby beam, then turned to face her, hands on hips.

"All done?" he wanted to know.

"Just about." Moving farther into the wide open space of the barn, she wrapped her fingers around the sides of the ladder that led to the loft and said, "I want to check on a new litter of kittens before we leave."

She scurried up the ladder in a matter of seconds,

creeping quietly across the straw-strewn floor in search of
the kittens. The light up here was even weaker than down
below, but she could still make out the shapes of stray
bales and—hopefully—tiny bundles of fur.

A second later, a board squeaked behind her and she
turned her head to see Mitch standing at the top of the
ladder. Her stomach did another one of those queer flip-
flops at the sight of him, then settled down to a dull simmer.

"You didn't have to come up," she whispered.

"I wanted to," he said just as softly, but didn't elaborate.

Deciding Mitch pretty much did what he wanted,
whenever he wanted, she went back to looking for the
kittens. She found them tucked together in a tight ball,
nestled into a pile of loose straw in the corner. They were
adorable, and so small she thought she could probably
hold the entire brood of them in the palms of both hands.

There were five in total—two tabbies, one calico, one
white, and one black with white feet and a streak of white
on its nose. She'd been playing with them on an almost
daily basis since she'd discovered them. They were old
enough that their eyes were open but young enough that
they still wobbled when they tried to walk.

Not wanting to disturb their rest, she intended to simply
back away and leave them be, but then the mama cat
appeared, rubbing between Emma's legs before moving to
her babies and lying down to let them feed. They immediately woke up and started nuzzling around their mother's
belly, and Emma took the opportunity to stroke their soft
little heads and backs.

Most barn cats were afraid of people because they didn't
get handled as much as house cats, but from the time she
was old enough to toddle around in her father's footsteps,
Emma had loved the odd collection of felines running

around the property. Her father used to tell her to be careful or she'd stroke them all bald, but so far that hadn't happened. Instead, they had a barn full of friendly cats that often came running when they heard the doors open and would pester for attention while you were trying to work.

"Cute," Mitch murmured just above her left ear, startling her.

She straightened, covering her heart with her hand. For a moment, she'd forgotten he was there but wondered now how she ever could have made such a grievous error. His tall frame and broad shoulders filled the space around them like a sponge in a glass of water. His presence alone seemed to suck all the oxygen out of the air and make her short of breath.

"Well," she said nervously, backing a step or two away, "I just wanted to see how they were doing. We can leave now."

Instead of heading for the ladder to climb back to the main floor of the barn, Mitch moseyed over to a couple of bales of straw stacked against the far wall and sat down.

"What's your hurry?" he asked, leaning back on his elbows until he was nearly lying flat. "If we wait for the kittens to fill their bellies, you might get to pet them again."

Stuffing her hands into the hip pockets of her jeans, she rocked back on her heels. She could play with the kittens anytime, which he probably knew perfectly well. But he seemed to want to hang around a while longer, and she didn't get the chance to talk to him very often anymore, especially alone. Besides, as tired as she'd been only half an hour ago at the picnic area, she didn't feel at all sleepy now.

Feet dragging slightly through the loose straw that covered the loft floor, she took a seat beside him. She kept her spine straight, her hands on her knees as she searched for something to say. The problem was, she'd already ex-

hausted her list of small-talk topics on the drive home. She
didn't have a clue what else to say that wouldn't sound
forced or too probing into his personal life.

Thankfully, Mitch kept the moment from turning
awkward.

"So how'd you enjoy the celebration today?"

"It was fine," she said. "The Fourth of July picnic is
always fun."

"Yeah." He picked up a long strand of golden-yellow
straw and twirled it between two fingers, casting shadows
in the dim light. "I got a slice of your cherry pie before it
was all gone. It was good."

"Thanks."

"You made some of the other food, too, right? I
thought I heard somebody mention you always cook a lot
for the picnic."

She nodded, remembering all the times she, Mitch and
his brother, Chase, had hung out together just like this. On
those long summer days when it was too hot to run or play,
they'd found a shady spot to do nothing more than lie
around and shoot the breeze. The happy childhood
memories eased her nerves and she began to relax.

"Mom used to cook up a storm for all the town celebrations, you know. After she died, I guess I picked up where
she left off. I had her recipes, and I didn't want anyone to
be disappointed."

"I think people would have understood," he said seriously.

"Probably. But I enjoy it, and I think it makes Pop feel
more like Mom's still around."

"She did make the best potato salad in Texas."

"Yes, she did," Emma agreed with a smile.

"Yours was pretty tasty, too."

She met his storm-gray eyes and grinned. "How do you

know it was my potato salad you were eating?" There had to have been at least four or five bowls of the stuff, all prepared by different cooks.

He sat up and leaned closer to her, one corner of his mouth quirked with amusement. "Because I saw you arrive and watched you set the bowl on the table with the rest of the food. Then I made sure to get there early before it was all gone."

His face was inches from her own, hovering over her, smelling of some crisp, clean aftershave she couldn't quite identify. Whatever it was, it made her think of waking up in the arms of a strong, sexy man. This man, in particular. Running her fingers over his stubbled, unshaven jaw… kissing his warm, pale lips…feeling the full, bare length of him pressed against her while they slowly stirred each other's arousal.

"I didn't see you," she responded quietly, unable to tear her gaze from his tempting mouth. "Not until much later."

"I was hiding out to avoid those nosy questions I get whenever I show my face in town. But I could still see every move you made."

She shivered with awareness at his words. He'd been watching her at the picnic and she hadn't even known it.

Instead of feeling unnerved that he'd essentially been spying on her all day, she was flattered…and suddenly incredibly turned on.

"I wish I'd known you were there," she said, boldly lifting her hand to caress the strong line of his jaw. "I would have asked you to dance."

He wrapped his fingers around hers, pulling her hand away from his face and turning it to press a kiss to the center of her palm. Tiny flames of desire flickered to life in her belly and started to spread outward.

"We could dance now," he offered softly.

She shook her head. "There's no music."

"I don't know," he murmured, brushing her bottom lip with the pad of his thumb, "I definitely hear something in the air."

And then he leaned forward, covering her mouth with his own.

Emma's heart kicked up, pounding in her chest like the hooves of a galloping horse. Mitch Ramsey was kissing her. Finally. Gloriously.

His lips were firm, skillful. He knew exactly where to press, where to move, when to open his mouth and encourage her to do the same. While his tongue darted over and around hers, she tasted the coffee with just a touch of cream and sugar that he must have drank before bringing her home.

Her nipples turned hard and pressed against the inside cups of her bra as he stroked her from hip to breast. The heat of his touch burned through her blouse, raising goose bumps along her flesh and sending her core temperature soaring.

She ran her hands over his back, feeling the sleek muscles beneath his shirt, the way they rippled and flexed as he moved. Using her nails like claws, she tore at the tail of his shirt, dragging it out from the waistband of his jeans until the pads of her fingers encountered smooth, bare skin.

Between them, he was loosening the buttons of her blouse from top to bottom, opening her to the night air. And Emma let him…more than let him. She moved however she thought was needed to grant him the best access.

It was amazing, wonderful, spectacular. Everything she'd ever imagined and more.

She was panting for breath when Mitch grasped her shoulders and pushed her slightly away. His own chest heaved as he stared down at her, his eyes dark with desire.

"Don't stop," she blurted out, thrusting her fingers into the hair at his temples and drawing him near once again.

She was so afraid he'd stop. So afraid the tight line of his lips meant he was about to apologize and say that kissing her was a mistake.

But it wasn't a mistake; it was what she wanted. Had wanted, more than anything, for years.

"Please," she said again, more softly this time, uncaring that she likely sounded desperate and pathetic, "don't stop."

"Not a chance," he murmured, just before he lowered his head to kiss her again and sent her world back to the realm of temporary perfection.

TWO

Mitch's body was on fire, throbbing with need and straining to get closer to Emma.

Four years. It had been four years since his divorce from Suzanne and four *long* years since he'd been with a woman. The time had taken its toll and stretched his control to the breaking point.

And now here he was, with a warm and willing woman in his arms.

Never mind that it was Emma, childhood friend and neighbor, a woman he shouldn't even be contemplating sleeping with.

But she tasted like peppermint and smelled like flowers and reminded him of a time in his life when he hadn't been miserable. Back when they were kids, without a care in the world, when he was first married to Suzanne, head over heels in love and believing they would always be that way.

Emma was safe and familiar…and sexy as all get out.

How had he never noticed that before? The way her small, firm breasts filled out the front of her blouse and her soft lips formed a seductive little moue. Or the way her strawberry-blond hair fell to her shoulders and perfectly framed her heart-shaped face.

He shouldn't be thinking of her in those terms, shouldn't be touching and kissing her. But she felt so good, so right, he couldn't seem to stop.

She made soft mewling sounds as their tongues tangled and her body writhed against his. He pushed her shirt the rest of the way off her shoulders, letting it fall to the bale of straw behind her.

Her chest rose and fell with her breathing, as rapidly as his own. But he didn't let it keep him from sliding his right hand over her left breast, beneath the lacy material of her bra. His fingers caressed the pillowy softness while his thumb teased and flicked the hardened nipple.

She moaned in pleasure, sending shockwaves rippling through his bloodstream. Her head fell back, exposing the long, smooth column of her throat, and he couldn't resist kissing her there, licking the pulse point and nibbling at the taut line of muscle.

He used his free hand to unhook the latch of her bra and skim the loosened straps down her arms.

In the back of his mind, he hoped she would protest. If she asked him to stop, suffered a sudden bout of embarrassment, he was gentleman enough not to pressure her to go farther than she felt comfortable. But on his own…

On his own, he wasn't sure he was man enough to let her go.

He had full access now to her bare chest and took a moment to admire the pale splendor of her small, pert breasts with their tiny cherry nipples. They reminded him of ice cream sundaes, sweet and delectable and good enough to eat.

Shifting around on the bales of straw, he supported her back with one arm while leaning in for a taste. He kissed the side of her breast, then opened his mouth to sample the silken skin.

She raked her hands through his hair, grazing the scalp and anchoring her fingers near his nape. His tongue drew circles around her tightened areola, the movements growing smaller and smaller until he engulfed the entire tip.

She straddled his thighs like a champion rider, tilting her hips, straining for a more intimate touch. And he wanted to give it to her, was desperate for it himself. Sweating, shaking, more aroused than he could ever remember being before in his life.

Releasing her breast, dragging in great gulps of air, he returned his mouth to her lips. At the same time, he tried to get his trembling fingers to work on the snap and zipper of her jeans.

With the denim loose around her waist, he slipped his hands inside, palms flat against her skin as he slid them down, beneath the elastic edge of her panties. He skimmed her hips, then moved around to cup her buttocks.

When she moaned and ground herself into the hard bulge behind the zipper of his own jeans, he knew he couldn't wait much longer to be inside her. Not without embarrassing himself and depriving them both of something he was beginning to suspect would be earth-shattering.

Laying her back along the bed of straw bales, he sat up only long enough to yank off her shoes and drag her pants down her legs. Then he was with her again, tearing off his shirt, unbuckling his belt and opening his fly before covering her with his body.

He lifted her legs around his waist, gently probing her warm, moist folds. Brushing thin strands of strawberry-blond hair away from her face, he met her eyes and offered her an encouraging smile. She returned his grin and lifted her hands to his shoulders, applying just enough pressure to tug him down for a kiss. While his tongue plumbed the depths of her mouth, he cocked his hips and entered her in one long, strong stroke.

The instant friction and intense sensation made them both gasp. Mitch held himself perfectly still, feeling her tight inner muscles flexing around him, all but blowing off the top of his head. He knew if he moved, if she shifted even a millimeter, things between them would be over much too soon.

So he gritted his teeth, concentrating on his breathing until the blaze in his gut sputtered to a low forest fire and he thought he could open his eyes, gaze down at Emma's angelic features without exploding. She was staring up at him with liquid blue eyes, the same stunned expression on her face that he suspected mirrored his own.

Taking a deep breath, he let the air shudder out of his lungs, and then brushed his lips across her mouth.

Her breasts brushed his chest, her arms and legs locked around him like tentacles. With a minor shift, just a small forward movement, he was inside her, buried to the hilt.

He groaned, the sound rumbling up from his diaphragm even as she flexed around him and he began to move. Short, slow strokes growing slightly longer and faster as the tension built. Blood pumped through his veins, hot and flowing like molten lava to pool between his legs.

Emma threw her head back and he kissed her throat,

nibbled her ear, trailed his lips down to her breasts. His belly clenched at the noises she was making. Low, erotic mewling sounds that drove him senseless and made him thrust harder, faster, striving for completion.

Sweat dripped past his temples and down the middle of his back. Her fingers tangled in his hair, caressing and keeping him close as her hips rose and fell to meet him.

"Emma," he growled out.

She met his gaze and smiled even as her mouth opened on a rush of ecstasy. "Mitch," she breathed in return.

And that was all it took to send him over the edge. White-hot pleasure pounded through his pores, filling every cell of his being to near bursting.

With a deep groan, he drove into her one last time, relieved to feel her pulse and shake, following him over the cliff into mindless pleasure.

Emma couldn't keep her lips from curling up in a grin as she ran her hands over Mitch's silky-soft hair and sweat-slickened back, his strong, muscular bicep and broad chest.

His face rested in the hollow of her neck, his body still covering hers after the most intense session of lovemaking she'd ever experienced.

She still couldn't believe it had happened. Her body hummed with recently released passion, the lingering effects causing her muscles to twitch and a delightful warmth to spread all over.

And she knew, without a shadow of a doubt, that with anyone but Mitch Ramsey, the sex might have been good, but it wouldn't have been phenomenal.

So many times, private wishes and forbidden fantasies lost their luster in the bright light of day. She'd dreamed of being with Mitch for so long that when he'd begun to kiss her, a part of her had been worried she'd be disappointed.

Or perhaps she'd been worried that she would disappoint him.

Instead, being with him had been everything she'd hoped for and more. So much more.

He'd been gentle and caring and…amazing. Not only in the way he touched her—although the memory of that alone was enough to curl her toes and cause a renewed warmth to pool deep in her belly.

No, he'd been kind and considerate all evening. Offering her a ride home, helping her tend to the livestock, climbing into the loft with her to check on the kittens.

It was a side of him she hadn't seen in a very long time. Since Suzanne had ripped his heart out and stomped it into the ground, leaving him an empty husk of his former self.

Mitch thought he'd handled his ex-wife's infidelity and the subsequent divorce well. He thought he'd been impervious to the pain that woman had caused him and had recovered quickly to return to his normal life.

But everyone around him knew it was a lie. He pretended to be okay while his insides remained shriveled and cold.

Emma often thought that if she ever ran into Suzanne again, she would slap the cheating bitch for what she'd done to Mitch.

But then, Emma had never liked the woman. From the moment Mitch had brought her home to Gabriel's Crossing, having met her at a truck stop in Abilene, Emma had known that every dream she'd ever had of spending her life with Mitch was destroyed.

Suzanne was tall and blond and built like a 1920s pin-up girl, while Emma had always had a more boyish figure. Small breasts, narrow hips, no feminine curves to speak of.

She was a bit of a tomboy, and had always been proud of the fact, until Suzanne Yates had waltzed into town and reminded her of all the things she wasn't, stealing Mitch in the process.

It had been a silly dream to start with, thinking that just because she and Mitch had grown up together he might fall in love with her. She'd grown up with Chase, too, but had never had an erotic or ever-after thought about him.

And until tonight, she'd truly thought she was over Mitch Ramsey. Or, if not over him, at least had come to terms with the fact that he was never going to completely heal from Suzanne's betrayal. He was off the market and more out of her reach than ever before.

Now, though, she wasn't sure what to think. Her heart wanted to believe this was the start of something permanent. That by driving her home tonight and making love to her in the barn loft, he was showing that he was recovered from his lousy marriage and willing to love again.

But her rational, more somber brain warned her to be careful. Reminded her that one night of passion did not a marriage proposal make.

She would keep that in mind, play it safe and follow his lead, whatever it may be.

"Mmm." He moaned low in his throat like a man waking from a good night's sleep and pushed himself up on one elbow.

Cool night air washed over her skin where his body no longer covered, and she fought not to shiver. Not because she was cold, but because she missed the intimate contact.

"You okay?" he asked, still leaning over her, staring down at her with those slate-gray eyes.

She nodded, biting the inside of her lip to keep from saying more.

He shifted again, rolling farther away on the bales of straw. She felt bereft without his touch, but curled her fingers into fists at her sides and took deep breaths until she got the urge to reach for him under control.

"We should think about getting dressed before your father gets home and catches us out here." He shot her a wicked grin. "I've made it almost forty years without getting chased off by an angry, pitch fork-wielding father. There's no sense in starting now."

Moving around her, he climbed to his feet and began gathering their discarded clothes from the straw-strewn floor. She sat up and accepted her things when he handed them to her, taking her time putting bra and panties then her jeans and blouse back on.

She ran her hands through her hair, picking out pieces of straw and wishing for a brush to smooth the tangled mass. When she looked back at Mitch, he was dressed and just fastening his belt.

When he was finished, he slapped his hands against his thighs and fixed her with a lopsided smile. "Should we head down?"

She glanced around, surprised to find no visible signs of what had happened between them. After their explosive joining, she'd expected to see burn marks, singed straw, smoke still rising from the ashes. But, instead, there was just plain yellow straw, a little flat in places, but ordinary enough, and the litter of kittens curled up sleeping around their mother.

Turning back to meet his gaze, she nodded, then climbed down the ladder ahead of him.

Just as they reached the door of the barn, they heard tires crunching on the dirt and gravel drive, and saw headlights headed their way.

"That'll be Pop," she told him.

"Looks like we made it just in time." He stuck his hands in the front pockets of his jeans, his thumbs hooked over his belt and waistband.

If he was nervous about coming face-to-face with her father only minutes after having her naked and writhing beneath him, he didn't show it.

Her father pulled his pickup into the yard and cut the engine. A second later, the door opened and he climbed out.

He didn't look completely steady on his feet, and she rushed forward to take his arm, hoping he'd kept his word about only finishing off that one last beer.

His head snapped up when he felt her hand on his elbow, and he smiled through his shaggy gray beard and mustache.

"Well, there you are. I thought you would have been in the house, asleep by now. What are you doing out here?"

"Mitch and I were just…um…"

"Checking the livestock," Mitch offered, stepping out of the shadows of the barn and into the glow of the house's front porch light.

"Good, good," her father said. "Thanks for helping out my girl, Ramsey."

Emma's cheeks heated, but she hoped neither her father nor Mitch would notice in the dark.

"My pleasure, sir," Mitch answered, rocking back on the heels of his well-worn boots, hands still in his pockets. "Anything else I can do for you tonight before I get going?"

"No, no, you go on." Her father started toward the house, slipping out of Emma's hold and looking more steady on his feet now that he'd had the chance to stand for a few minutes. "Have a good night. We'll see you soon."

"Yes, sir. Good night, sir."

"Emma, I'm going to bed. I'll see you in the morning."

"All right. 'Night, Pop. I love you."

"Love you, too, sweetheart."

The screen door slammed closed behind him and she waited several long seconds before speaking. Once she was sure he was out of earshot, she turned to face Mitch.

"Went a little overboard with the 'yes, sir,' 'no, sir,' 'have a good night, sirs,' didn't you?"

She thought she saw him wince and bit back a chuckle of amusement.

"Maybe," he answered shortly, his face a mask of inexpression. "But it sure beats the alternative."

"What's that?"

"Letting him know I spent the last half hour rolling around in the loft with his daughter."

It was Emma's turn to wince, and she cast a quick glance over her shoulder, afraid her father might have been close enough to overhear Mitch's declaration.

She was a grown woman, so what she did with her body and with whom was no one's business but her own. But talking about sex in front of her father—or worse, having him know she'd just finished having hot, extremely satisfying sex in his barn—was still something that made her keenly uncomfortable.

"Point taken."

Gravel crunched beneath her feet as she crossed to him, then followed as he stalked to his truck.

"Thanks for your help with the horses and cattle," she said.

He nodded, opening the door and climbing inside.

Watching him get ready to leave made her stomach clench. But what had she expected? That he would ask to stay the night or suggest they sneak back into the barn for seconds? That he would declare his undying love and fall to one knee, asking her to marry him?

She might harbor fantasies of happily-ever-after with him, but she wasn't delusional. She was realistic enough to accept that sex was just sex, even if it had been with the one man she'd always secretly had a crush on.

"So I guess I'll see you around," she offered. The perfect opening for him to ask her out on a date, tell her he'd call, anything to imply that what had passed between them would be more than a one-night stand.

"Yeah," he replied, and nothing more.

A beat passed before he started the engine, then turned his head to meet her gaze. "'Night."

Forcing a smile to her lips, she swallowed back the bubble of disappointment swelling in her belly. "Right. Good night."

He put the truck in gear, turned around and rolled slowly down the drive. She stood watching until his taillights disappeared, rubbing her arms to stave off a chill that centered in her chest and had nothing to do with the still night air surrounding her.

Three

Emma glanced at her shopping list. She had everything she needed except bread flour.

Turning down the baking aisle, she scanned the shelves for the brand and type she wanted, groaning when she spotted it on the uppermost shelf. The store had apparently rearranged items since the last time she'd purchased bread flour. And at five foot three, that left it just a couple of inches out of her range.

Pushing her cart to the side, she used the toe of her shoe to nudge cans of pie filling on the lowest shelf out of the way, then grabbed hold of a shelf at waist level and hoisted herself up. Her fingertips brushed the front of the bag, but she still couldn't get a good enough grip to lift it down.

"Need some help?"

With a yelp, her hold on the shelf slipped and she fell

backward. Strong hands and an even stronger chest caught and steadied her.

She turned, looking up into Mitch's hard, gray eyes. Not that she'd needed to see him to know who'd spoken to her. She would know his voice anywhere.

"Hey," she greeted him, feeling slightly out of breath, and not because of her graceless pirouette from the grocery store shelves.

It had been two weeks since the Fourth of July picnic, since that night in the barn. Two weeks without seeing or even hearing from him again.

She hadn't been surprised. She would have been more surprised if he'd called or shown up on the doorstep, but that didn't mean she wasn't disappointed.

Disappointed that he could walk away without a backward glance after what they'd shared but also that their sleeping together might have ruined a perfectly good, lifelong friendship.

And now here he stood, staring at her from beneath the rim of his black Stetson. He didn't seem particularly pleased to see her, but then Mitch hadn't looked happy since Suzanne had left. A thin layer of stubble shadowed his square jaw, and lines bracketed his flat mouth.

"Hey, yourself. Is this what you were after?" He reached up with one hand and plucked a bag of bread flour from the top shelf with ease, holding it out to her.

She took it, cradling the five-pound weight to her chest while she swallowed and tried to think of something witty to say to break the tension and attempt to return them to the easy camaraderie they'd shared before sex had muddied the waters.

"You headed somewhere after this?" he asked without preliminaries.

"Just home to put groceries away," she answered.

"Got time for a cup of coffee? Maybe a bite to eat?"

She glanced over her shoulder into the basket of her cart. Nothing cold. Nothing that would go bad if she didn't go straight home.

Her stomach gave a little lurch at the possibilities of what he might want to talk about, but she nodded. "I guess that would be all right."

"Good. Need anything else?"

She checked her list one last time, then shook her head. "No, I'm ready."

They moved down the aisle together, Emma pushing the cart as Mitch followed a step behind. The heels of his boots clicked rhythmically on the hard, tiled floor, matching the nervous beat of her heart.

He stayed with her while she went through the checkout line, then helped to carry the bags to her car.

"Where are we going?" she asked, standing in the open driver's side door.

"Rosie's Café." He tipped his hat down a fraction to shield his eyes from the midday sun. "I'll meet you over there."

Ten minutes later, they were seated across from one another in a red vinyl booth near the back of the café. Located in the center of town, Rosie's was Gabriel's Crossing's most popular restaurant. A greasy spoon where folks came for home cooking and the latest gossip.

The lunch crowd had cleared out already, and dinner customers wouldn't begin to trickle in for a few more hours. When the waitress came, they asked for pie and coffee, then sat in uncomfortable silence while the young woman went to fill their order.

Emma folded and refolded her napkin until the paper edges began to flake and fall away. Finally, she took a deep breath, laid her palms flat on the Formica tabletop, and faced Mitch head-on.

"So, what did you want to talk about?" she blurted out, deciding it was better to simply come to the point than sit here imagining worst case scenarios. Like tearing off a Band-Aid in one quick swipe rather than toying and tugging and prolonging the agony.

"Us."

As much as she'd braced herself for his answer, she hadn't expected that.

She waited until the waitress set slices of pie and steaming cups of black coffee in front of them before responding, using the much-needed time to calm her erratic pulse and get her scattered thoughts in order. He took a sip of black coffee while she stirred a sugar packet and dollop of cream into hers.

Once they were alone, she took a deep breath and kept her tone low so no one would overhear. "What about us?"

"I think there should be one."

She knit her eyebrows. Mitch had never been the easiest man to talk to, but at the moment he was giving new meaning to the word *confusing*. "One what?"

"Us. I think there should be an us."

Picking up his fork, he dug into his slice of blueberry pie as though they were talking about the weather instead of…them.

Before she could reply, he swallowed and went on. "You know what happened between us, Emma. It shouldn't have. It shouldn't have happened the way it did, and for that I'm sorry."

The flush of embarrassment she'd felt at his mention of the night they'd made love flared into sudden anger and more than a little hurt.

How dare he apologize to her for what she conside
one of the most special nights of her life? If he was sorry,
if he regretted what they'd done, then he should have kept
it to himself instead of cornering her like this.

"That's what you brought me here to tell me?" she
demanded, her knuckles turning white as she clutched the
edge of the table. "You're sorry we slept together? I hate
to break it to you, Mitch, but you're not the first man I've
had sex with. You didn't seduce me, you didn't take my
virginity, you didn't do anything that requires an apology.
I'm a big girl. I can make my own decisions and sleep
with whomever I want. I don't need your permission or
your approval."

A beat passed while he held her gaze, then he nodded.
"You're right. You can make your own decisions."

He took another bite of pie and washed it down with a
gulp of coffee. "The thing is, I'm not the type to have a one-
night stand with a neighbor and childhood friend. It
feels…sleazy."

Her eyes narrowed in warning. He wasn't calling her
sleazy or even what had passed between them, she knew
that. But it was a close thing, and in her current mood she
wasn't sure she was willing to split hairs.

"My point is," he continued, "I think maybe we should
keep seeing each other. See where it leads."

Of all the things he might have said, that shocked her
the most. It also made her heartbeat—which had slowed
to a crawl at the direction the conversation was taking—
speed up and thump against her rib cage.

She swallowed hard, praying she wasn't hearing things.
"Excuse me?"

"I think we should…date. Go out a couple of times and
see what happens."

, anyway. But the suggestion wasn't driven
ch as nobility. And, he admitted, guilt.
eks since the Fourth of July picnic…since
e in the loft of her father's barn…he hadn't
been a op thinking about her.

Partly because the sex had been incredible and every
fiber of his being wanted to be with her again. And partly
because she was his neighbor, a friend since childhood.
They'd gone through school together. Climbed trees and
ridden horses together. Survived the prom and graduation
and the death of a parent—her mother, who had been a
second mother to him as well—together.

She wasn't some casual acquaintance to be used to slake
his lust. Even if it had been four long, lonely years since
he'd been with a woman.

So far, this was the best solution he could come up with.
His personal code of honor wouldn't allow him to just
walk away and pretend that night had never happened.
That might be all right for a stranger he'd met in a bar, but
he couldn't treat Emma that way.

Emma deserved better.

Using her for a one-night stand was unacceptable. But
dating her for a while wasn't.

Nothing would come of it, he knew. Nothing could ever
come of it, and he didn't want it to. But if they dated for a
while and then split up, he could justify having slept with her.

And he wouldn't sleep with her again, that was a promise.

Even if the memory of kissing her, touching her soft skin,
heated his blood and tightened his trousers across his groin.

He'd known Emma all his life, but this was the first time
he'd been distracted by her as a woman. The first time he'd
noticed how sexy and attractive she was.

Physically, she was the opposite of Suzanne in every

way. Where Suzanne had an hourglass figure, with full breasts and wide hips, Emma was proportionally well-balanced. Small, but still shapely.

Her hair was more strawberry-blond than peroxide-blond; her look more natural than painted on; her clothes stylish but comfortable, rather than skin-tight and meant to attract attention.

She certainly had succeeded at catching his attention, and not a day went by that he didn't regret it.

"So?" He took a swig of coffee to wash down the last of his pie, taking note that Emma had yet to touch hers. "What do you say?"

What could she say? What *should* she say?

This had to be the most bizarre date invitation she'd ever received. And if it were coming from anyone other than Mitch, she'd have probably laughed the poor guy out of the restaurant.

But it *was* Mitch, which left her torn.

Did she accept because her feminine heart had dreamed of this moment a million times? Or did she turn him down because she suspected the offer stemmed more from guilt than an actual interest in seeing her socially?

Wrapping her fingers around the mug of still-warm coffee in front of her, she lifted it to her mouth and took a sip, buying herself a little more time.

But in the end, she knew what her decision would be. Knew that her heart and her sense of possibility would drive her to at least see where things could lead.

Maybe it would lead only to a couple of dates, dinner or a movie. Or maybe it would lead to more—to Mitch realizing he'd never belonged with Suzanne, but with a woman more like Emma. If she was lucky, with Emma herself.

The sensible side of her brain knew it was too much to

hope for, but she was willing to take a chance. It was a small one, after all, and if things did work out, the payoff would be big. Everything she'd ever dreamed of.

And if it didn't, she was the only person who would ever know her wishes had been for more than a casual relationship. She was the only one who would be hurt.

Taking a deep breath, she returned the cup to its saucer, then lifted her eyes to his. "All right."

"Good." He shifted in the booth, digging his wallet out of his hip pocket, peeling off bills and dropping them onto the tabletop. Then he slid out and got to his feet. "I'll pick you up at six."

Without a backward glance, he stalked out of the diner, leaving her alone with her coffee and uneaten pie.

If she were smart, she told herself for the fiftieth time, she would have called Mitch up and told him to forget about tonight.

He hadn't exactly acted like Prince Charming back at Rosie's when he'd walked out on her. And he hadn't *asked* her out tonight, so much as *told* her when to be ready. For that alone, he almost deserved to be stood up.

Yet here she was, poised in front of her full-length mirror, checking her appearance one last time before he arrived.

She'd already fixed a supper plate for Pop and warned him she would be gone for the evening. She had no idea where Mitch intended to take her, but she assumed dinner would be involved, so she hadn't bothered eating herself.

Then she'd come upstairs and torn apart her closet in search of something decent to wear. Without a destination in mind, it made dressing difficult, but she'd finally settled on a denim skirt and pale-yellow peasant blouse.

Looking at her reflection now, she adjusted the gold

chain at her neck and tucked back a few thin strands of hair that had slipped out of its clip.

Through the open bedroom window, she heard Mitch's truck pull up to the house and her father's greeting as Mitch got out, slamming the door behind him.

She took a deep breath, straightened the hem of her top, then slid her feet into the black mules she'd pulled out of her closet earlier. Regardless of the butterflies tap-dancing through her belly, she'd agreed to go out with him. Beneath the layers of nerves that had her all but jumping out of her skin, she was even looking forward to it.

"Emma, honey," her father shouted up the stairs. "Mitch is here."

As though she wasn't already keenly aware of his presence. Her arms had broken out in gooseflesh the minute he'd turned into the drive.

"Coming," she called, when she found her voice.

He was waiting just inside the kitchen, near the front door. His black Stetson was in his hand rather than on his head, tapping against the side of his denim-clad thigh.

"Hi," she said when his gaze lifted to hers.

"Hi." He scanned her from head to toe, then met her eyes again. "You look nice."

As compliments went, it wasn't the best she'd ever received, but knowing that Mitch didn't dole them out very often to anyone, she decided to accept.

"Thank you. You, too."

He was dressed in jeans and a plaid button-down shirt, the same as usual, but he always looked good to her, so the compliment still fit.

"Ready to go?"

She nodded, grabbing a light jacket from the coatrack beside the door.

"You two have a good time," her father called out from his seat at the kitchen table. He waved them off, barely sparing them a second glance as he dug into his dinner.

Mitch closed the door behind them, then walked her to the passenger side of his truck and helped her climb in.

"So, where are we going?" she asked once he was behind the wheel and they were headed down the long dirt driveway to the main road.

"You'll see."

She raised an eyebrow at his less than enlightening answer, but he kept his eyes on the road and couldn't see the look of consternation she shot him.

Ten minutes later, they pulled into the parking lot of the Silver Spur, one of the most popular honky-tonks in Gabriel's Crossing. Lights blinked on the roof and bright neon signs shone in the windows, advertising a dozen different brands of draft and bottled beer.

Emma had only been to the Spur a couple of times before and always with a group of friends because the bar tended to get rowdy on the weekends. But this was a weeknight, and even though it was a strange place to go for a first date, she was with Mitch, so she had nothing to worry about.

He came around to help her down from the truck, then held her hand as they walked into the bar. Loud country music blared, filling the early evening air and hitting them like an ocean wave when they pushed open the front door.

Men and women, most wearing cowboy hats of all sizes and colors, filled the wide, open room. Dancing, milling around, sitting at the tables and bar with longneck bottles of beer and bowls of peanuts in front of them.

Sawdust was scattered in clumps across the scarred wood floor, and antlers decorated the walls, along with a dartboard and assorted alcoholic beverage posters and signs. At the far end of the room, a live band played on a raised stage and a group of people—mostly made up of couples—line danced to the tune of a Texas two-step.

"So, what do you want to do first?" Mitch asked, leaning over her shoulder and speaking close to her ear to be heard over the volume of the music. "Dance, find a table and order some nachos, or sit at the bar and order a drink?"

She scanned the crowd, weighing her options. This was a far cry from the movie or dinner at a quiet restaurant she'd expected of tonight, but it could still be fun.

"Let's get a drink," she yelled back, tipping her head toward the bar.

With his hand at her back, Emma eased her way through the crush of bodies and hopped up on one of the tall stools lining the long mahogany bar. Mitch took a seat beside her and ordered two cold beers.

Since she hadn't had anything to eat yet that evening, she sipped her drink slowly and tried to avoid their images in the mirror that lined the wall behind the bar.

It wasn't her reflection that made her uncomfortable, but Mitch's. He was too darn handsome, too tall and sinewy and masculine in all the right places.

Beneath the wide rim of his black hat, he looked like some hardened Clint Eastwood character. His eyes glittered in the low lighting, his mouth a thin line of indifference.

And yet he took her breath away. Every strong, familiar inch of him.

She dragged her gaze away, staring intently at the colorful label that circled the brown glass bottle in her hand until her pulse slowed to an almost human rate of speed instead of that of a hummingbird.

Even in a rowdy, crowded bar, surrounded by strangers and the teeth-rattling thrum of a noisy band, she was still unaccountably attracted to him. He hadn't touched her intimately since that night in the barn two weeks ago, yet she still felt the whisper of his hands and mouth on her naked flesh.

She shivered at the memory and took a long swallow of her light beer to extinguish the fire sparking to life low in her belly.

When Mitch's hand closed on her arm, she jumped.

"Sorry, didn't mean to startle you."

He was talking at a near-normal volume now, and she realized the band had slipped into a much slower song.

"Let's dance," he said. Then, without waiting for a reply, he slid off his stool and pulled her down to the floor beside him.

Fingers linked together, he led her to the dance floor, then swung her around and into his arms.

He held her entirely too close…not too close for society's standards, especially in this place, but too close for her peace of mind. For her body to maintain its natural calm.

One of his hands clutched hers. The other rested at the small of her back, his arm wrapped around her waist. His tall form brushed against her in all the right spots—chest to breasts, stomach to stomach, pelvis to pelvis. Everywhere they touched, rockets went off beneath her skin.

If he hadn't been holding her up, she thought she probably would have melted to the floor. As it was, her feet felt like they were barely touching the ground.

The music flowed all around them, and for the moment she let herself pretend this was more than their first date, more than two old friends who were toying with the idea of getting more seriously involved.

She imagined they were old lovers, maybe even a married couple, still very much in love. Out on the town for their anniversary, or perhaps just for an evening away from the kids.

The hand on her back shifted slightly lower, caressing the upper curve of her buttock and drawing her snug against his arousal.

It stunned her still that he was so obviously attracted to her. After all the years she'd pined for him from afar, to suddenly have him notice her as a woman and show sexual interest left her feeling confused and off-balance. Especially when he could make love to her with abandon one minute, then leave her hanging for two full weeks without so much as a phone call.

But he was trying. His suggestion that they try dating might not have been the smoothest invitation she'd ever received, and this might not be the greatest first date she'd ever gone on, but she gave him an A for effort.

And an A-plus for the way he made her heart beat faster, her knees turn to jelly, and her insides feel like she was riding up and down in an elevator car.

She sighed and closed her eyes, forgetting that they were in the middle of a crowded dance floor. As far as she was concerned, there was only Mitch and herself and the electricity arcing between them.

His rough jaw scraped her cheek as he leaned in close, his warm breath stirring her hair as he leaned in to speak above her ear.

"Want to get out of here?"

She blinked, raising her head to meet his gaze. His gray eyes burned with barely banked desire, and it was all she could do to remain upright.

She didn't think, didn't weigh the pros and cons, she simply responded in the only way her heart and body would allow. "Yes."

Four

Even as he half-dragged Emma out of the Silver Spur and across the gravel parking lot, Mitch called himself seven kinds of fool.

He'd purposely brought her here, knowing the bar would be noisy and crowded. Knowing there would be no chance of him being overcome by lust and making a move on her.

Ha! So much for that theory. His brilliant plan had back-fired almost at the speed of light.

It had started innocently enough. Sit at the bar, sip a beer. The decibel level of the music and surrounding conversations made small talk impossible, which he considered a good thing.

But then he'd gone and asked her to dance. What a colossal mistake.

What had he been thinking? If he was going to make such a blunder, he could have at least made the offer during a fast song or while people were two-stepping in a synchronized group.

But, no, he'd gone and asked her to dance to a slow song. One that required them to stand close, to touch just about everywhere.

And he'd willingly taken her into his arms, set them both to swaying. Only when he felt her breasts with their semi-erect peaks brushing against his chest had he realized he was in trouble.

But by then, it had been too late. The scent of her freshly washed hair and spicy floral perfume had invaded his nostrils. The brush of her hands and belly and hips had turned him hard in an instant.

And despite his best efforts to maintain control, to cool his jets and remind himself that he'd promised he wouldn't sleep with her again, he found himself leaning in and asking her to leave with him.

To hell with their drinks. To hell with his vow to keep things platonic. He wanted her...now, with a single-minded determination that made him feel like a bull charging a red flag.

Their feet crunched on the gravel of the parking lot as he led her to the pickup and lifted her inside. Slamming the door, he stalked around the front of the truck and climbed behind the wheel.

Before the sound of his door closing had finished echoing through the cab, he was on her. Reaching out, dragging her across the vinyl seat and kissing her sense-less. His hands were everywhere, groping, yanking, tearing her clothes away so he could get to her naked flesh.

She tasted of the beer she'd drunk earlier but also like Emma. Sweet, womanly, innocent.

Her lips met his, matched him move for move as though

she could read his mind. Her tongue teased and tangled, parried when he thrust and thrust when he parried.

And her hands...her hands were at the buttons of his shirt, the belt at his waist, every bit as eager to strip him bare as he was to do the same to her.

Her willingness, her eagerness drove him, let him know he wasn't the only one raging with passion, scrambling to get closer, faster, now, now.

He let her push the shirt off his shoulders and fumble with his heavy busting bronco belt buckle while he yanked her denim skirt up around her hips. He whispered a prayer of thanks when he discovered only a pair of sheer panties, with no stockings to bar his way, and wasted no time shucking them down her slim legs.

She had his belt undone by then and was working on the button and zipper of his jeans. He released her long enough to cover her hands and help her along.

As soon as he was free, hard and aching, he stopped, took a deep breath, lifted his head and looked into her eyes. She was staring back, chest heaving, her expression one of impatience and longing.

He felt like he should say something...compliment her, tell her she was beautiful or he cared about her. But he couldn't think of a damn thing that wouldn't sound fake or forced, and his mouth was full of cotton, anyway.

So he scrapped the idea of trying to be romantic or chivalrous and simply leaned in to take her lips. She kissed him back, wrapping her arms around his neck and weaving her fingers through his hair.

Keeping his mouth firmly on hers, he laid her back along the seat of the cab and knelt between her legs. A small shift of her skirt and his pants, and he was inside her.

She was gloriously tight and wet and felt like heaven.

He let out a groan of pleasure, resting his brow against hers for a moment until his breathing and heartbeat returned to normal. Well, as normal as they were likely to get when he was this close to Emma, this close to pure bliss.

"You okay?" he asked, his voice strained. He sensed rather than saw her nod and felt her slick inner muscles tighten around him in assent.

It was all he could do not to moan in sweet agony.

She was amazing. Open and eager. Fluid and graceful, but at the same time wild and uninhibited.

Holding her was like holding a live wire. And that charge, that jolt of high-voltage electricity, rocked him to his core.

He'd been celibate ever since he found out Suzanne was cheating on him, so it was no small wonder he was ravenous for a woman's touch. It had almost been easier to simply grit his teeth and white-knuckle his way through the lack of sex in his life.

But now that he'd been with Emma, had had a woman's silky skin beneath his hands and feminine body enveloping his, he couldn't seem to get enough. He wanted her naked and writhing for him twenty-four hours a day.

One would think that for a man who'd been without a woman's company as long as he had, any woman would do. But something told him that wasn't quite true. Some part of him knew that if his dry spell hadn't been broken by Emma…it might not have been broken at all.

In all the time he'd been divorced from Suzanne, no one had even tempted him to break his celibacy.

No one until Emma, up in that loft.

And now here she was again, letting him take her. In the cab of his truck, no less.

If he were any kind of man, he would stop what he was

doing and let her up. Apologize and take her home. Or at the very least, take her somewhere decent to finish what they'd started—his place or a motel. Somewhere with a bed and clean sheets.

But he was too far gone, and he obviously wasn't that noble because instead of pulling away, he tugged her legs more snugly around his hips and pressed forward until he was as deep inside her as he could go.

Emma couldn't think, could barely breathe with Mitch's weight on top of her. His heat, his intensity, the feel of him filling her to overflowing.

She wanted him to move, to give her what she needed before the urge to scream became unbearable.

"Mitch, please," she whimpered, tightening her hold around his hips and neck.

Ripples of pleasure coursed through her and she gave a sigh of relief when he began to rock, thrusting into her with power and purpose. He wasted no time with added foreplay or spare caresses, and she didn't need them. All she wanted was him—hard, fast, now.

He sped up, driving into her with increasing force until her vision turned blurry around the edges and bursts of color went off behind her eyes and in her bloodstream. She bit her lip to keep from crying out…then cried out anyway when her orgasm broke and washed over her in a giant wave of sensation.

Mitch thrust once, twice more, before giving a shout of completion and stiffening above her. His breath panted in her ear, his heart pounding against her chest.

Long minutes passed before feeling returned to their limbs and they were able to move. Mitch hoisted himself off of her with a reluctant groan, then helped her sit up and rearrange her clothes. Once everything was back in order, they sat on opposite ends of the wide bench seat, staring straight ahead.

After a moment of awkward silence, she said, "Boy, we really fogged it up in here, didn't we?"

The windshield and side windows were smoky with condensation, blocking their view.

A beat passed, and then he let out a rough laugh. "Yeah, we sure did."

He leaned over to retrieve his Stetson from her side of the cab's floor, where it had fallen during their wild groping, dusted it off and jammed it back on his head.

"You hungry?" he asked, fingers flexing on the steering wheel.

Now that both her nerves about their first date and the intense passion of their quick joining had passed, she realized she was starving.

"Definitely."

Brushing his shirt sleeve across the glass so he could see, he started the engine and pulled slowly out of the parking lot. Ten minutes later, they were back in one of the red vinyl booths of Rosie's Café.

The diner was open till ten, but evening wasn't a busy time, so only one waitress and one cook were working, and Mitch and Emma were the only customers. They sat on opposite sides of a booth near the rear of the restaurant and ordered glasses of iced tea and two plates of the special— spaghetti and meat sauce, with garlic bread on the side.

Normally, Emma would have avoided any type of garlic, onions and the like on a date, but since Mitch was having some, too, and they'd already gotten all the hot and heavy business out of their systems before dinner, she thought she was probably safe.

They made small talk while they wound pasta around

their forks and sopped up red sauce with the chunks of garlic bread.

"So, how's your family?" she wanted to know.

"Good. Mom and Dad keep themselves busy with the ranch, and I help out when I can."

"And Chase?"

Chase was younger by four years but every inch as handsome and charming. Even though he'd grown up on a horse and cattle ranch and knew the workings of one as well as she and Mitch, his interests had always lain elsewhere. Instead of working the land, he found greater pleasure in the business world, buying up struggling companies to either help them revamp and have a second shot at success or breaking them up to sell off for profit. From what she'd heard, he was doing quite well for himself.

"He's fine. You know Chase, he's off working on some kind of deal again. Last I heard, he was in Chicago, but we expect him back soon."

She nodded and wiped the corners of her mouth with her napkin before taking a sip of tea.

"You know, what happened tonight...I didn't plan it that way."

He kept his eyes glued to his plate, so she had no doubt what part of the evening he was referring to.

"I told myself I wouldn't touch you, no matter what. We were just supposed to go out and have fun."

She let a moment pass, deciding how best to respond. Finally, she said, "I had fun," before taking another bite of tender spaghetti.

She had the pleasure of watching his eyes widen and his mouth drop open slightly. But only for a second. In the blink of an eye, he caught himself and once again schooled his features into a mask of stern control.

Honestly, he was the most rigid man she'd ever met.

He'd always been serious but not *this* serious. She blamed Suzanne for the change, and it wasn't a positive one.

Which was why it was almost amusing to do or say things that knocked him off balance and broke through that steely exterior. Lord knew someone needed to.

"Relax, Mitch," she said on half a laugh. "For heaven's sake, you're acting like you personally escorted me to the lion's den. It was sex. Incredibly good, incredibly hot sex. But I wish you'd stop apologizing…. You're starting to give me a complex."

He studied her from across the booth, and she could see the wheels turning in his mind.

"What do you suggest we do?" he asked in a low voice. "Continue having incredibly good, incredibly hot sex every chance we get?"

At his words, a bolt of heat lightning shot straight to her feminine core. "Yes." *God, yes. Please.*

This time, he didn't bother trying to control his reaction as he goggled at her.

"Are you crazy?" he hissed. "How can you be so cavalier about this?"

"How can you be so uptight about it? We're hardly strangers; we've known each other since we were kids. If any two people should be comfortable around each other in just about any situation, it's us."

She waved her fork at him while she chewed. "And I don't know about you, but I'm enjoying myself. The sex is great, very satisfying, and I like being with you. We haven't spent this much time together since before you married Suzanne."

As soon as the name passed her lips, Emma wished she could take it back. His mouth flattened into a thin line and his eyes turned dark. Just as they always did at the mention of his ex-wife.

"Sorry," she mumbled, letting her gaze skitter away.

After playing with her food for a minute or two, she took a deep breath and lifted her head, determined to look him straight in the eye.

"All I'm saying is that I've missed hanging out with you. And if I'd known the sex was going to be so good, I'd have probably seduced you way back in high school."

At that, one dark eyebrow winged upward. "You would have, huh?"

"Oh, yeah," she said with a nod. "Either you or Chase. I figure since you're so alike in other ways, you're probably equally talented in bed."

That brought a deep scowl to his face, and she nearly chuckled.

Note to self. Don't tell the man you're sleeping with that you can find another man who can satisfy you just as well as he does. Especially if the two are related.

"Look," she said when he remained stoically silent for so long, she feared smoke would seep out of his ears. "You're the one who said we should go out for a while, see where things lead. So why can't we keep doing that?"

"Because every time we go out," he told her through clenched teeth, "we end up rolling around like…like… monkeys in heat."

Monkeys? In heat? She wasn't sure she appreciated that particular imagery.

"Most men would be thrilled to have all of their dates end with them getting lucky."

"Is that so?" His eyes glittered, but she couldn't tell if it was with amusement or warning. "I guess I'm not like most men, then."

Well, that was certainly true. For better or worse, Mitch was unlike any man she'd ever known before.

With her heart pounding in her chest, she licked her lips nervously and asked, "Does that mean you don't want to sleep with me anymore?"

A muscle in his jaw jumped as he contemplated his answer. "I didn't say that," he replied finally, sounding reluctant.

Emma hoped her face didn't show her intense relief, but it washed over her all the same, causing her stomach to flutter.

"Do you not want to go out anymore at all?"

"I didn't say that, either."

"Then may I make a suggestion?"

She was loathe to press her luck, to push him into a corner or evoke a response from him that she might not care for quite as much as the ones she'd gotten so far. But she also didn't want to continue having this conversation with him or know that every time they were together, he'd suffer a bout of postcoital guilt.

"What's that?" he asked.

"Let's go back to your original plan. We go out, we enjoy ourselves. If we feel like having sex, we can, but without any pressure *or guilt*," she stressed, "on either side. And we'll see where it takes us, just like you suggested."

His eyebrows drew together and lines formed around his frowning mouth. "Throwing my own words back at me, huh? Guess I should be more careful of what I say around you."

She smiled, reassured by his comment that he wasn't going to cut her loose and demand they go back to being just friends and neighbors.

"Guess you should."

His lips curved up on one side and he pushed his empty plate aside, folding his arms in front of him on the tabletop. "So, what do you want to do on our next date?"

"Maybe a movie," she offered. And then, with a straight face, she added, "Followed by hot, sweaty, monkey sex."

This time, her mention of sex didn't set his eyes or jaw to twitching. Instead, he met her gaze and said, "How does Saturday sound? I'll pick you up at eight."

Five

Mitch pushed his plate away and released a breath that only seemed to tighten the waistband of his pants. Once again, he'd eaten too much. But it was Emma's fault for being such a damn fine cook.

They'd been following their dating plan for three weeks now, and this was the third time he'd had dinner at her place. It was becoming something of a weekly custom.

And though it had made him nervous at first to sit across the table from Wyatt, wondering if the man was going to jump up at any moment and threaten to castrate Mitch for taking advantage of his daughter, he had to admit he was starting to enjoy the evenings he spent in the Davis household.

Each meal Emma fixed tasted better than the last. He didn't miss the fact, either, that she made a point of preparing his favorite dishes on the nights he came over, like meatloaf and pork chops. And she always had homemade biscuits, fresh out of the oven, ever since his first visit when he'd eaten six and told her how good they were.

"Would you like any more?" Emma asked before pushing back her chair and collecting the bowls of mashed potatoes and green beans.

"No, thank you. I couldn't eat another bite." He patted his belly and slumped in his chair with an appreciative smile on his face.

"My girl sure can cook, can't she?" Wyatt asked, beaming proudly. "She takes after her mother."

"Yes, sir," Mitch agreed. "I can't remember the last time I tasted such good food."

His dinners these days pretty much consisted of single-serving microwave meals or leftovers his mother sent over when she got worried he wasn't eating right.

"Don't tell my mother I said that, though," he added.

Wyatt chuckled. "Don't worry, your secret's safe with me."

Then he turned to Emma, who was busy transferring the remainder of the meal into smaller containers and slipping them in the fridge.

"If you don't need any help, honey, do you mind if Mitch and I step outside for a few minutes?"

Mitch was a little surprised by the request, but judging by the friendly expression on the older man's face, he didn't think Emma's father planned to take him out to the barn and shoot him. At least he hoped not.

"No, I'm fine," she told them, piling dishes into the sink and running hot water over them. "You two go ahead. But no smoking, all right?" She shot her father a warning look. "I mean it, Pop. Mitch, don't let him light one of those filthy cigars."

Wyatt winked at Mitch, his blue eyes twinkling as he

pushed to his feet. "A man can't have any fun around here," he pretended to grumble.

Mitch didn't know that he would agree with that statement. Considering the number of times in the past few weeks that he and Emma had sneaked out to the barn or up to her room when her father wasn't around, he could reliably say a man could have a great deal of fun around this place.

But he didn't think it would be very smart to point that out to Wyatt. Not when he was doing his damnedest *not* to let the man know he was sleeping with his daughter.

Emma, up to her elbows now in sudsy water, shook her head but chose not to respond to her father's complaint.

The legs of Mitch's chair scraped the floor as he got up and followed Wyatt onto the front porch. The older man took a seat on the solid wooden swing to one side of the kitchen door and pulled a plump brown stogie from his front shirt pocket. He ran the cigar under his nose, inhaling deeply, then tucked it away again with a sigh of regret.

"A couple of puffs after dinner, that's my limit. But she worries about me, so most of the time all I get to do is sniff the damn thing."

Moving to a spot in front of Wyatt, Mitch leaned back against the porch railing, feet crossed at the ankle, hands resting on either side of his hips.

After several more minutes passed in silence, he said, "You wanted to talk to me, sir?"

"Yes. Yes, I did."

Wyatt slapped his hands down on his knees and rose to his feet, coming to stand beside Mitch, facing the other direction.

"Emma is my pride and joy, you know that."

"Yes, sir."

"And I worry about her, just as much as she worries about me."

"Yes, sir," Mitch murmured again, not sure where this conversation was headed.

"I worry especially about what will happen with her after I'm gone."

It took a moment for that to sink in, and when it did, Mitch's gut clenched. "Is something wrong, Mr. Davis? Are you sick?" He couldn't quite bring himself to ask if the man was dying, but that was the message flashing across the front of his brain.

"Hell, no," Wyatt denied firmly. "Healthy as an ox, according to the doctor. But I'm not getting any younger, and accidents happen. There's no telling how long any of us will get to be on this earth. And when my time comes, I'd like to know my girl is taken care of."

Mitch's breathing had returned to normal, but his heart was still beating just a little faster than it should. "I can understand that."

"That's where you come in."

One eyebrow lifted in curiosity. "Excuse me?"

"I've got a proposition for you, my boy." Wyatt twisted to face him more fully and slapped him on the arm. "Emma's an only child, and as sexist as it might sound, I don't have any sons to deed this land to when I die. My girl loves this place and is great at helping me out with the business end of things, but she won't want to run the ranch after I'm gone."

Mitch made a noncommittal noise, still not sure what Wyatt was getting at.

"Our families have always been close, you and Emma grew up together, and your land borders ours. So I'll come right out and say what I'm thinking, Mitch. I'd like you to marry my daughter."

He blinked, stunned into speechlessness. Where his

heart had been running a bit too fast only minutes before, it now seemed to slow almost to a stop.

"I know, I know," Emma's father continued. "It's an odd request. Not to mention extremely meddling of me. But I've watched the two of you together these past weeks. Emma's happy, and it does my heart good to see the two of you getting so serious.

"I don't mind telling you that your parents and I have always sort of hoped our two families would end up connecting this way. We never wanted to pressure you kids in any way, but there were many nights that we discussed the possibilities over a couple hands of cards."

That was news to Mitch. As close as their families had been and as much time as he and Chase had spent with Emma growing up, it had honestly never occurred to him that either he or his brother might wind up interested in Emma romantically.

Not that there was anything wrong with her. On the contrary, she had always been a nice, good-looking girl. But she'd practically been their sister.

He wondered if Chase had ever thought of her in any other way and made a mental note to ask the next time he saw his brother.

"I know it's a strange thing to ask, and you'll want to think it over. But I'd feel more comfortable leaving the Double D to you, as my son-in-law, knowing you'll keep it in good shape. Emma would do her best, but she'd have to hire on a lot more help, and I'm just not sure her heart would be in it.

"You're a responsible man. Decent and trustworthy. If you married my Emma and took over the running of this ranch, I'd know Emma was being taken care of."

Mitch rubbed his jaw, briefly entertaining the notion that

he was hallucinating. It just didn't make sense that in this day and age, a father was standing beside him, trying to work out the details of an arranged marriage for his daughter.

And yet, he understood Wyatt's motivation, the love and concern behind the offer. The Double D had been in Wyatt's family for generations. Wyatt had lived here all his life, loving and working the ranch. He'd grown up, married, and raised a family all in the same house, on the same land.

Mitch understood the man's desire to make sure the ranch was taken care of after he was gone. To see that his *daughter* was well taken care of, as well.

It might sound callous or overly chauvinistic to some, but Wyatt only wanted the best for Emma and his homestead.

Not that Mitch was honestly considering saying yes. When his marriage to Suzanne had ended, he'd sworn never to get lured into that trap again. He and Emma might have been heating up the sheets these past few weeks, but being good together in bed didn't mean they had to get leg-shackled.

"I'm sorry, Mr. Davis," he said, returning his hands to the porch railing, "but I don't think—"

"Now, now," Wyatt interrupted. "Don't answer just yet. Take some time, give it some serious thought. I understand the significance of my proposition and don't want you agreeing to anything you aren't absolutely sure about. Emma deserves better than that, and so do you."

The older man slapped him on the back and took a few steps away, heading toward the kitchen door. "But just so you know, I'd consider it a personal favor if you and Emma got hitched. I can't think of anyone I'd rather have running this place and looking after my girl after I'm gone."

Shaking his head in puzzlement, Mitch pushed off of the railing and followed Wyatt back into the house.

The arresting aroma of fresh-brewed coffee hit him the

minute he stepped into the kitchen. Emma had set a platter of homemade cookies in the center of the table and was pouring coffee for the three of them.

As they returned to their chairs, she slid a mug toward him and his heart lurched to realize how much care she'd taken with everything. The meal, the hominess of the room they were sitting in, the cookies on the table, and each cup of coffee doctored just as the drinker liked it.

As wives went, he could do a lot worse than Emma, that was for sure. She was kind and considerate, a terrific cook and sexy as all get out.

He didn't imagine everyone would think so. She didn't possess the fantasy hourglass figure, and what she did have, she tended to hide beneath blue jeans and button-down blouses.

But she wore those jeans like no one he'd ever see before. She didn't pour herself into them the way Suzanne had, but they weren't loose and baggy, either. They fit just right—snug where a man could appreciate it most and roomy enough in other places to plague his imagination.

And since he'd seen her naked, *felt* her naked beneath him on many recent occasions, he happened to know that her less than fashionably ideal form was actually quite perfect.

Her breasts were pert and pretty and just large enough to fit his hands. Her waist was slim, tapering down to narrow hips that made his mouth water. And her legs were as long and muscular as a colt's.

He'd come up with that particular analogy the last time she'd sat astride him and ridden him into a foaming lather.

The memory sent blood shooting to all the wrong places—at least while he was sitting across the table from her father—and he immediately tried to redirect his wayward thoughts. Wyatt's invitation to marry her and take over his land pretty much did the trick.

The only problem was, this time, the idea didn't seem quite so repugnant.

As he sipped his coffee and listened with half an ear to what Emma and Wyatt were saying, he pictured himself standing in front of a preacher again, speaking those holy vows that had backfired on him once. A skitter of icy fear snaked down his spine.

But then he imagined being married to Emma. She wouldn't be like Suzanne, that was for sure. She was the homey type and would take great pride in taking care of him and their household. He would have piping-hot meals to look forward to on a daily basis, and even hotter nights spent in her arms. She would laugh and maybe even make him smile in return.

That was certainly something he could get used to. And he knew that he could be married to Emma, be a good husband, without getting too emotionally attached to her.

Men were blessed that way. He'd married once for love and been kicked in the crotch for his trouble. No way was he interested in a repeat performance. But he could live with her, sleep with her and make her happy without risking his heart.

His only concern was that Emma might not. Women were different, and she was perhaps more sensitive than most. What if she developed feelings for him that he couldn't reciprocate? What if she read too much into their arrangement and ended up getting hurt?

But she seemed to understand that he was once bitten, twice shy. In all the time they'd been dating and sleeping together, she'd never once asked more of him than he was willing to give. She didn't bring up Suzanne or ask him to pour out his soul so she could analyze his feelings and try to fix them. She simply accepted their relationship—and him—for what it was.

If she could handle a marriage to him in the same way, then they might just have a shot at building some sort of life together and fulfilling her father's wishes, as well.

And it was no small consideration that if he took Wyatt up on his offer, his own parents would stop pressuring him to get over his ex's betrayal, get on with his life, and find a better woman to settle down with.

Emma's and Wyatt's voices buzzed in his ears, his thoughts seeming to race faster than his brain could process them. What he was contemplating made his temperature rise at the same time a cold sweat began to trickle between his shoulder blades.

Suddenly, he realized his companions had stopped talking. The room was eerily silent, and, when he raised his head, he found two nearly identical sets of eyes gazing back at him.

"Sorry," he said, feeling like an idiot. "Guess my mind wandered."

"That's all right," Emma replied softly, gifting him with a comforting smile. "Pop was just fishing for compliments on my behalf, anyway."

Still smiling, she floated up from her chair and made her way to the sink to rinse her coffee cup. He watched her cross the room, mesmerized by the fluid grace of her movements, by her long, slim limbs and tight, round bottom.

His gut tightened and a sensation like warm melted butter crawled through his veins.

Before he could talk himself out of it, he pushed his chair back and got to his feet. "Care to take a walk with me, Emma?"

Her head whipped around, startlement in her clear blue eyes. She reached over to turn off the water, then dried her hands on a nearby dish towel before turning to fully face him.

"Um...okay." Her gaze skittered to her father for a brief second. "You don't mind if we leave you alone for a while, do you, Pop?"

"'Course not," he answered quickly, waving them away. "You two go on. There's plenty around here to keep me busy."

Mitch opened the front door and held it while Emma passed through. He waited until she'd crossed the width of the porch and stepped down into the yard before tipping his head back in Wyatt's direction.

"I thought about it," he said in a low voice, not wanting Emma to overhear, "and I've decided to take you up on your offer."

He stepped outside, closing the door behind him, but not before he caught the grin of pure delight on Wyatt Davis's bearded face.

Emma turned in time to see Mitch come down off the porch steps and catch up with her. Without speaking, he took her hand and started walking.

They moved away from the pale streaks of yellow light shining through the windows of the house, but the moon overhead shone brightly enough to illuminate their path.

"Where are we going?" she finally broke the silence to ask.

"Nowhere special. I just thought we'd find some place private to talk."

"Just talk?" she shot back with a teasing grin. From her experience, he was fine with talking in public. It was other things he preferred to do in private.

"Just talk."

His tone was so serious, so unyielding, a ripple of fear caused her stomach to tighten.

This was it, she thought. He was getting ready to break up with her.

She shouldn't be surprised. She'd known it was coming—eventually.

But that didn't keep her heart from twisting, didn't keep regret from tensing her muscles and slowing her step.

Just a little longer. That's all she'd wanted—just a little longer to be with him, to love him, to pretend he loved her, too.

A few more days, a few more weeks…then she'd have been able to let him go. She might even have been the one to end it before he had a chance.

Breathing deeply, she tried to remain calm, tried to tell herself it was inevitable and probably for the best. She was a big girl, she could handle it.

She would miss being with him, but they could still be friends. Instead of going out as a couple, they would run into each other on the street and make small talk. Instead of making love, they would smile and pretend they'd never seen each other naked, never made each other pant and scream in ecstasy.

Piece of cake.

And maybe next she'd attempt to leap tall buildings in a single bound.

When she felt a tug on her arm, she realized Mitch had stopped walking. Looking around, she decided they must be out behind the house. She hadn't been paying enough attention to know how far.

"So…what did you want to talk about?" she prompted, even though she knew perfectly well. She swallowed hard and blinked, telling herself not to cry.

He leaned back against the bark of a tall catalpa tree and took her other hand, pulling her close. Their bodies brushed and she reveled in his warmth, even as she wondered why he was bothering when he just planned to dump her, anyway.

"Our future," he said.

Here it came. By *our future*, he meant the lack thereof.

Her heart was racing, her palms turning damp with nervousness. And she knew that when she spoke, her voice would quaver. "What about our future?"

"I've been thinking."

Of course he had, and he'd decided he'd had enough of her.

"These past few weeks...we've had fun. We've been pretty good together."

Yes, they had been. More than good. At times, they'd been phenomenal. But apparently that didn't matter to him.

"And I've been thinking..."

Yes, yes, he'd said that already.

"That maybe we should make it permanent."

Of course. Ever since Suzanne had left him—

She stopped. Stopped thinking, stopped blinking, stopped breathing. Had he just said...?

What had he just said?

"Excuse me?" she practically wheezed with what little air was left in her lungs.

"Emma," he said slowly, his eyes dark and solemn as he stared into her own. "Will you marry me?"

Six

Emma had heard of being struck speechless before, but she'd never actually experienced it until this moment. Her head was spinning so fast, she feared she might pass out, and, even though her lungs burned for air, she couldn't seem to inhale.

He'd just asked her to marry him. Mitch. Had asked *her.* To marry *him.* When she'd thought for sure he was about to dump her instead and had been bracing herself for the worst.

Finally she managed to suck in a long, much-needed breath. "But—"

"It may not be a love match," he said, running his hands up her arms to cup her shoulders and essentially cutting off whatever she'd been about to say. "I know that, but we get along well enough to make a marriage work. I like you, you like me. There's no doubt we're good in bed. And I'll take care of you, no matter what. You can trust me on that."

In the space of a heartbeat, she went from being elated

that he might have feelings for her after all…enough to propose to her…to being crushed by his blatant admission that he didn't love her at all but merely saw a marriage to her as something that would be convenient and comfortable for both of them.

Her first instinct was to tell him what he could do with his less-than-inspiring offer. But then she began to think of how much courage it had taken for him to even ask.

Suzanne had done a real number on him, and she knew exactly how bitter he still was over her betrayal. It was a huge step for him to come to her now and ask her to marry him…even if it wasn't her idea of a dream proposal.

And she *had* been in love with him for as long as she could remember. This was her chance to be with him, regardless of the circumstances.

Maybe he didn't love her. Maybe he never would. Or maybe he just didn't love her *yet*. People changed. And people most especially healed after painful breakups.

If she married him, then every day would be another chance for her to erase a little more of Suzanne from his mind and heart and instill herself there instead. Not all women were like his scheming, two-timing ex, and all she needed was an opportunity to prove that to him.

A small voice inside her head warned her not to get her hopes up. That a woman couldn't change a man, and there was no use trying.

But Emma didn't want to change Mitch. She liked him just the way he was…or she had before he'd married up with that tramp.

And now, she simply wanted to be around when his battered heart finally healed and he got over his ex. For that, she could put a couple of years into a marriage that lacked the emotions she so dearly craved.

As long as she believed there was a chance he'd come around, a chance he could grow to love her as much as she already loved him.

A shiver of anticipation raced through her, settling low in her belly and spreading warmly outward.

She was doing the right thing. She knew she was.

Leaning close, she put her hands on either side of his waist and pressed her lips to the corner of his mouth. "Yes," she whispered. "Yes, I'll marry you."

His fingers tightened on her shoulders and she thought she felt him shudder against her.

"Good," he said with a matter-of-fact nod. He kicked himself away from the trunk of the tree and took her hand. "Let's go back to the house and tell your dad."

Her eyes widened in surprise and she let out a nervous chuckle. When he tugged at her arm, she tugged back.

"Wait a minute. Don't you want to celebrate?"

Since he was standing as still and immovable as a stone statue, she went to him, pressing herself along his tall frame and raising her face to his.

"Yeah, right. Celebrate." He bent in to kiss her, just a quick, hard peck on her lips, then he straightened again and dragged her after him.

She laughed, increasing her steps to keep up and thinking that from now on, her life—her life with Mitch— was going to be very interesting, indeed.

Emma took a sip of her wine—her second glass of the evening, and she'd only arrived an hour ago.

The Ramsey's sprawling one-story house was filled with guests, family and friends gathered by Mitch's mother to help celebrate their engagement. Flowers and balloons decorated the large, hardwood living room, and a banner that said Congratulations Mitch And Emma! hung over the stone fireplace.

It was all very thoughtful…and very intimidating.

But as soon as Theresa Ramsey had heard the news, she'd insisted she be allowed to throw a party for them, inviting half the town to what had transformed from wine, cheese and classical music to louder country tunes and free-flowing alcohol.

Ironically, it was his parents' enthusiasm about their engagement and all the plans his mother immediately began to launch that had seemed to turn Mitch off. From the time they'd announced their plans to marry—first to her father and then to his mom and dad—the same night he'd proposed, he'd seemed to shut down, showing no interest whatsoever in their engagement or upcoming nuptials.

He'd reluctantly agreed to his mother's arrangements and told Emma to do whatever she wanted as far as the wedding was concerned. He was leaving it up to her to set the date and decide on all of the preparations.

She understood him not wanting to get involved. How many men really wanted to play a part in deciding on flowers and color schemes and girlie things like that?

But she'd at least expected him to help her choose a place for the ceremony—the church or his parents' backyard?—and maybe offer suggestions for the guest list. Instead, he'd washed his hands of the entire situation, leaving her feeling very much alone.

They'd arrived tonight together, at his mother's prompting. Theresa had mapped things out so that everyone else arrived before the guests of honor, and when Mitch and Emma walked through the door, it was to mingled shouts of "Surprise!" and "Congratulations!"

She hadn't seen Mitch since.

Swallowing past the lump of emotion threatening to

clog her throat, Emma forced a smile to her lips for the gentleman who'd just told her a supposedly amusing story of which she hadn't heard a word.

It was Mitch's way, that's all, she told herself. He was a private person who didn't like crowds or parties and especially didn't like people making a fuss over him.

He'd also been married before. A marriage he'd been eager for and expected to last forever. Going through all of this again couldn't be easy for him.

He was probably being flooded by painful memories and might even be considering what all of these guests were thinking about his latest engagement. *Here he goes again. Maybe this time it will work out. Wonder if Emma will end up stepping out on him, too.*

Emma didn't believe any of their friends and neighbors would think such things about him, but she knew how Mitch's mind worked these days. He'd become incredibly sensitive and prickly since Suzanne's infidelity. As Emma imagined most men would.

But she would never hurt him that way and only needed a chance to prove it. She only needed time for him to begin to believe it.

That didn't mean she wasn't still nervous about the entire situation, however. Couples who were madly in love and one-hundred-percent dedicated to having a happy, healthy marriage suffered from butterflies and cold feet. Emma was positively petrified.

As much as she loved Mitch already, as much as she wanted to be his wife, having a fiancé who treated her coolly and was indifferent to their wedding plans was enough to bring doubts the size of Texas to the forefront of her mind.

The room around her felt suddenly too small, packed

with people to a claustrophobic degree. Her chest tightened and her breathing became slightly labored.

She needed some fresh air and just a few minutes alone to calm her nerves.

Keeping a smile on her face and nodding to acquaintances as she passed, she made her way into the kitchen and out a side door. The Ramsey home had a great wraparound porch that connected to three sides of the house, with three different entrances. The better to slip away without being seen than if she'd been forced to leave through the front door.

Once outside, she stepped to the railing, set her wineglass aside and took a deep breath as she stared across the darkening landscape. Nails digging into wood, she studied the colors streaking the horizon as dusk drifted into night.

The cool air felt nice on her heated skin, and she finally relaxed her grip on the railing enough to reach for her glass and take another small sip.

"Getting a little crowded in there, isn't it?"

Emma jumped at the sound of the deep male voice coming out of the darkness and turned to find Mitch's brother, Chase, standing just a few feet away. Her heart pounded as she watched him step out of the shadows.

He was dressed in jeans and cowboy boots like just about every other man in attendance but was also wearing a tan jacket over his blue chambray shirt. The highball glass in his right hand was half filled with amber liquid and three rapidly melting ice cubes.

"Chase," she said, still somewhat breathless from the shock of having him sneak up on her. "I didn't know you were here. Mitch told me you were in Chicago or some such place on business."

"I was. But I couldn't miss my brother's engagement party to my favorite neighbor." He smiled gently and leaned in to kiss her cheek. "How are you, Emma?"

"Fine," she replied letting her gaze slide away from his. "How are you?"

"That's funny," he said, taking a sip of his drink and completely ignoring her polite question. "For someone who's supposed to be celebrating her upcoming marriage, I'd expect you to be a little more than just 'fine.' In fact, I'd expect you to be fairly vibrating with excitement."

"I'm excited," she told him, eyes still riveted to the porch floor. Her response sounded lame even to her own ears.

He gave a short huff of amusement. "If this is excited, I'd hate to see you depressed. Come on," he said softly, reaching out to knuckle her chin up and force her gaze to his. "You can't fool me, Emma. We've known each other too long. What's wrong?"

"Nothing," she tried to assure him with an overly bright grin, even as tears prickled behind her eyes.

"Emma…"

His tone was so soft, the look he gave her so sympathetic that she buried her face in the soft fabric of his suit jacket and burst into tears.

For several long minutes, he simply held her and let her cry, patting her back and murmuring nonsensical words of comfort. When she finally got hold of her emotions and lifted her head, he handed her a handkerchief to wipe her eyes and nose.

"Thank you," she said with a sniff, knowing she would have to slink back inside to fix her makeup and make sure her eyes weren't all red and puffy before anyone else got a look at her.

"Now are you ready to tell me what the problem is?"

She shook her head. "I shouldn't. You're his brother, and I'm sure I'm just overly nervous and emotional about the wedding."

"But…" he prompted. "My brother has obviously done something typically stupid or insensitive."

"That's just it," she said quietly, glancing at the handkerchief she was worrying with her fingertips. If it had been made of tissue rather than a sturdy cotton weave, she'd have shredded it into a million pieces by now. "He hasn't done anything. Ever since he proposed, he's been acting like he doesn't even *want* to get married. He hasn't shown a single bit of interest in the wedding plans or our future or even this party that your mother is so excited about and put so much time and energy into."

She waved a hand toward the crowded house, then dabbed once again at her flooding eyes. "I thought that being engaged to Mitch, being married to him, would make me happy, but now I wish we'd stuck to just sleeping together."

Chase's eyes widened at that declaration, but she ignored it. Obviously, Mitch wasn't the only person in town who expected her to be an innocent virgin until her dying—or wedding, as the case may be—day.

"Look," Chase said, rubbing her arms, left bare by her sleeveless dress, in a comforting gesture. "The reason for all of this is simple. My brother is an ass. His first mistake was hooking up with Suzanne, which anyone who was paying attention could have told him was a situation that had *disaster* written all over it. His second mistake was wasting so much as a minute being sorry when she left. And his third mistake…"

He paused to brush a lock of hair behind her ear and

offer a gentle smile. "His third and by far largest mistake, was making you cry when he should be holding on to you with both hands and letting you know every minute how much you mean to him."

At that, Emma's lungs hitched and tears started rolling down her face again.

Chase pulled her into his arms and patted her back. "*Shh.* He doesn't mean to hurt your feelings, he's just a little mixed up right now. You know what a number Suzanne's infidelity did on him. He doesn't know what he wants anymore."

She understood what he was saying, but it didn't make her feel any better. She was still in the distressing predicament of being engaged to a man she wasn't at all sure wanted to be with her.

Behind her, she heard the side door of the house open and footsteps echo on the wooden planks of the porch floor. Pushing away from Chase's embrace, she wiped her nose and cheeks, embarrassed to have been caught crying at her own engagement party.

When she turned, it wasn't a random guest standing a few feet away, but Mitch, who was glaring at her with dark, angry eyes.

"Well," he drawled, his voice as sharp as a knife edge, "I guess it's a good thing I found out about this before the wedding rather than after. It would be pretty stupid of me to marry *another* liar and cheater."

She felt Chase tense behind her a second before he growled, "Now, wait just a damn minute—"

"And with my own brother." Mitch stared past her, a sneer twisting his mouth.

"Mitch…" she said quickly, hoping to diffuse the situation before it got any worse "…it's not what you think."

Taking a step forward, she stretched a hand toward his chest only to drop it when he moved back and gave her a look that could have cut through glass.

"It never is, is it?" he replied nastily.

"Watch it, Mitch," Chase murmured from behind her in a threatening tone. "I'm not above bloodying your nose at your own engagement party."

Mitch took a menacing step forward, his furious gaze locked on his brother, completely ignoring Emma, who stood between them. "You're not above making time with my fiancé, either, are you?"

"Enough," she snapped, turning sideways and holding her arms out to stop both men in their tracks. "That's enough. Chase, I appreciate your help, but I think Mitch and I need a few minutes alone."

Chase relaxed his stance enough to meet her eyes. "You sure?"

"I'm sure."

"All right, but I'll be just inside. Yell if you need me."

She nodded but kept her mouth shut, knowing that if she said anything, Mitch would take it as a further sign that she was siding—not to mention cheating—with his brother.

Chase moved around them to the door, keeping a wary eye on his brother the entire time. With his hand on the knob, he said, "Hurt her and I'll make you sorry," before returning to the crowded house.

"Too late," Mitch muttered, even though his brother was no longer there to hear him. "I'm already sorry."

Her heart squeezed at his implication, but she lifted her chin and forced herself to face him head-on.

"Mitch, what you saw… Chase was only comforting me because I was upset. We weren't involved in some clandestine meeting. I'm not Suzanne," she added with feeling. "I would never betray you like that, and neither would your brother."

His eyes narrowed, jaw tightening, and he lifted his hands to his hips. "I know what I saw."

"You saw me crying on your brother's shoulder, that's all."

But even as she said the words, she knew they were falling on deaf ears. No matter what she said, he wasn't going to believe her. He thought the worst because he'd been cheated on before and was still raw and aching from the experience. She could talk herself blue...for heaven's sake, she could show him photographs *proving* her faithfulness and he still wouldn't believe her.

A stab of regret pierced her belly and her heart began to ache as she realized this would never work. She couldn't marry Mitch. Couldn't maintain a relationship with him when it was obvious he would never trust her.

His reaction to her innocent conversation with his brother was enough to convince her of that. And she didn't want to be with someone who was automatically going to think the worst of her in every situation.

She couldn't live like that, always being watched, always being suspected and accused.

Taking a deep breath, she closed her eyes and prayed she wouldn't break down in front of him the way she had with Chase.

"You know, I don't think this is going to work," she told him, glad when her voice came out solid and self-assured, because her insides were shaking like the San Andreas Fault. "There's nothing going on between Chase and me. That's the God's honest truth. But you'll never believe it, never believe a word I say because you're still not over Suzanne. And I can't marry a man who doesn't trust me."

She opened and closed her hands at her sides, not

knowing what else to do with them and half-afraid she would reach for him, effectively ruining any resolve she had about calling things off.

"I'm sorry, but I think it would be better if we called off the wedding."

For several long seconds, Mitch stared at her, gaze intense, a muscle jumping in his clenched jaw. "You're right. Things never would have worked out."

Turning on his heel, he stepped off the porch and disappeared into the night. Emma watched him go, knowing she'd made the right decision but hating it all the same.

Mitch was the one man she'd always loved. And now, she realized, he was also the one man she could never have.

Seven

Emma pushed herself up from the bathroom floor, using the edge of the tub as leverage. Still shaky and weak, she made her way to the sink to rinse her mouth and splash a bit of cool water on her face.

This was the fourth day in a row that she'd been sick, and she fully expected to feel better by midafternoon, just like all the other times.

At first she'd thought she was just coming down with something—a cold or the flu. She'd even considered that the headaches, nausea and tiredness were simply symptoms of stress due to her breakup with Mitch. Lord knew she'd been upset every one of the eight-and-a-half days since that night.

She'd left the engagement party right after he had, without bothering to go in and explain her absence to anyone else, and spent the rest of the evening crying into her pillow. If she had her choice, she'd still be crying, but since she hadn't wanted her father to begin to suspect anything was wrong, she'd cleaned herself up and tried to maintain a strong outer facade.

She would have to come clean eventually and admit to her father—and everyone else—that the wedding was off. But she just couldn't seem to bring herself to do it yet. Her emotions were still too raw, the pain still too deep and acute.

And judging by her father's comments and behavior, no one seemed to have a clue. They all thought she and Mitch were still engaged, still making plans to be married. Apparently, Mitch hadn't returned to the party or mentioned their split to anyone, either.

At the moment, though, that wasn't her biggest concern. She had worse problems than what people did or didn't know about her personal life.

Namely, she was late.

And now, she was beginning to believe she was in much worse trouble than just having to fight off the flu.

She was beginning to suspect she was pregnant.

Two weeks late for her period, morning sickness, moodiness and sensitivity…it might as well be written in neon across her forehead.

Then again, maybe she was wrong. Maybe she was overly emotional from the recent ups and downs with Mitch and was letting her imagination run away with her.

Meeting her reflection in the mirror above the sink, she noted the dark circles beneath her eyes and the sallow pallor of her skin.

There was only one way to find out if she needed an extra dose of vitamin C…or a bassinet.

She straightened away from the sink and stood perfectly still for a moment to be sure the room wasn't going to spin around her the way it so often did of late. Then, taking a deep breath, she opened the bathroom door and stepped out.

The house was quiet, and she sincerely hoped her father was busy outside so she could slip away without having to give an explanation or risk his noticing that she looked like the walking dead.

Grabbing her purse and keys, she slipped out the front door and headed for her car, which was parked only a couple of yards away. Just as she reached the driver's side door, her father stepped out of the barn and gave a shout of greeting.

"Morning, sleepyhead," he said, teasing her over her recent habit of waking up late, going to bed early and even taking naps during the day. "Where are you headed?"

"I need to run into town," she called back without elaboration. Then she yanked open the car door and jumped inside.

"Be back soon," she added before starting the engine and tearing down the drive so quickly, her rear tires sent gravel flying.

Pop would think she was crazy, she knew. Or at the very least, be very wary that something was wrong.

But how could she tell him that she might be pregnant? Even if she were happily married and had been attempting to procreate, the announcement would have made her blush. Telling him that she'd gotten herself in trouble *before* marriage and with a man who was now her *ex*-fiancé, would be positively mortifying.

A burst of hysterical laughter broke past her lips, and she blinked rapidly to keep tears from clouding her vision.

Dear God, how had her life gotten so out of control in such a short amount of time?

And what would she do if she really *was* pregnant?

Images of digging a deep, dark hole in the ground and burying her head in denial ran through her head. Oh, if only it were that simple. But if a baby was on the way, there would be nothing she could do to hide or refute the fact.

She made it to town in record time and aimed the nose of the car into the first available space near the drugstore. Leaving the keys in the ignition, she slammed the door and walked as fast as she could without breaking into a run.

Her breathing was labored by the time she reached the right aisle, from both anxiety and exertion. Rows of home pregnancy tests stared back at her, mocking her with their bright colors and promises of immediate results.

She wished even one of them promised the result she was hoping for. But life—and over-the-counter pregnancy tests—didn't work that way, and she had a sneaking suspicion this was one test she was destined to fail, no matter which brand she chose.

After studying the boxes a few moments longer, she grabbed one with a flashy yellow star announcing one hundred percent accuracy and headed for the checkout counter.

Relief washed through her when she saw a teenage boy behind the register. He wore a ratty black T-shirt advertising some heavy metal band she'd never heard of, his dirty blond hair stuck out in seventeen different directions, and he was leaning back against the cigarette rack reading an automotive magazine.

She didn't recognize him and prayed to God he didn't recognize her. If he did, word that Wyatt Davis's unmarried daughter had bought a home pregnancy test would likely spread through town like a brush fire. And that was one more problem she *did not* need.

Nose still buried in his magazine, the boy scanned the item without even glancing at it and stuffed it into a plain paper bag before checking the total and taking her money.

She carried her purchase out of the drugstore, stopping on the sidewalk for a split second and taking a deep breath before crossing the street and entering the local library. At this time of day, the place should be fairly empty. And she knew she could slip in, pretend to be perusing the stacks, then slip into the restroom at the back of the building and take this stupid test.

She smiled and said hello to Mrs. Alderson, the librarian, doing her best to shield the drugstore sack with her body. Making an effort to tamp down the urgency thrumming through her veins, she stopped at the New Arrivals section, then headed for the paperback rack, where she could disappear between the shelves.

Two minutes later, she was in the bathroom, peeing on a stick…and then she began to wait. With the little plastic wand balanced on the edge of the sink, she paced the tiny, tiled room and told herself not to panic.

She re-read the instruction sheet, checked her watch, read the instructions again. When she looked down at her watch a second time, her stomach plummeted.

This was it. The point of no return.

Stumbling forward, she closed the lid of the toilet and sat down, afraid she might fall otherwise once she got a glimpse of the results. With her eyes squeezed tightly shut, she reached over and grasped the plastic test strip. Holding it up in front of her face, she slowly opened her eyes…and was glad she was sitting.

Right there, in screaming aqua-blue was a plus sign as big as her thumb. *Plus means pregnant, minus means not pregnant.*

She was definitely, positively, plus-sign pregnant.

A wave of nausea rolled through her and she spent a long minute breathing through her nose until the sensation passed.

What in God's name was she going to do?

Emma didn't know how much time flew by while she sat there, numb, staring at the test wand in shock. But finally, she got shakily to her feet, grabbed her purse from the floor and stuffed both the pregnancy test box and the test itself inside.

Making as little noise as possible, she left the bathroom and stalked back between the shelves of books toward the front of the library. Mrs. Alderson was still behind the counter as she passed.

"Didn't find anything?" the woman asked politely.

"Nothing today," Emma forced herself to say in a voice that didn't tremble. "But I'll stop in again soon."

"All right, dear. Have a nice day."

Walking back to her car, she climbed in and started toward home. She wasn't even remotely ready to face her father—or anyone else, for that matter—but didn't know where else to go.

She thought about running away. To Europe or Hawaii or even just the other end of Texas.

But what good would that do? She didn't have the money to start over on her own somewhere else, even if she had been willing to leave her father and the only home she'd ever known. And at the end of the day, she would still be pregnant with Mitch Ramsey's child.

How could this be happening? She'd only recently begun to accept the fact that she and Mitch would never be more than just neighbors, and now this. Talk about a streak of bad luck.

Preoccupied, her mind swirling with a million scattered thoughts, she zipped past the turn to Mitch's ranch. A second later, she stood on the break, bringing her car to a screeching, skidding halt in the middle of the road.

She'd been going home—or at least heading in that direction—but now the idea of stopping off at Mitch's place first seemed to rise up and overshadow everything else.

Why should she be the only one plagued with this new knowledge? The only one suffering from a healthy mix of fear, panic, hysteria...

It was his child, after all. He'd played an equal part in its creation, however unplanned.

And—if she was feeling generous, which she was only about five percent of the time lately—she would admit he did have a right to know. Especially before she showed up in town with a growing belly, and word of her predicament got around.

Shifting the car into reverse, she backed up, turned right and drove slowly down Mitch's lane.

Her stomach was rolling, her palms sweating on the steering wheel. Lord, she wasn't looking forward to this. It had to be done, but she wished she could be anywhere else, doing anything else.

Pulling up in front of the house, she cut the engine and grabbed her purse off the passenger side seat. Her feet felt like lead weights as she crossed to the porch, wiping her damp palms on the legs of her jeans before lifting a hand to knock.

It was nearly lunch time, so she had a chance of catching him here. But if she had to, she would go out to the barn to look for him.

She was about to knock again when the inside door opened and she found Mitch standing on the other side of the outer screen door, staring down at her.

"Emma."

He sounded surprised to see her, even though his dark

eyebrows knit over storm-cloud eyes. It was obvious he still thought the worst of her.

Instead of bothering with pleasantries, she said simply, "We need to talk."

"About what?" The lines around his mouth lightened slightly, but he looked otherwise disinterested.

Reaching into her purse, she pulled out the test wand and held it up, big blue plus sign turned in his direction.

"What's that?" he asked.

"What does it look like?" she tossed back, her words laced with more than a little annoyance.

"I don't know," he drawled. "One of those fancy thermometers?"

Rolling her eyes heavenward, she heaved a frustrated breath. "No, not a thermometer. I wish."

Digging into her bag one more time, she came up with the flattened pregnancy test box. She waved it in front of his face, right beside the test stick.

"See this?" She was moving it back and forth so fast, he probably couldn't make out what it was, so she elaborated.

"This is a home pregnancy test," she said, thrusting the box against the screen. "And this is the little plus sign that means the test came out positive." She shoved that up right beside the other so there could be no confusion.

That, at least, elicited a reaction. The stern expression on his face washed away, replaced by a look of stunned disbelief.

"What...you mean..."

"I'm pregnant."

Mitch stared stupidly at Emma through the screen, then pushed the door open and moved onto the porch, forcing her back a step.

"You're pregnant," he repeated, feeling as though he was losing IQ points by the second.

"Yes."

She held out the pregnancy test pieces again, and this time he took the stick. That little blue plus sign she'd been talking about sure looked a hell of a lot bigger now. Ominously, toweringly bigger.

"When…" The word came out strangled and he stopped to clear his throat and lick his suddenly parched lips. "How did this happen?"

"The usual way," she snapped, fixing him with a freezing-cold, narrow-eyed glare. "And I'm not sure when. We were together a lot before calling it quits, and I guess we weren't quite as careful as we should have been."

He didn't say anything, still trying to wrap his mind around the fact that he was going to be a father.

A father.

He'd barely been ready to get married again, even knowing it was more as a favor and for the sake of convenience than anything else. The idea of having children had never occurred to him.

He'd thought that marriage to Emma would be easy and uneventful. One of those things that simply *was* and wouldn't require too much of his input or attention.

He'd been willing to marry her because her father had asked, but his decision had been underlined by the knowledge that they'd been friends since childhood and cared for each other already. Maybe not in the way most married couples cared for one another, but in his estimation it was a decent enough basis for a relationship.

It didn't hurt, either, that the sex was phenomenal. To him, that was an added bonus and one more sign that a marriage between them could work, even if there was no love involved.

When he'd pictured their future as man and wife, he'd seen them sharing a house, sharing a bed, working his ranch—and then someday her father's, too—together.

But nowhere in those pictures had he ever imagined children.

He probably should have. With all the sex he'd intended to have with her, the topic of pregnancy was bound to come up eventually. Emma might even have *wanted* children, which was another possibility he'd never considered.

In retrospect, he realized just what an oversight that had been. Of course, she'd have wanted children. Emma was a woman, and women loved kids.

But even if that had been the case, he'd have fought her on it. He had no idea what kind of father he'd make. The very idea terrified him. And having a child with her would only have risked evoking stronger emotions on Emma's part than he was ready to deal with, making more of their marriage than there was meant to be.

He scraped a hand over his face, stale air leaving his lungs in a huff of breath. The shock of her announcement was still reverberating through his system, chilling him down to the bone.

The Fates, it appeared, were having a field day. At his expense.

He'd been ready to marry her with no thought of children, even though they were a normal progression of an average marriage. Yet the minute they split up and despite all the precautions they'd taken to prevent this very thing from happening—at least after those first two hurried, spontaneous couplings—she wound up pregnant with his child.

Good God, what the hell was he going to do?

"Well," Emma prompted in a less-than-polite tone, her

fists propped angrily on her hips. "Don't just stand there. Say something."

If only he could *think* of something to say...other than asking again how the heck this had happened.

But then, he knew. The only question was how they planned to deal with it.

Clearing his throat to be sure it would work, he said the first thing that came to mind. "Why don't you come on in the house. I don't know about you, but I could use a drink."

He held the screen door open and waited for her to precede him inside. She did so reluctantly, her movements stiff, a mutinous expression on her face.

They headed for the kitchen and Emma took a seat at one end of the wide oak table while he took down two glasses from the cupboard and opened the refrigerator.

"What would you like?" he asked, leaning on the door to look inside. "I've got milk, orange juice, tea. Although you probably shouldn't have tea. I'm pretty sure it's caffeinated."

When he turned his head to glance in her direction, he found her arms crossed beneath her breasts and a frown marring her brow that was definitely aimed in his direction.

The problem was, he couldn't blame her. If she was half as mixed up about this new predicament as he was, then she had to be confused, scared, angry...basically tied in knots with no clue of how to untangle them.

He grabbed the jug of milk and poured her a glass, then poured tea for himself. But before he carried the drinks to the table, he opened another cupboard, pulled out a bottle of Jack Daniel's and topped off his tea.

"Sorry about this," he told her, replacing the cap and returning the bottle to its spot at the back of the shelf. "You could probably use a shot of this as much as I can, and it's not fair that you can't have any. But this is just going to have to be one of those things you hold against me, because if I don't get some liquor in me soon, I doubt I'll be much use to you at all."

Setting the milk down on the table in front of her, he pulled out another chair and took a seat, already downing half of his own drink in great, gulping swallows.

Not bothering to touch her own glass, she shifted slightly on her seat and said, "Aren't you going to ask me?"

He set his glass aside with a small clunk and met her bright, steady gaze. "Ask you what?"

"If you're the father."

The words hit him like a punch to the gut. Deservedly so, he supposed, after the way he'd acted at their engagement party.

He'd had no reason to suspect she was fooling around on him, especially with his own brother. But then, he'd never suspected Suzanne of cheating on him either, even though she'd been sleeping around almost the entire time they were married.

It was that knowledge, the realization that he could be blind to a woman's betrayal, that put him on his guard. No way in hell was he going to wind up married to another liar, another unfaithful woman.

So, yeah, he had trust issues. Anyone who knew him— or had known Suzanne was cheating on him, while he was left standing in the dark like an idiot—was aware of that.

But even with all of that hanging over his head, when Emma had told him she was pregnant, it had never once occurred to him that it might be another man's baby.

He didn't know why, except that just because a woman was *capable* of cheating didn't mean she had, and he simply didn't believe Emma had been sleeping with anyone else at the same time she'd been sleeping with him.

"No, I'm not going to ask. I don't think I need to."

If she found his behavior now odd as compared to the night of their broken engagement, she didn't say so. Instead, some of the tension seemed to seep from her body and her rigid posture began to relax. She sat up a bit straighter on the chair and leaned against the table, lifting her glass of milk to take a small sip.

Mitch took the opportunity to take another drink of his own odd mix, wishing it could be straight whiskey, even as the small amount in his tea warmed its way down his throat to his stomach.

"So how long have you known?" he asked quietly, concentrating on putting his glass back directly over the water ring it had left the first time.

She looked at her watch, then said, "About forty minutes."

He raised an eyebrow in surprise. Somehow he'd thought she'd had a few days to come to terms with this new turn of events.

"I haven't been feeling well," she explained, in answer to his unasked question. "After I'd been sick three or four mornings in a row, I started to think maybe I wasn't suffering from just a cold or a touch of the flu. I drove into town this morning, bought the home pregnancy test and took it in the bathroom of the library. Then I was on my way home and thought I should stop by to let you know…what was going on. It's bound to be all over town before long, anyway."

Her blue eyes flitted to the side, away from him, her fingertips worrying the rim of her glass. Then, without warning, the legs of her chair scraped the floor as she got abruptly to her feet.

"I don't want anything from you," she told him, backing through the kitchen and toward the door. "I didn't come here to make you feel guilty or rope you into anything. I just…thought you should know."

She'd reached the front of the house and stood with her back to the screen, one arm behind her, already pushing the door open a fraction.

"So I'll see you later. Have a good day."

Have a good day? Did she really think she could waltz up to his house, say, "Hey, I'm pregnant. Just thought you should know," and then waltz off again with a simple *have a good day?*

Uh-uh. Not with his child. Not while he still had breath left in his body.

"Emma," he called out, rising and moving to stand close enough that he could have reached out and touched her. To keep himself from doing just that, he stuffed his hands in the front pockets of his jeans and rocked back on his heels. His heart was pounding a mile a minute, sweat breaking out across his brow at the thought that was echoing through his brain.

"Yes?"

He blinked, bringing his attention back to Emma's face. Her soft complexion, bachelor's button eyes and wavy, strawberry-blond hair.

It might not be ideal. It might not even be what he really wanted. But it was right, and it was a necessary.

Lifting his gaze, he met her eyes, took a deep breath through flared nostrils and uttered the six words he knew would change his life forever.

"I think we should get married."

Eight

Emma managed not to snort rudely at this latest pronouncement of Mitch's, but just barely.

"We tried that once already, remember?" she muttered tiredly. "It didn't work out."

She saw the flash of memory cross his face and was struck with a fresh wave of pain at their short-lived engagement.

The muscles of his throat worked as he swallowed. "I think we should try again."

Closing her eyes for a brief second in weariness, she let her chin fall to her chest and then lifted it again. "Why?"

"Because you're pregnant, that's why."

Yes, because she was pregnant. Not because he was in love with her or wanted to be married to her but because she was pregnant. And, judging by the determined expression hardening his eyes and flattening his mouth, he wasn't going to listen to reason.

"This is my baby, too, Emma," he continued, apparently reading an equal amount of determination on her own face. "He—or she—should have my name and grow up with two parents who love and care for him. Or her."

He was trying, she knew that. And yet… "That's no reason to get married, Mitch."

"Around here, it is. You know how fast word will get around town that you're pregnant. You'll be labeled an unwed mother, and the baby will be labeled a bastard."

He pulled a hand from his pocket and moved it to the back of his neck, kneading as though trying to work out a particularly stubborn knot.

"Gabriel's Crossing is a good town, with good people living here, but we both know they can still be an opinionated, judgmental lot. They might never say anything to your face, but you know they'll whisper behind your back. Behind our child's back. How fair is that, to bring a child into this world with baggage like that to deal with?"

She shook her head, not because he was wrong, but because he was right…and the guilt trip was working.

Gabriel's Crossing *was* a good town, but it was also filled with citizens who held old-fashioned beliefs and values. And even though she didn't think any of them would truly treat her or an innocent child badly, Mitch was right about the gossip and the whispers. Eventually, in some way, their child would hear the word *bastard* or *illegitimate* and want to know what it meant.

Even if Mitch maintained an active role in their child's life, the stigma would still be there. And there was a difference between a father who was married to a child's mother and a father who dropped by once a week or picked the kid up for the occasional weekend visit.

"We can make it work," he pressed on, reaching a hand

out to touch her arm. "A lot of the wedding arrangements have already been made, and, unless you told people we broke up, no one even knows we called it off. We can go right back to being engaged and just move the date up a bit, if we need to."

He said it all so matter-of-factly, as though he were discussing his plans to buy a few more head of cattle. There was no emotion there, no eagerness or true desire to spend his life with her, merely his deep-rooted sense of responsibility that told him two people who were planning to have a child together should be married first.

She wished she could argue with him, offer a list of reasons his proposition was inferior to simply going on with their lives—separately, but sharing a child. The problem was, she had been raised the same way he had, with the same beliefs.

She didn't want to be a single mother. She didn't want to go home and tell her father that she was pregnant with Mitch's baby—but rather that the wedding was off. She didn't want to be the butt of gossip and condemnation, and she didn't want to raise her child on her own.

Mitch's thumb was making small, mesmerizing circles on the inside of her arm, distracting her even as his intense gray gaze burned into her, silently urging her to make the right decision.

If only he loved her, even a bit. The way she still loved him, despite everything. Childhood crushes, she supposed, were slow to die.

The worst part, though, was that she suddenly realized he'd never really felt anything for her. Not the way she'd hoped, at any rate.

Why he'd bothered to propose to her at all was a mystery. And she felt more than a little stupid for ever thinking she could help to heal his bitter, wounded heart.

Not that it mattered any longer. Necessity had taken the place of what either of them might have felt or wanted before. Now it had to be about the baby, about the best interest of their child.

As much as she hated the idea of being married to a man who didn't love her...or being married to a man who didn't *want* to be married at all...he was right about the need to give their child a name and let him or her grow up with a reputation free of labels or scandal.

Closing her eyes and feeling her shoulders slump slightly, she resigned herself to what she knew had to be done. She would sacrifice her own happiness, her own peace of mind for that of her unborn child.

Opening her eyes, she raised her gaze to Mitch's and prayed she wasn't making the biggest mistake of both their lives.

"All right," she said softly. "We'll go through with the wedding."

He didn't smile, but she felt the tension leave his body, loosening his muscles and lightening the rigid lines of his face.

"Good," he said with a firm nod. "We'll set the date as soon as possible and won't mention the baby to anyone before then. Agreed?"

"Agreed."

With that settled, she pushed backward through the screen door and stepped onto the porch. "I'll be seeing you, then," she said, heading toward her car.

He followed her across the yard. "Let me see you home."

"That isn't necessary," she told him, shaking her head and climbing behind the wheel.

Before she could slam the door closed, he caught it, rested an arm along the window frame and leaned over. "Is there *anything* I can do?" he asked quietly. "You know, about…" He waved a hand up and down to indicate her midsection. "Anything?"

She warmed a little at his offer and the obvious awkwardness that accompanied it. "No, thank you. I think we're okay for now."

"You'll let me know if that changes?"

"I'll let you know," she said, cocking her head to look at him, giving a small smile.

With a silent nod, he stepped back and closed the car door, then stood where he was while she started the car, turned around and drove off. She watched his unmoving form grow smaller in her rearview mirror as she headed down the long dirt driveway toward the main road.

She was engaged again, she thought, not sure whether to be relieved or disheartened. She was going to marry the same man she'd been set to marry before, the same man she'd fancied herself in love with.

Only two things had changed—she was pregnant, and this time she knew it was all for show.

Emma spent the next several weeks fighting morning sickness and making hurried wedding plans. Where they'd once intended to wed a few months or even a year down the road, the date had now been moved up significantly, the guest list whittled down to only family and very close friends.

Instead of getting married in the church, they were now going to exchange vows in his parents' backyard. They had made arrangements with the minister and rented a gazebo, folding chairs and most of the decorations that would make an outdoor ceremony complete.

Yet all of the things she should have enjoyed—deciding on flowers, addressing invitations, picking out a dress—

were merely duties to be done while pretending she was both nervous and excited about her upcoming nuptials.

In reality, she was just plain nervous. She was about to walk down the aisle in front of her father and friends and promise to love, honor and cherish a man she was marrying only to protect her unborn child.

She'd seen Mitch a handful of times since that day at his ranch when she'd told him about the baby. He was checking up on her, she knew, even though he'd never said as much, and they'd also agreed that they needed to be seen together both by their families and in town at least occasionally to keep up the pretext of being the happily engaged couple.

It hadn't been easy, and Emma was keenly aware that the rest of her life would be much the same—an act put on in public to convince people she was happier than she really was.

But she would have her child, she reminded herself.

Her hand slipped down to cover her still-flat abdomen. They would have each other, and she would do all she could to make her child's life a joyous one.

As for the rest…she would simply have to make the best of it.

A soft knock at the guest room door brought her head up, dragging Emma from her deep, dismal contemplations. She inhaled sharply and glanced in the mirror above the vanity table to be sure there were no telltale signs of her reluctance to walk down the aisle.

The door opened and Mitch's mother poked her head in.

"It's nearly time," she said with a gentle smile. "Your father is just outside, waiting to walk you down the aisle. Is there anything I can do to help?"

Not for the first time, Emma noticed in Theresa's face where Mitch had gotten his soulful eyes, high cheekbones and several shades of his dark, dark hair. The rest had come from his father, which only meant that he'd been twice blessed.

If all else failed, Emma thought, at least their child would benefit from the attractive gene pool on Mitch's side of the family.

Theresa stepped forward to fuss with the flowers in Emma's hair. Emma was wearing a plain white dress with no straps or sleeves, and more flounce in the knee-length skirt than she'd have liked. But there were only so many wedding dress options in downtown Gabriel's Crossing on such short notice.

She felt guilty enough even wearing white, considering her current condition and the things she and Mitch had done to get her there.

"I think I'm ready," she said, her voice somewhat scratchy with emotion and disuse.

Her future mother-in-law took a step back, still fingering the ends of Emma's reddish-blond hair, left loose around her shoulders.

"You look beautiful," she said, gazing at Emma with undisguised love and happiness. "My son is a very lucky man."

Unshed tears clogged Emma's throat and she fought to swallow them back. If Theresa only knew what a sham this entire ceremony was, she wouldn't be nearly so eager to see this wedding take place.

"All the guests are here and seated, and everything else is set. The only thing left is for the bride to make an appearance."

Taking a deep breath, Emma got to her feet. She smoothed the skirt of her dress, tugged the bodice up a fraction and reached for the bouquet of flowers at the edge of the vanity table. An assortment of simple wildflowers to match the blossoms in her hair, tied together with long strips of pale yellow ribbon.

"I'm ready," she murmured with a determined nod.

Theresa beamed, then opened the door and rushed out, leaving Emma to follow.

Her heart was pounding in her chest, fast and erratic, and her feet felt like bags of sand, dragging her down and slowing her steps.

As she rounded the corner from the guest bedroom, she spotted her father at the bottom of the stairs, dressed in a dark gray suit and grinning widely. She offered him her best reassuring smile and carefully descended the steps to meet him.

"I can't believe it's my little girl's wedding day," he said, his voice sounding suspiciously thick. Taking her hand, he lifted it to his mouth for a brief kiss. "You're just as pretty as a picture."

"Thank you."

"You remind me of your mother on our wedding day. She'd be so proud of you."

The mention of her mother immediately brought tears to her eyes, and she tipped her head back, hoping to keep her mascara from running.

She so wished her mother could have been there. Not just to see her get married, but as someone to confide in about everything that was going on in her life right now. Her mother was the one person she knew she could have talked to about Mitch, her unexpected pregnancy and this wedding that she knew neither she nor Mitch were a hundred percent ready to go through with.

But her mother was gone, and there was no one else to turn to. She had to do this, and she had to do it alone.

Forcing a smile to her face that she didn't quite feel, she let her father lead her to the rear of the house, with its wide-open back door. She could see the cloth aisle laid across the grass-sprigged yard and the rows of chairs covered with white fabric, filled with guests dressed in their Sunday best.

And there, at the end of that long aisle running between the two clusters of seats, stood Mitch beneath a white latticework trellis climbing with pink and white wild roses.

Her racing heart stuttered for a second as she studied him. He always had that effect on her—stopping her heart, slowing her breathing, sending her senses on red alert.

And today, he looked exceptionally handsome in his black suit and newly shined black boots. His black hair gleamed almost blue in the midmorning sunlight, and he'd spotted her. His intense gaze pinned her in the doorway, making her shiver.

Even though they weren't marrying for love, she had to admit that the lust was still there, at least on her part. One glance from those smoldering gray eyes, one touch of his strong, callused hands, and she was putty.

She only hoped he never figured that out or she would be in big, big trouble.

"Ready, sweetheart?" her father whispered, patting her arm where it linked with his.

Swallowing hard, she inclined her head, praying she made it all the way to the end of that long, long pathway without fainting or throwing up or screaming.

The music began, and everyone got to their feet, turning toward the house, waiting for the bride to begin her walk down the makeshift aisle.

Mitch watched Emma hover for a moment just inside the house, looking as though she planned to bolt, regardless of her father's hold on her arm.

He didn't blame her. If it weren't for his brother standing on his one side, the minister on the other and fifty of his closest friends and relatives seated all around, he might have made a run for it himself.

Not for the first time, he ran a finger around the inside of his too-tight shirt collar. Damn. He'd wanted to keep things simple and get this over with as quickly as possible, but he was beginning to think a daytime wedding, in Texas, in the middle of September, was a mistake. The sun was beating down like a heat lamp, threatening to make him sweat through his suit jacket before he even said "I do."

And Emma still hadn't moved. If she didn't come out of the house soon, people were going to start wondering just how eager she was to be marrying him.

Catching her eye, he smiled and gave her an encouraging nod.

That was all it took, it seemed, to jump-start her. She raised the collection of flowers that had been hanging at her side to the center of her waist and started forward, stepping onto the porch and then down into the yard, her movements in perfect alignment to her father's.

Despite her obvious reluctance, she looked lovely. He'd been through all of this before—albeit on a larger scale—but that didn't diminish Emma's natural beauty.

The simple white dress hugged her curves and left her slim shoulders seductively bare. Her wavy hair framed her delicate face, one side pulled up and held in place by the small bunch of flowers that matched those in her hands. The strawberry-blond strands shone like a new penny in the sun, and her skin glowed with a slight tint of pink beneath the surface.

She and her father reached the trellis and stopped. His eyes damp with emotion, Wyatt kissed her cheek and placed her hand in Mitch's with an approving nod before moving to take his seat in the front row of the folding chairs.

Emma turned more fully to face him so that they both

stood sideways directly in front of the minister, hands clasped between them. Her fingers squeezed around his, but he suspected it was more from nerves than as a gesture of closeness. Still, he squeezed back, offering what comfort he could and silently trying to let her know that everything would be all right.

They may not have planned for things to turn out quite this way, but they would make the best of it. They would have a child together and do their best to raise that child right.

And he would be a good husband. It might not have been his idea to get married again—not when her father had brought it up, at any rate—but he would still do the best he could to take care of her and see that she was happy.

The minister's words droned on, speaking of love and commitment. Things Mitch believed in but hadn't had much experience with—at least not the first time around.

He had no illusions that this time would be better. Emma was a different person, different from Suzanne in a lot of ways. But she was still a woman, and that meant she wasn't to be trusted.

Hadn't he caught her in his brother's arms the night of their engagement party? Seen it with his own two eyes. Both Emma and Chase claimed the embrace had been innocent. But he'd heard claims of innocence before and was no more sure he could believe them now than he could then.

Even if Emma and his brother were being honest…even if there had been nothing going on between them and never would be…he simply wasn't willing to take the chance. To open himself up to that vulnerability ever again.

But that didn't mean he couldn't be a good father and decent husband.

Finally, the minister had reached the important part.

"Do you, Mitchell Alexander Ramsey, take this woman to be your lawfully wedded wife?"

A few seconds later, after the rest of the vow, Mitch looked directly into Emma's cornflower-blue eyes, still clouded with uncertainty, and said firmly, "I do."

Emma slipped a ring on his finger and the minister asked her the same question.

"Do you, Emma Louise Davis, take this man as your lawfully wedded husband?"

She may not have looked certain and her fingers might have involuntarily contracted around his once more, but her voice didn't quaver as she answered.

"I do."

The minister pronounced them man and wife and, as he added that Mitch could kiss his bride, a cheer went up from the crowd of guests.

Before they were surrounded by well-wishers, he leaned in and pressed his lips to hers. To his surprise, she kissed him back, her delicate fingers curling into his forearms as she leaned closer.

As much as he might have liked to continue kissing her, he didn't care for an audience, and guests were moving in to hug them and pat him on the back. Reluctantly, he released her mouth, but kept her at his side, feeling oddly more comfortable with his new wife than he would have expected.

Nine

The wedding and small reception that followed went off without a hitch…if one didn't count the fact that neither the bride nor groom particularly wanted to be there.

Emma couldn't help but be amused by the irony of the situation as she left the reception—also held at Mitch's parents' house—with her new husband and headed for her place.

Or rather, her father's place now. It only made sense that after they were married she and Mitch would live together, and the obvious choice was for her to move to his ranch.

So, after dancing and eating and staying only as long as they felt necessary to keep up the pretense of the happy couple, they left to begin moving her things from one house to the other.

After three trips back and forth, she was exhausted, even though Mitch hadn't let her carry anything heavier

than a grocery bag full of clothes and assorted toiletries at
any one time. There was still a lot to go...larger things, like
her hand-carved hope chest and a few sentimental
items...but she had enough to get by. And if she discovered that she needed something, her father's ranch was
only a couple of miles away.

Stifling a yawn, she made her way slowly upstairs,
Mitch following close behind with his share of the last
load. At the top of the stairs, she turned left and entered
the extra bedroom, directly across from his own, where
they'd been piling her possessions.

The bed was still clear, neatly made with a patchwork
quilt coverlet, and as soon as she set aside the cloth tote
she'd been carrying, she took a seat at the edge of the
mattress. She was still wearing her wedding dress...
another testament to Mitch's insistence that she not overdo
it. He hadn't let her work hard enough to get so much as a
smudge of dust on the soft white material.

"You look tired," Mitch commented from just inside the
door. He leaned over to place the box in his arms on the floor
before straightening to face her. "Why don't you take a nap."

It would certainly be easy enough to fall asleep. The
stress and exertion of the day were taking their toll, making
her eyelids droop and her limbs heavy.

But it was her wedding day. Technically, her wedding
night, she thought, glancing at the bedside clock. It was
barely 7:00 p.m.

When she didn't respond, Mitch tucked his hands into
the front pockets of his black dress slacks, then tipped his
head and left without another word, closing the door
quietly behind him.

So much for being ravaged. Or passions overtaking
them and spending a week in bed.

Hmph.

She fell back on the bed with a groan of frustration. There had been only one thing she was even remotely looking forward to in this marriage, and now it seemed Mitch intended to deny her even that.

Well, she'd just see about that.

Shaking off the traces of lethargy that urged her to stay in bed and drift off to sleep, she sat up and started digging through her bags and boxes of things. She knew she'd packed it. She even thought she'd put it somewhere on top for easy access.

"Ah-ha," she breathed when her hands closed on what she'd been looking for.

A slinky, satiny negligee, perfect for her wedding night. Or so she'd thought when she'd bought it on impulse soon after Mitch had asked her to marry him the first time.

Opening the bedroom door a crack, she looked out, checking for signs of Mitch. She didn't hear anything but noticed that his bedroom door—which had been open when they'd made all their trips upstairs—was closed. And the bathroom door was open.

She darted across the hall and locked herself in, setting the folded gown and robe on the closed toilet lid as she began to strip. First she removed the flowers from her hair, then reached behind her back to lower the zipper on her dress. Once she'd stepped out of the gown, she made quick work of her shoes, stockings, panties and bra.

Turning the water on in the shower, she stepped under the strong spray, quickly washing her hair and scrubbing every inch of her body. She wished she'd bothered to unpack some of her more feminine bath salts and hair care products, rather than having to make due with Mitch's all-purpose soaps. Maybe something in rose or lemon.

Then again, Mitch always smelled exceptionally good, and having his scent on her body from his soap was a decent substitute until—with any luck—she could get it to rub off directly from him.

She used a towel to create a turban for her hair, then rubbed herself dry with another. Once her skin was no longer damp and the delicate material of the negligee wouldn't stick, she shrugged the gown on over her head and checked herself in the mirror over the sink.

The cream-colored satin set off the red in her hair and the rosy hue the hot water had brought out in her skin. Quite a bit of skin had been left bare by the spaghetti straps and low, lace-trimmed bodice, too.

But that was the goal, after all. To leave just enough uncovered, and to wrap the rest in a seductive package to attract Mitch's attention.

With her hair hanging in damp tendrils around her shoulders, she slipped into the robe that matched the gown and ventured into the hall, leaving her other clothes behind. Mitch's bedroom door was open now, but there was no sign of him, which meant he was either downstairs or outside.

Feet bare, she padded down the steps, the hardwood floor creaking occasionally beneath her weight. As she reached the bottom of the stairs, she heard noises in the kitchen and headed that way.

Mitch was moving back and forth along the rows of cupboards, putting dishes away. She stood in the doorway for a moment, watching him. Admiring his smooth movements, the sinewy flow of muscle in his back and arms.

He'd changed out of his suit and was now wearing his usual jeans and a plaid work shirt. A few stray pieces of straw clung to the cuffs of his pants, making her think he'd been out to the barn already.

But at least she'd caught him inside. It would save her having to either sit in the living room waiting heaven knew how long for him to return…or traipsing out there in her wedding night negligee, risking the lewd stares and ribald comments of his hired hands.

She wasn't sure she'd have actually had the courage to do the latter, so it was just as well he'd been out there and back already.

He turned from organizing silverware in the drawer beside the sink and spotted her. His gaze flitting from her head to her toes and back again, and for a moment his grip on the countertop tightened, turning his knuckles white. Then he let go and straightened, deliberately going back to what he was doing.

"Hey," he said, and she was delighted to hear a noticeable hitch in his voice. At least she'd succeeded in getting his attention, even if he was doing his best to ignore her.

"Hey, yourself."

He grabbed a couple of coffee mugs from the top rack of the dishwasher and moved to put them away. "I thought you were resting."

"I'm not tired," she told him, and prayed an ill-timed yawn wouldn't out her as a liar.

"Still, you've had a long day. You shouldn't overdo it."

She shifted slightly to rest against the framed opening that separated the kitchen from the dining area, aiming for a nonchalant pose.

"You had as long a day as I did," she pointed out.

He finished emptying the dishwasher and clicked the door closed with his hip.

"I'm used to it. And I'm not pregnant," he added pointedly, still leaning on the edge of the counter.

Well, he had her there. But she'd only spent the day getting married, not hauling horse feed or climbing Mount Everest.

"In case you missed it," she said, deciding to get right to the point, "this is our wedding night. We aren't supposed to fall asleep for quite a while yet."

Pushing away from the wall, she took a few slow steps forward until she stood directly in front of him. She held his gaze, but her fingers were busy teasing up and down the buttoned front of his shirt.

"But we can go to bed any time we like."

Going up on tiptoe, she pressed her lips to the underside of his jaw. It was like brushing against small grain sandpaper, even though he'd just shaved that morning.

She kissed his cheek, then the corner of his mouth, her fingers curling into the waistband of his jeans as she rubbed her body close to his, letting the friction build.

Only when she kissed him full-on, mouth to mouth, did she realize he wasn't responding. Oh, there was some definite action taking place below his belt buckle, but otherwise he held himself perfectly still, not moving, not kissing her back.

Pulling away slightly, she opened her eyes and looked up at him. His face was impassive, his lips drawn into a tight, flat line.

"Mitch?" She frowned, wondering if she'd done something wrong, been too aggressive for his tastes.

Wrapping his hands around her upper arms, he set her back a step. "You should get some rest. It's been a long day," he said without inflection.

She stood frozen in the middle of the kitchen, blinking in utter confusion. "Excuse me?"

"It's been a long day," he said for what had to be the hundredth time. "You look tired. You should be in bed."

So rather than making love to his new wife on their wedding night, he was telling her she looked *tired* and that she should go to bed *without him*.

She didn't know whether to be hurt or angry, but a fair share of both were building up in her bloodstream, threatening to send smoke shooting out of her ears. And all she could think to say was, "You're kidding, right?"

He gave a quick shake of his head, then busied himself with nonsense stuff around the room, like wiping down the already clean counter or moving the dish detergent on the windowsill an inch to the left.

"Get some sleep," he said, not bothering to meet her gaze. "I have some work to do in the barn."

And then he turned on his heel and walked out of the house. Leaving her alone. On her wedding night.

Mitch stalked straight across the lawn, climbed over the paddock fence and bent forward, immersing himself up to the shoulders in the cool water of the horse trough.

Dammit. Was she trying to drive him crazy?

It had been hard enough to resist her all day while she'd been dancing around in that snow-white dress that showed off her smooth, pale arms and drool-inducing legs. But did she have to get cleaned up and come downstairs in next to nothing?

She might as well have been naked. Oh, the robe and nightgown were long, running almost to her bare ankles, but the material was sheer and slinky and so thin, he could see the dusky circles of her nipples, the flare of her waist, the dark shadow between her thighs.

Her hair had been damp from her shower, and she smelled fresh and clean, with the scent of his soap clinging lightly to her skin. He'd gone hard in an instant, and it had taken every ounce of control he possessed not to take her right there on the kitchen floor.

And then, to feel those gentle curves pressed against him, burning through his clothes, her mouth hot on his own. He'd had to get out of there or risk doing something he'd regret, something he'd promised himself he wouldn't.

He *was not* going to sleep with his wife.

It was expected, he knew, especially on their wedding night, and Emma had made it clear she was more than willing. But to Mitch, touching her now felt too much like taking advantage of the situation.

She hadn't agreed to marry him this time because she wanted to but because she was pregnant. That didn't exactly make him feel like a typical groom.

He also didn't want to risk getting too close to her, physically or emotionally. Not after seeing her in his brother's arms and having all of his ex-wife's betrayals come flooding back.

And not now that they were legally joined, forced to live together. There was too much chance of getting more involved, of beginning to care too much. More chance than he was willing to take.

Keeping his distance was the best way he could think of to prevent that from happening and to prevent her from getting too attached or wrapped up in their sham of a marriage.

He lifted his head from the trough and shook himself, sending droplets of water flying in every direction. Stomping toward the side entrance of the barn, he ran his hands over his hair to squeeze out excess water.

The only problem with his brilliant plan, he thought as he entered the dim interior of the large, weather-beaten structure, was that Emma didn't seem to be on the same page as he was. She seemed more than willing to jump in with both feet and make this a real marriage, in every sense of the word.

And if she took it into her head to seduce him the way she'd tried in the kitchen…how the hell was he going to resist? How long could he hold out?

If his reaction to her today was any indication, not long. His blood was still simmering in his veins, his libido urging him to turn around, stalk back into the house and make love to his wife.

His gut gave a lurch at the image that popped into his head of Emma sprawled on his bed in that ivory nightie, writhing beneath him, curling around him. For a moment, he couldn't move, the longing thrumming so thickly through his system.

Drawing a deep, shaky breath, he forced himself to take a step forward and then another. He grabbed a bale of hay from the stack at the back of the barn and carried it closer to the empty horse stalls.

He would just have to be stronger, more determined. And he would have to avoid being near his new wife as much as possible.

Marriage, Emma decided, was not all it was cracked up to be.

She and Mitch had barely spoken in the month and a half since their wedding, and if they did it was only about the most mundane topics. The weather, the livestock, dinner with their parents. It was enough to make her want to scream.

Any time she tried to get close to him or even brushed close enough to touch as they passed in the hall, he acted like she'd scalded him with a burning hot brand. As often as not, he quickly made up some excuse to go out to the barn and get away from her.

He didn't seem to notice the changes her body was going through, either. They might not be major changes, but they were dramatic—at least to her.

Her pregnancy was starting to show in all the typical ways. Her breasts were growing larger and more sensitive, her stomach rounding out to a tiny mound that no longer fit beneath her pants unless they had an elastic waistband. And her tops, which used to be somewhat loose, were now snug, making her condition more obvious to anyone who cared to look.

Unfortunately, Mitch wasn't one of them. It was almost as though they were roommates—roommates who didn't particularly care for each other—instead of husband and wife. And it was beginning to get on her nerves.

Her father and Mitch's parents had been delighted at the news that they were going to be grandparents, though. And so far, none of them had brought up the fact that she was three months along in her pregnancy and only one month along in her marriage.

But even though it had only been six weeks since she'd exchanged vows and moved in with Mitch, she was becoming almost insanely bored. The few times she'd wandered out to the barn, hoping to find something to break up the monotony of her days, Mitch not only made it clear he didn't want her there, but if she so much as fondled the handle of a pitchfork, he immediately moved it out of her reach and reminded her that she was pregnant and shouldn't be working too hard.

Working too hard? She wasn't working at all. She was barely doing anything beyond cooking and keeping the already neat house free of dust and stray magazines. At least when she'd lived with her father, she'd had ranch business to keep her busy.

Maybe that's what she should do now that she was living here. Mitch spent so many hours outside, in the barn, working with the cattle and horses, she couldn't imagine he had much time for bookkeeping and organizing his records. He had a home office, complete with a computer monitor on the desk and file cabinets along the far wall, but she couldn't remember ever seeing him in there.

Of course, for all she knew, that could be where he spent his nights. It wasn't like they were sharing a room…or a bed.

But she still needed *something* to occupy her time and her quickly stagnating brain. So first thing that Monday morning, she got up, dressed and fixed breakfast as usual, not surprised when Mitch sat across from her, eating the food she'd prepared without speaking two words to her. She considered it progress that he grunted in response to a couple of her benign comments, uttered more to break the silence than because she actually expected any interaction with him.

Then, after he'd headed out the door, she made her way to his office and started snooping around. Not that she was looking for anything private or incriminating but to familiarize herself with his business.

Just as she'd suspected, he hadn't updated his records in quite a while. She found piles of receipts that hadn't yet been filed, as well as lists of livestock and records of sales and purchases.

Instead of being overwhelmed by the work that needed to be done, she felt a distinct sense of excitement. Finally, she had something to devote her time and attention to, a purpose for her married life other than being a so-called wife and glorified housekeeper. And maybe, if she was lucky, she might even prove herself to be an asset to Mitch and the Circle R.

It wouldn't solve all her problems… Heck, it might not solve any of them, especially where Mitch was concerned…but at least getting back to some office work would help her feel useful and keep her mind off of her miserable, failing sham of a marriage.

Ten

Two weeks later, Emma couldn't sleep. It had to be close to two in the morning, and rain was pelting the roof and windows by the bucketful, bringing with it the rumble of thunder and the occasional flash of lightning.

Normally, she enjoyed storms. The cool breeze, the relaxing rhythm of the rain, the fresh brightness and clean smell they brought to everything the next day.

But tonight, all those things only made her feel more alone.

With a sigh of defeat, she sat up in bed, threw back the covers and reached for her robe. Maybe a glass of warm milk would help.

Her slippers scuffed along the steps as she made her way downstairs and into the kitchen, turning on the dim light over the stove to illuminate the room without half blinding herself. She pulled a cup from the cupboard and the milk from the refrigerator, pouring enough for several healthy swallows before setting the heavy ceramic mug in the microwave and punching numbers.

While she waited for the buzzer to go off, she returned the milk jug to the fridge, then stood with her arms crossed, hip resting against the counter as she gazed out the front kitchen window. It was dark, the glass streaked and spattered by the rain, but still she could see a light on in the barn on the other side of the yard.

Her brow knit as she frowned. It was odd for anyone to be in the barn at this time of night—even Mitch, with the number of hours he spent trying to avoid her.

Out of curiosity, she wandered into the other room and halfway up the stairs until she could see his bedroom door standing open. She hadn't noticed it on her way past, but Mitch normally closed his door when he went to bed at night. The better to keep her out, she supposed.

The microwave beeped and she returned to the kitchen to retrieve her warm milk. As she sipped, she moved to the window to stare at the pale light showing through the half-open barn door, her curiosity piqued.

If Mitch wasn't in his room and didn't seem to be anywhere else in the house, that meant he very well could be out in the barn.

But why? She couldn't imagine any chores needing to be done so badly that they couldn't wait until morning. The obvious answer, of course, was an emergency with one of the animals.

Suddenly concerned, she set her mug on the kitchen table and moved to the front door. She slipped on a pair of tennis shoes and a jean jacket, then opened the door and ran out into the rain.

The ground was wet and muddy, the rain plastering her hair and clothes to her body almost the minute she stepped outside. She crossed the lawn in less than a minute, ignoring the soggy earth trying to suck down her shoes and splattering on her bare legs and the hem of her long nightgown.

Slipping through the crack in the barn door, she shook herself, wiped the water and clinging strands of hair away from her face, then glanced around to see if she could find Mitch.

The center of the barn was empty, filled with nothing more than the usual bales of hay, bags of feed and assorted equipment for cleaning stalls and currying the horses. But she heard noises at the far end of the building and started toward them.

One of the stall doors was open, and as Emma got closer she realized that what she'd heard was Mitch's voice, speaking in low tones. When she got close enough, she saw him hunkered over a dappled gray mare who was on her side on the stall floor, plainly in the final stages of giving birth.

Careful not to make a sound for fear she would distract him or disturb the horse, Emma stood at the edge of the stall and watched. Mitch continued to murmur encouragements, patting the mare's haunches and neck when he could, offering hands-on assistance when it was needed. In only moments, tiny hooves and a tiny nose appeared, and, when the time was right, Mitch tugged on the long, slippery legs to help pull the foal's body free of its mother.

On the final tug, Mitch fell back and the foal landed almost completely on top of him. Tears sprang to Emma's eyes as she heard his deep laughter and saw his wide smile as he made sure the foal's nose and mouth were clear, then helped get the baby on its feet.

The mare was back on her feet, too, licking the baby clean, and it only took a few minutes longer for the foal to start nudging around, searching for its first meal.

Mitch wiped his hands on the legs of his jeans and she quickly ran the back of her hand over her cheeks before he turned and caught her crying.

When he saw her, he froze for a second, then continued brushing the straw from his pants as he moved slowly toward her, his gaze raking over her body.

"What are you doing here?" he asked, stepping out of the stall, closing and latching the door behind him.

She shifted backward to stay out of his way, tugging the sides of her denim jacket closed and crossing her arms to keep them in place.

"I saw the light on and thought something might be wrong."

She glanced over the edge of the stall door at mama and baby, and he followed her gaze.

"Nothing wrong," he said, "just a mare in labor."

"I can see that." She smiled and stepped just a fraction closer. "He's beautiful. Or is it a she?"

"He. It's a colt."

Several seconds ticked by in silence while they watched the pair.

"You shouldn't be out here," Mitch told her, breaking into the moment. "You're soaking wet, and you should be in bed."

"I couldn't sleep." She turned, taking in his damp hair and the stains marring the front of his shirt and pants. "And I think you're in worse shape than I am."

He looked down at himself and grimaced. "Yeah, I guess a shower wouldn't be out of the question."

"Come on. Let's go back in the house." She slipped her arm through his, ignoring his protests that she would get dirty and tugged him forward. "I'll make us some hot cocoa while you get cleaned up."

Mitch turned out the lights and dragged the heavy door

closed before they set out across the yard at a jog. The rain soaked them through again and they hit the covered porch already shaking droplets from their hair and clothes. Just inside the door, they both kicked off their shoes and hung their jackets.

Emma padded barefoot across the kitchen and began digging in one of the low cupboards for the right size saucepan. When she realized Mitch hadn't moved from his spot by the door, she straightened to face him.

"You go ahead upstairs. Get a hot shower and change into some clean, dry clothes. I'll have the cocoa ready by the time you get back."

"Maybe you should take a shower first. You're just as wet as I am, and—"

She scowled and started tapping the bottom of the stainless steel pan in her hand against her leg. "If you say 'you're pregnant' one more time, I swear, I'll bean you. Yes, I'm pregnant, but no, that doesn't mean I'm as fragile as a china doll. It hasn't started to get cold out yet, and a little bit of rain isn't going to kill me. I'm not even cold, and I'll dry. You, however, are both wet and dirty. So go."

His eyes darted to the pan at her side, then back to her face, apparently reading the annoyance there quite clearly. He stuffed his hands in the pockets of his jeans, his shoulders slouching forward just a touch.

"Right. I guess I'll go get that shower then."

Struggling not to laugh, she forced her mouth to remain tight, knowing that he would hear the amusement in her voice even if her expression remained stoic. "Good idea."

He spun on one stockinged foot and marched out of the entryway in the opposite direction. She listened to the squeak of boards and the sound of his footfalls as he passed through the living room, then up the stairs.

When he reached the bathroom and she began to envision him stripping out of his damp clothes, down to nothing but skin, she knew she had to get busy making the cocoa or risk melting into a puddle in the middle of the kitchen floor.

He might have made it clear he had no interest in sleeping with her, but that didn't mean her hormones had gone off to hibernate. If anything, they were more charged and raring to go than ever. She blamed it on pregnancy, sending her libido into overdrive.

Or maybe it was simply a matter of wanting something even more once she'd been told she couldn't have it.

Either way, looking at him made her feel like a dieter faced with an all-you-can-eat dessert buffet. She was famished, salivating and more than ready to cheat.

She winced, then blew out a huff of breath and turned for the stove. That was probably not the best analogy, considering Mitch's biggest fear was just that—that she, or any woman he got involved with, would cheat on him.

But while she was definitely eager to cheat on her no-sex diet, she would never, ever cheat on him.

Even if he never touched her again. Even if he insisted that their marriage remain a cold, passionless one.

She might have to resort to a dozen cold showers a day or investing in a battery-operated self-pleasuring device, but she would never be unfaithful. Not when it was the one thing that would hurt Mitch the most.

And regardless of anything else going on between them or in their lives, that was something she would never intentionally do.

Measuring out milk, sugar and cocoa powder, she mixed them together in the saucepan and set it on a burner over low heat. Just about the time the water turned off upstairs and she heard him moving around again, the cocoa was ready. She turned off the stove and took down an extra mug, filling both with steaming chocolate.

Before setting the drinks on the table, she dropped a few slices of bread in the toaster and pressed the lever. A minute later, Mitch came down the stairs and reappeared in the kitchen doorway.

His hair was still wet, but this time, she assumed, from being freshly washed. And, instead of changing into pajamas or boxers, he'd opted for another pair of denims and a long-sleeved plaid work shirt. He was barefoot, though, and had left the tail of the shirt out rather than tucking it into the waistband of his jeans.

A jolt of awareness zinged through her body, settling warmly between her legs. Swallowing hard, she made a mental note to do some discreet online shopping…and pick up extra batteries the next time she was in town.

But outwardly she tilted her head toward the table and smiled. "Cocoa's ready. And I'm making toast to dunk. I don't know about you, but I love hot buttered toast with my cocoa."

Without saying a word, he passed behind her and took a seat, wrapping his hands around the still-hot coffee cup. She thought about warning him not to burn his mouth, then decided he was a big boy and could certainly tell by the temperature of the ceramic mug and the steam emanating from the liquid inside that it was too warm to drink right away.

The toast popped and she buttered it, then cut the slices in half before setting them on a plate and carrying them to the table. She sat in the chair nearest him, put the plate between them and reached for her own cocoa.

Mitch watched Emma drifting around the kitchen, as comfortable and proficient as ever. Almost immediately after moving in, she'd made herself at home as though she'd always lived under his roof.

Without a word of discussion, she began cooking three meals a day and tidying up. He'd even had to phone his once-a-week housekeeper on the sly and ask her not to come until further notice. He didn't want Emma thinking he didn't appreciate her efforts or that she wasn't doing a good enough job. Especially when he was well aware there was too little to keep her busy around the place otherwise.

Although he made a point not to be around her any more than he had to, he'd noticed the work she'd done in his office and was secretly glad. Not only that she had found something she enjoyed to occupy her time but that she'd taken it upon herself to deal with a part of the ranch business he hated. From what he'd seen, she had managed to organize and complete all of the bookkeeping he had been avoiding for weeks.

Having her here, taking over so many household duties, was somewhat disturbing. It was almost too domestic for his tastes, too strong a reminder that he and Emma really were married and likely to stay that way for a hell of a long time, regardless of the circumstances.

But it wasn't Emma's ability to make a damn fine cup of coffee or balance his books that set him most on edge. It was *her.*

Her presence. Her voice and her scent. Her hair and the sound of her footsteps as she moved around the house. The way she sometimes hummed while she cooked, or the warm, steamy feel of the bathroom after she finished one of her long bubble baths.

Everything about her heated his skin and sent his temperature rising. He awoke each morning with the smell of her in his nostrils, so strong he could swear she'd spent the night beside him in bed.

And her body…her body was enough to make a godless man pray. Especially now, with the changes her pregnancy was making.

They were subtle, to be sure, but he noticed every last one. The slight swell of her small breasts, the gentle rounding of her formerly flat abdomen.

And he wanted, more than anything, to rest his hand on her stomach and feel the place where his child was growing. He dreamed of it, ached with it.

But touching her even that much, to share in the development of the baby they'd made together, would be too dangerous. Because he knew that one touch of her belly would never be enough. He would want to touch her face and her neck and work his way down. He would want to kiss her and make love to her.

As it was, he lay awake at night, remembering what it had been like to hold her, caress her, be inside her. Before, when their relationship had been casual instead of complicated, temporary instead of permanent.

He lifted his mug with both hands and took a long slug of hot chocolate, wishing it were something ice-cold to cool his ardor. Not that it would make much difference. With Emma around, he was in a constant, near-painful state of arousal.

In between bites of toast and sips of cocoa, she was talking about the new colt that had just been born. Her voice was light and upbeat. It washed over him and soothed his jagged nerve endings, even as it turned him on.

She had that effect on him. Hand in hand with his desire for her came a deep level of comfort. Like a roaring fire on a cold winter's night or the kind of ease he would expect to feel after living with someone for fifty years.

But it had always been that way with Emma. Maybe because they'd grown up together and had seen each other through the chicken pox and gawky teen years, broken bones and broken hearts.

Or maybe it was just Emma, with her soft smile and kind eyes and her gentle demeanor that seemed to accept everyone for who they were, warts and all.

And God knew he had enough warts for a garden full of toads. It hadn't always been that way, but it sure as hell was these days. Frankly, he didn't know why she'd gotten involved with him in the first place, let alone agreed to marry and move in with him.

"Mitch?"

He blinked, suddenly aware that her stream of chitchat had ended and she was looking at him as though waiting for an answer.

Shaking his head, he set his cup on the table with a small clunk and said, "Sorry, guess my mind drifted there for a minute. What was the question?"

She smiled and shook the hair back from her face. It was still damp from the storm, falling in dark, stringy strands around her shoulders.

And her hair wasn't the only thing that was damp. Though they'd been indoors for nearly half an hour, her long white nightgown was still wet in patches. The thin cotton material had been no real barrier to the pounding rain, and despite her claims that she wasn't cold, her nipples had beaded into tight, rosy points.

He could see them clearly through the transparent fabric. Or perhaps it was just his imagination, his memory of how her breasts looked, felt in his hands, tasted against his lips and tongue.

Dammit, he was as stiff as a fence post. If the wide tabletop hadn't hidden the lower half of his body from view, Emma would no longer have had a single doubt about his feelings for her. He may have been able to *tell* her he wasn't interested with a straight face, but his physical response to her was bound to give him away if he wasn't careful.

Inhaling and exhaling with almost surgical precision, he fought to get his longing under control. His fingers tightened around the mug in his hands until the knuckles turned white, and he made himself meet Emma's gaze head-on rather than drifting toward her alluring chest.

"It was nothing," she said, still smiling, oblivious to the war that was raging in his bloodstream. "I was rattling on about nothing very important."

And then she stood, carrying her empty cup to the sink. "You're probably tired and don't need to stay up with me just to be polite."

While she rinsed her mug and brushed crumbs from the plate she'd used for toast, Mitch seized the opportunity to rise from the table. With her back to him, he could slip out and away before she noticed the rather prominent bulge in his jeans.

"Here you go," he said, standing as far away as possible while at the same time reaching around to set his own mug in the sink.

His plan was to dump the glass, then hightail it out of the kitchen and up to his bedroom, where he could lock the door and be safely away from Emma's unintentional seduction.

But at the same moment glass clinked on stainless steel, she turned, the front of her body coming flush with his own.

The tiny expanse of her belly brushed just above his belt buckle, the loose fabric of her gown across his groin, and he groaned. It was like setting a hot branding iron to naked flesh. In a flash, his diaphragm clenched, his heart lurched and his blood reached the boiling point.

Her blue eyes stared up at him, wide open and swimming with an odd mix of uncertainty and longing.

He swore, cursing himself for being the one to make her doubt her beauty, her desirability. He'd meant to keep his hands off of her, yes, but never to lessen her self-esteem or self-assuredness.

She was beautiful, amazing. Any man would be lucky to have her. He just happened to be the poor sap who'd gained her affection when he was neither worthy of nor able to return her feelings.

"Emma…" He ran a hand over her tangled hair, cupping the back of her head in his palm.

Her tongue darted out to lick her lips and he almost exploded. He pressed closer, rubbing sensually against her where he needed her touch the most.

In a soft, shaky voice, she whispered, "I thought you didn't want me anymore."

With a moan, he let his head drop until their brows met. "I always want you," he told her in a gravelly voice. "I didn't *want* to want you, I tried to fight it, but it's still there. Every day, every night, awake or asleep. I've taken more cold showers since you moved in here than ever before in my life, and not a damn one helped."

Her eyes welled and for a moment he feared she was about to burst into tears.

"You could have fooled me," she said with a hint of anger, her tone stronger and more confident than before.

"I *tried* to fool you. I tried to fool myself. But this doesn't lie." He pushed the hard ridge of his erection into the apex of her thighs, letting her know exactly how much he craved her.

Something flashed in her eyes for a brief second, a hint of lust to match his own. But then she tamped it down and her expression grew serious.

"What if I told you that I'm only willing to sleep with you if I know you love me and are serious about making this marriage work?"

His jaw clenched, his fingers tightening where they wrapped around her delicate forearms. "I'm serious about making this marriage work," he responded carefully.

"But you don't love me."

She said it matter-of-factly when he would have expected her to make it sound more like an accusation. Before he could answer, she shrugged a slim shoulder and a ghost of a smile began to play on her lips.

"It's all right," she told him. "If you'd said you did, I'd have known you were only doing it to get me into bed. At least this way, I know you're being honest with me."

"I've never lied to you," he said firmly. There may have been a few occasions when he hadn't told her the entire truth, but he'd never lied.

She leaned closer, letting the heat of her body mingle with his and running her hands over the taut muscles of his biceps.

"If we do this," she said in a low voice that poured over his skin like aged whiskey, "there's no going back. Consummating our marriage means we can't get an annulment if we change our minds in a few weeks. We would have to divorce."

"The thought never entered my mind," he told her truthfully. "And there won't be any divorce. When I said 'till death do us part,' I meant it."

He'd married her for better or worse, with his eyes wide open. It may not have been for love, may only have been to give their child a stable home and protect Emma's reputation, but he'd always intended it to be a forever thing. No matter what.

Her fingers moved from his shoulders to the back of his head, tangling in the short strands of his hair. "Then I guess it's about time we had our wedding night."

Eleven

She lifted her mouth to his, sighing with contentment as their lips met and he kissed her like she was a bountiful oasis and he was a man left too long in the desert without a drop to drink.

His hands framed her face as his mouth threatened to devour her. She might have been frightened by the desperation in his kiss, his touch, if she hadn't been equally desperate and aroused.

Without breaking the kiss, he stroked down the sides of her throat, over her breasts, coming to rest with his hands on the slight swell of her abdomen. His thumbs moved up and down as though testing the shape and texture of her expanding figure.

He pulled away, his chest heaving with each ragged breath he struggled to take into his lungs. She was gasping, too, and shaking so hard she was surprised she was able to stay on her feet.

"Is it all right?" he asked. "With the baby...is it all right if we do this?"

"Oh, yes." She ran her hand over the rough line of his bristled jaw and smiled encouragingly. "It's fine, I promise. You won't hurt either one of us."

"Thank God."

It was the most heartfelt declaration she'd ever heard from him, and she might have laughed if he hadn't leaned in and scooped her off her feet so fast, all she could do was yelp and hold on tightly.

"What are you doing?"

"Taking you to my room," he told her, his long strides eating up the floor as he stalked through the kitchen, dining room and up the stairs, carrying her as effortlessly as he would a bag of grain.

"Ever since you moved in, I've dreamed of having you in my bed. I can't sleep at night for wanting you so bad."

"I was right across the hall," she whispered softly, using her teeth and tongue to tease the lobe of his ear. "Why didn't you ever come over and get me?"

"I was trying to do the honorable thing." He groaned low in his throat, a sound that came much closer to a growl. "Dammit, I didn't want to use you. Just because we had to get married, I didn't want you to think I was taking advantage of you."

"It's not taking advantage if I want you back," she said as they reached the bedroom and he kicked the door closed behind them, heading directly for the wide, king-size bed.

The covers were pulled down and tangled, as though he hadn't made the bed in several days. Not that she cared. She had a feeling the sheets would be in much worse shape by the time they finished with them.

"In the morning, I hope you'll remember you said that.

Because I am going to make love to you tonight, and I won't regret it for a second, even if you think I should."

He set her gently in the center of the bed, before stepping back to loosen his belt and pop the buttons of his shirt. Shrugging his arms out of the sleeves, he let the soft plaid flutter to the floor, then went to work on the front of his jeans. He shoved the denim and his underwear down his legs, kicking them aside.

He strode back to her, delectably naked and fully aroused. She only had a moment to appreciate his long legs and broad, muscular chest before the mattress dipped and he was stretched out beside her, kissing her lips and caressing the flesh of her arm, left bare by her sleeveless nightgown.

His fingers trailed upward, around the lacy edge of material near her collarbone, then over the rise of her breast to the line of tiny pearl buttons lining the front of her gown.

As he began slipping them through their holes, he lifted his head and murmured against her mouth, "Did anyone ever tell you how beautiful you are? And that you have lousy taste in sleepwear? These buttons are too damn small."

Her heart leapt at his compliment, then settled back in her chest as she chuckled at his complaint. If she'd known the evening was going to lead to something as wonderful as this, she'd have worn a robe—and not a stitch more.

"Please tell me this isn't one of your favorite nighties," he said, his head bowed now as he concentrated. He had six buttons undone and was still only halfway down her chest.

"No, not at all, it's just—"

"Good. I'll buy you another one, I swear."

And then the sound of tearing filled the room, followed by the soft ping of tiny plastic buttons hitting the floor, headboard, nightstand. Cool air hit her chest as he laid her bare.

When he moved to push the gown down her arms, she

sat up to help him, then lifted her hips and legs so he could get rid of the offending garment altogether. It landed on the floor near his own pile of quickly discarded clothes.

He covered her once again with his own long, hot body, and she wrapped her arms around his back, loving the feel of his warm, smooth skin beneath her hands, his hair-roughened chest abrading her nipples, the hard, throbbing length of him pressing between her legs.

She opened for him, more than ready to take him inside her. Yearning for it, aching with all the pent-up passions she'd been struggling with since their ill-fated wedding night.

But Mitch seemed to be in no rush. Instead, he kissed her, ran his hands through her hair, over her breasts. His thumbs teased the tightened peaks until she writhed beneath him, and then he followed the action with his lips. His tongue licked and swirled before he drew the entire tip into his mouth to suckle.

She whimpered, holding tightly to the back of his head even as the sensations became almost too painfully plea-surable to bear.

With one final swipe, he moved away, only to stare down at her with his own dark, smoky-gray gaze.

"They're bigger. Not by much, but I could tell just by looking. The same here."

His hand moved down to cover her belly and a shiver of awareness rippled through her.

"The baby's growing." With his eyes still locked on hers, he said, "Do you have any idea what that does to me? Watching your body change, knowing I played a part in it?"

He slipped down until his face hovered just above her abdomen. Leaning in, he pressed his lips to the minor bulge, then lifted his head and grinned. "I've been wanting to do that for weeks now."

She returned his smile, blinking rapidly and swallowing hard to keep emotion from clogging her throat. "I've wanted you to do it."

That and so much more. She'd wanted him to touch her, kiss her, hold her. She'd wanted to fall asleep in his arms and wake up the same way. She'd wanted to talk with him and laugh with him and share some of the changes her body was just beginning to go through.

And now he was doing at least some of those things. It gave her hope and lifted her spirits for the first time in months.

He continued to dribble soft, ticklish butterfly kisses over her stomach before moving lower. She squirmed, suddenly shy, and tried to pull him back up by tugging at his hair. But he ignored her, continuing his quest and shifting her legs so her thighs were balanced on his shoulders.

She pushed up on her elbows, attempting to slide backward, away from what she thought he was trying to do. "Mitch, you don't—"

Slapping the side of one bare buttock playfully, he raised his head and gave her a determined, lascivious look. "Hush. This is something else I've been dreaming about, and you're going to let me. All you have to do is lie back and enjoy."

The first touch of his mouth on her warm, swollen flesh set off bursts of color behind her closed eyelids. Her fingers curled in the sheets on either side of her hips as she panted in pure, unadulterated pleasure.

His tongue licked, stroked, flickered and swirled. He started slowly, then sped up, bringing her to the precipice of climax before slowing down again and making her whimper.

When he began to concentrate on the tiny bud of desire buried within her slick folds, she didn't even try to hold back but let the sensations overtake her.

Her body bowed, lifting off the mattress for several long seconds before her bones melted like hot candle wax and she slumped back down. She was breathing hard, amazed that she'd managed to remain conscious.

Mitch pushed himself up, a smug, self-satisfied smile curling the corners of his mouth. "Can I take that to mean you enjoyed yourself?"

She made a noise that might have been a laugh, but even she wasn't sure. Grabbing him by the ears, she yanked him up until they were once again face-to-face. "Shut up and kiss me, you big jerk."

His chuckle of amusement was swallowed by her lips. She tasted herself on his tongue and moaned, letting her hands drift down his sides and between their sweat-slick bodies. Her fingers closed around his stiff, pulsing member and it was his turn to gasp and writhe.

She teased him, running her hand back and forth, squeezing, skimming the pad of her thumb over his sensitive, dew-kissed tip.

Finally, he grabbed her wrist, putting a halt to her erotic ministrations. "That's enough, I can't take anymore."

"You did it to me," she shot back.

"Yeah, but I can't recover as quickly as you can, and I want to be inside you when I come."

With that, he got to his knees and sat back on his haunches, pulling her up with him. She was poised directly over his rampant erection, and as she crossed her legs behind his back, she slipped down, taking him into her eager, waiting body.

They both sighed at the glorious friction their joining created, remaining still for a moment to let the ecstasy pour through them. And then his hands closed on her buttocks. He lifted her slowly and she watched a muscle in his jaw jump at the same time the muscles in his arms rippled and bulged.

He let her down slowly, only to lift her again, then let her down. Over and over until her limbs quivered, her belly contracting with the anticipation of what was to come.

She dug her nails into the meat of his shoulders as her inner sheath tightened around him with the first signs of orgasmic spasms. Mitch's lips peeled back from his teeth, telling her he wasn't far behind. With her heels digging into the mattress, she rose and fell on him faster and faster, while his hips tilted to meet her thrust for thrust.

In a flash, the building pressure reached its limit and spilled over. Beneath her, he tensed and gave a low growl of completion. A second later, she followed him over the edge with a keen cry of her own.

For long minutes, they stayed that way, the sounds of their ragged breathing filling the room. Then he circled her waist with one arm and carefully lowered her back to the mattress.

She almost groaned in disappointment when he slipped out of her, but he quickly rolled to his side, drew the covers up over them both and hugged her close.

Feeling happier than she had since the first time he'd proposed, she fell asleep cocooned in his warmth, wishing she could whisper the three words singing through her soul.

I love you.

The moment Emma opened her eyes early the next morning, she knew something was radically different. It took a few seconds for the fog to clear from her brain and the previous night's events to come flashing back.

As soon as they did, a wide smile split her face and she started to stretch. *This* was what she'd expected marriage to be. *This* was how she'd wanted to feel on her wedding night and every day thereafter.

"It's about time you woke up."

The low, rumbled voice near her ear made her jump. Only then did she feel the strong male forearm around her waist as Mitch drew her back against his chest, which vibrated with laughter.

"I expected you'd be out at the barn by now," she said, tipping her head until his face came into view. His gray eyes sparkled and a dark shadow lined his tanned jaw.

"I thought about it but couldn't seem to drag myself out of bed without you."

Goose bumps broke out along her skin at his words. This was a side of him she'd never seen before, playful and romantic.

"Won't the cows get hungry without you?"

He chuckled. "Nah. I've got hired hands to pick up the slack."

She rolled the rest of the way around, mimicking his position of propping her head on one bent arm. Beneath the covers, their legs rubbed together and she could feel her blood begin to heat.

"Does that mean you're taking the day off to stay in bed and satisfy your sorely neglected wife?"

One black eyebrow winged upward. "After last night, can you really say you've been neglected?"

"No, I suppose not." Her cheeks heated at the memory of the things they'd done together each of the three times they'd awakened throughout the night. "But if you abandon me now, I might."

His hand moved from the small of her back to the curve of her bottom and he pulled her close so she could feel his arousal growing between them.

"Well, we can't have that, now can we?"

His kiss set off brush fires in her bloodstream and it was a long, long time before either of them made any attempt to get out of bed.

Hours later, they were downstairs. Showered, dressed and full from a quick brunch that they'd prepared together between feather-light touches and lingering kisses.

Mitch's hand enfolded hers on the table all the while they ate, and then, after his last sip of coffee, he gave a heavy sigh and pushed back his chair.

"As much as I hate to, I really should go out and check on things. Would you mind?"

The way he'd been acting since last night, she wished he would stay with her forever. Right there, touching her, kissing her, looking at her with such attentive devotion in his storm-dark eyes.

But she knew how implausible that was and knew, too, that if she clung too tightly to him, there was a chance he'd begin to feel smothered and pull away.

So as much as she didn't want to, she smiled and shook her head. "Of course not. Do you need any help?"

He stood, still holding her hand and pulling her to her feet. "I don't need help, no. And half of what I'll probably end up doing, I wouldn't let you take part in, anyway. Not in your condition."

The corners of his lips lifted in a gentle grin and his free hand slipped down to caress her belly through the layers of her slacks and top.

"But you're welcome to come out and see the new colt, if you want. Just make sure you wear boots and are careful around the mare. New mamas can get nasty if they think their babies are at risk."

She nodded, reaching up to meet him as he leaned down

to kiss her, then walking him to the door. He threw her one
last smile over his shoulder before crossing the lawn and
disappearing into the barn.

As she walked back to the kitchen and started clearing
the table, Emma caught herself humming. With any luck,
Mitch wouldn't get cold feet again, and they could go on
like this indefinitely.

He may not be in love with her, but phenomenal sex and
a positive outlook could make up for a lot. They certainly
respected each other and would soon have a child to bind
them together even more.

She could be happy with that, she told herself. And only
a very small voice in the very back of her mind whispered,
But maybe not forever.

For now, though…for now, she was more than willing
to take it day by day.

She finished in the kitchen and wandered back to
Mitch's office, deciding to spend a few minutes dealing
with paperwork before heading out to the barn. If she
waited long enough, perhaps Mitch would be done with his
work and could join her in admiring the newborn foal. She
liked the idea of watching the baby together, knowing that
they would soon have a baby of their own to share.

By the time she glanced up from the computer screen,
an hour had passed. She rubbed her eyes and rolled her
neck to work out the kinks, then pushed back the wheeled
desk chair and hopped to her feet.

Mitch would surely be finished by now, or close to it.
Hurrying to the front of the house, she stepped into her old,
worn work boots and opened the front door.

A woman was standing on the porch just in front of her,
hand raised to knock.

Emma gave a gasp of surprise and stepped back, then

felt her stomach lurch as she recognized the overly bleached, violently teased hair. The skintight, hot-pink, scooped-neck top revealing entirely too much cleavage. The white, painted-on spandex pants and bloodred toenails sticking out of three-inch high, platform slides.

It was Suzanne. Mitch's ex-wife and *the first* Mrs. Ramsey.

Twelve

Emma felt the earth lurch beneath her feet and her lungs seize painfully in her chest. She reached out a hand, grasping desperately for the doorjamb to catch herself before she fell over.

What in God's name was Suzanne doing here?

Why now, just when everything seemed to be going so well?

Crossing her arms beneath her well-endowed breasts, Suzanne hitched her hip and scowled. "Who the hell are you?"

The rude demand snapped Emma out of her near-catatonic state and was like a dousing with ice-cold water. She shook herself mentally and straightened her spine, now using her grip on the doorframe to keep from clawing at the woman on the other side of the screen.

"I'm Emma. Emma Davis," she said, using her maiden

name, since she thought it might be one Suzanne would recognize more easily than her married name. "We've met before at—"

Suzanne's gaze slipped past Emma to look deeper into the house before she'd even finished speaking. "Where's Mitch? I'm his wife and I want to see him. Where is he?"

Emma's eyes narrowed and an angry heat swept up from the soles of her feet. She fisted her hands at her sides, furious not only at the woman's obvious dismissal of her presence but at her false claims of being Mitch's wife.

"*Ex*-wife," Emma said just above a growl, surprised her teeth didn't shatter from the force with which she was grinding them together. "You're his *ex*-wife, Suzanne."

"Not for long," the woman replied lightly, tossing back her peroxide-enhanced hair. "The divorce was just a phase, one of those things newlyweds go through. We'll reconcile and be remarried in no time."

"Sorry to disappoint you," Emma said, still seething, "but that might not be as simple as you think. You see, *I'm* Mitch's wife now."

Suzanne's mouth fell open, her eyes flashing fire, and Emma braced herself for a knockdown drag-out. The screen door still separated them, but she had no illusions that the thin barrier would keep Mitch's ex out if she decided to go for Emma's jugular.

Nor was she afraid. She'd been raised on a ranch and suffered her fair share of kicks from horses and cows both, as well as falling out of trees, the loft, off the back of tractors. Fighting might not be something she was used to, but she could certainly handle herself, especially against one puffed-up, painted-on floozy.

But before Suzanne could respond or Emma could slam

the door in her face, Mitch's voice rang out from the center of the yard.

"I thought I heard a car in the drive. Do we have company?"

Emma had to lean to one side to see around Suzanne's big hair. Mitch's long strides were eating up the ground, but his head was down, the brim of his hat hiding his eyes and obscuring his view as he tugged off his leather work gloves.

He apparently didn't recognize Suzanne's car or he would have known immediately who their "company" was.

With his booted foot on the bottom porch step, he lifted his head and spotted Suzanne for the first time. His eyes went wide in startlement, and Emma almost expected his mouth to drop open like in the cartoons.

She found his reaction reassuring. Despite her own annoyance at his ex's unexpected arrival and her willingness to scratch the woman's eyes out if necessary, the butterflies in her stomach had never stopped their frantic flapping for fear he would be glad to see Suzanne again.

For a moment after turning in Mitch's direction, Suzanne remained frozen in place. Then suddenly, she let out a squeal and threw herself at his chest.

Emma raised an eyebrow as Mitch stumbled backward off the porch step, his arms flailing at his sides to keep from falling over.

"Oh, Mitchy, Mitchy, I missed you so much."

Suzanne's voice was high-pitched and saccharine-sweet. She kissed one cheek and then the other over and over again until Emma wanted to throw up.

"Suzanne." Mitch grabbed her wrists, finally managing to pry her hands from around his neck, and pushed her away. "What are you doing here?"

Emma wasn't sure, but she thought his tone held an edge

of irritation. She hoped so, anyway. She wasn't sure she would be able to handle it if she sensed he was happy about his ex-wife's return in any way.

"I missed you, Mitchy. I want us to get back together and be happy again."

"What about Kevin?"

"Oh, he's just an old pooh. I was an idiot for running off with him when I had you here to love me. Can you ever forgive me?"

Mitch was quiet for so long, a bolt of panic hit Emma in the solar plexus.

What if he did forgive Suzanne? What if he wanted her back?

Without any real intent in mind, she pushed the screen open and stepped onto the porch, letting the door close with a slam behind her. The noise sounded like a gunshot to her ears and caused Mitch's head to jerk up, his gaze to meet hers.

Releasing his hold on Suzanne, he moved around her and toward Emma. He climbed the porch steps, coming to a stop at her side and placed an arm around her waist, his hand resting on her hip.

"Suzanne, I believe you've met Emma. My wife."

Emma's heart swelled with pride at Mitch's pointed introduction, at the same time that relief made her feel lightheaded. He wasn't going to throw her over right here and now for his ex-wife.

The expression on Suzanne's face was nothing short of hateful—and aimed directly at Emma.

"I didn't know you got married again," she said with a distinct pout.

"You don't know a lot of things about me," Mitch retorted. "That's just one of the reasons *we* aren't married anymore."

Suzanne's arms took up residence beneath her breasts

again, thrusting them up and together, creating a bottom-
less chasm of cleavage that even Emma was having trouble
tearing her eyes away from.

"Well, can we at least talk for a minute?" she asked,
tapping one foot in frenetic agitation. *"Privately?"*

Emma stiffened at the sound of that. The woman couldn't
be planning to say anything good if she wasn't willing to
say it in front of Mitch's new wife, now could she?

Glancing up, Emma found Mitch staring down at her.
His eyes were dark and hooded, giving her no clue as to
his inner thoughts.

"Do you mind?" he asked.

Yes! she wanted to scream. Yes, she minded. Yes, she was
insecure and frightened and beginning to feel territorial.

But, of course, she couldn't tell him any of that. Not
without coming across as clingy and angst-ridden.

"No, go ahead," she answered, the words scraping past
her throat like rusty nails.

He let go of her waist and started down the porch steps,
following Suzanne as she sashayed her way across the
lawn. They didn't go into the barn but stopped a few yards
from the wide double doors.

Emma couldn't hear what they were saying, but she
certainly noticed the number of times Mitch's ex reached
out to touch him. The brush of her fingers along his arm,
pretending to pick a piece of dirt or lint off the front of his
shirt, leaning close enough for the tips of her breasts to
brush his chest.

A twitch started at the corner of Emma's left eye, and
she lifted two fingers to cover the stress-induced tick.

As she watched the couple with her good eye, she saw
Mitch shrug, Suzanne give him a smug smile, then both of
them turn and walk toward her. Suzanne headed for her car,

climbing in and driving away without another word to either of them. Mitch continued on his path to the house, coming to a halt directly in front of her.

He stuffed his hands in his pockets and rocked back on his heels. "Sorry about that," he said. "I never expected her to show up here."

Emma gave a small nod, not sure how else she was supposed to respond. Then she cleared her throat and ventured, "So what did she want?"

His mouth turned down in a frown and he shook his head. "I don't want to talk about it right now. I'm going for a shower, okay?"

Without waiting for her to respond, he brushed past her and into the house.

She turned, watching as he walked away and did the math in her head.

Fourteen hours. For fourteen hours, she'd had an almost perfect marriage. She'd actually been happy and thought Mitch had been, too.

For fourteen whole hours.

Mitch stood under the hot spray of the shower, wishing the pelting droplets could wash away the last twenty minutes of his life.

Just when he'd thought things were going pretty well. He and Emma had worked out a truce of sorts, which he could only be grateful for. And they'd spent the night and half the morning making love like bunnies.

Maybe if he hadn't gone out to the barn. If he'd stayed in bed with Emma, maybe the entire day wouldn't have been ruined.

But, no, Suzanne had a way of ruining things no matter what.

God, why the hell did she have to come back? Why now?

Oh, but he knew why, thanks to the little "private chat" she'd talked him into out by the barn. She'd left her beloved Kevin, the man she'd been sleeping with while still married to Mitch, and was looking for a reconciliation. She claimed to want him back, to still be in love with him, to be sorry she'd ever cheated on and left him.

Of course, he didn't believe a word that came out of her mouth. Not anymore.

There'd been a time when he had believed her, trusted her. He'd been stupid, blinded by lust and convinced he was in love.

Now, he knew better. Love didn't step out on you, flirt with other men in front of you just to make you jealous, do its best to alienate you from your family in hopes of getting more time, attention and money.

Suzanne used to flash that sultry smile, toss her hair over her shoulder and run her painted nails down the middle of his chest, and his groin would take over the thinking process from his brain.

He shook his head in disgust, ducking once again under the pulsating spray.

The question was, what did she really want?

It was completely possible that Suzanne *did* want him back, he just didn't buy the reasons she'd stated—love, regret, second chances. No, she was up to something, and he had no intention of giving it to her.

But that didn't mean her visit hadn't stirred up old memories.

He scrubbed his skin hard with the bar of all-purpose soap, trying to wash off both the sweat and grime of the day's work, as well as the stink of his ex-wife's untimely appearance.

He'd thought he was over her, and in a way he was. He was over *her,* but apparently he still wasn't past the heartache and hard feelings she'd caused by her betrayal. Which only pissed him off more.

Damn her. He wished she'd stayed with her precious Kevin and kept the hell out of his life.

Shutting off the water with a jerk of the knobs, he climbed out of the shower and began toweling dry.

And then there was Emma. He knew she was upset about Suzanne showing up on the doorstep, and he hadn't helped matters by refusing to talk to her afterward. But he'd just wanted to get away, to be alone, to lick his wounds and do his best to drive his ex-wife's voice and image from his mind.

Now, though, he owed her an explanation. Or at least some reassurance that Suzanne wasn't going to become a permanent part of their lives. Not if he had anything to say about it.

Padding barefoot and bare-ass naked to the bedroom, he climbed into a clean pair of denims, threw on some socks and grabbed a fresh shirt, buttoning the front and cuffs on his way downstairs.

He found Emma in the kitchen, starting on supper. She had a cast-iron frying pan on the stove and was rolling chicken parts in a spiced flour mixture before dropping them into the hot oil.

Her fried chicken was one of his favorite meals, but tonight he couldn't seem to work up an appetite for it.

She turned her head when she heard him enter the room. Her lips lifted up at the corners, but the smile didn't reach her eyes.

"Feel better?" she asked, returning her attention to her task.

"Yeah," he responded, although it wasn't quite true. The shower had gotten rid of the dirt on his body, but he couldn't say he actually felt any better.

"Look—" he said, taking a spot opposite her and leaning against the countertop with his arms across his chest "—I'm sorry about the way I left things after Suzanne took off."

She shot him a sideways glance without pausing the movements of her hands as they flipped a thigh in flour. "That's all right, I understand."

Maybe that was the problem, Mitch thought crossly. She was too damn understanding. If he'd done something similar to Suzanne, she'd have pitched a fit, screaming, yelling, crying, chasing him around the house and possibly even lobbing something at his head.

But, ironically, Emma's lack of reaction annoyed him almost as much as one of Suzanne's rages would have. Didn't she care that his ex-wife had shown up out of the blue? That Suzanne had left her second husband and now wanted Mitch back?

A little bit of jealousy wouldn't be out of the question. God knew he'd been jealous enough to chew glass when he'd found Emma in his brother's arms. His own brother, whom he never really believed would make a move on a woman he knew Mitch was interested in.

But Emma didn't seem to be jealous of Suzanne at all, and, on top of everything else, that just put him in a worse mood.

"Well, just so you know, she won't be coming around again." At least he hoped not.

Emma nodded, still facing the other direction, showing no reaction whatsoever. If she was in a snit, she'd just have to get over it because he didn't know what else he could do or say to set things right. Suzanne's visit sure as hell hadn't been his idea, and he'd be damned if he was going to grovel over something he'd had absolutely nothing to do with.

"So…is there anything I can do to help?"

"You could set the table," she said without looking at him.

He pushed himself away from the counter to collect plates and utensils.

Good. Great. That was that, then. It was over and they could all go back to their lives.

But the hard knot in the center of his stomach as he set the dishes on the table and went back for paper napkins told him that wasn't the case at all. He had a feeling things between Emma and him were going to get worse before they got better.

Things could have been worse, Emma decided a couple of weeks later.

Her relationship with Mitch had never returned to the happy, euphoric state she'd thought they'd accomplished before Suzanne's reappearance in their lives, but it hadn't gone back to that cold place where they avoided each other and walked on eggshells, either.

They shared meals and talked more than they had during the first weeks of their marriage. Sometimes, they worked together, when Emma asked him to go over some papers or figures with her in his office or the few times he let her help him in the barn.

Of course, she knew darn well that he didn't really need her help and that the jobs he allowed her to do were simple, lightweight tasks meant to make her feel useful. But then, she didn't need him to help her with any of the ranch's paperwork, either. She only said she did occasionally as an excuse to be near him and as a way for them to do something that made them feel—to her, anyway—like a team.

And they slept together every night, in his bed. She'd abandoned the guest room and all but moved into the master bedroom with him, where they made love, whispered in the dark and slept in each other's arms.

It was almost, but not quite, perfect.

Mitch still didn't love her. She lived with that knowledge every day, and in her own way had made peace with it.

Her biggest fear at the moment was Suzanne...Yates Ramsey Burnes, who was doing her silicone-breasted best to become simply Suzanne Yates Ramsey again.

She'd been back to the house four more times since that first visit. Every couple of days she showed up, staring daggers at Emma while batting her lashes at Mitch and taking every opportunity to touch him.

To Mitch's credit, he tried to fend off Suzanne's inappropriate caresses and to make it clear he didn't want her around. But she was deaf to his protests—or pretended to be. And the fact that Mitch was remarried...that his new wife was standing not three feet away the entire time... didn't faze her in the least.

Emma could tell Suzanne's visits bothered Mitch. After each one, he became stoic and withdrawn, barely speaking the rest of the night, sleeping on his side facing away from her, making no effort to touch or hold her.

She tried not to take it personally. Suzanne had cheated on him, left him for another man. And now she was back. That was bound to put any man in a bad mood.

But she couldn't help being afraid that he was pulling away, that Suzanne's presence was beginning to put a wedge between them.

He told her he was over Suzanne, that he had no desire for the reconciliation his ex-wife was pushing for, but how could she be sure?

He'd been in love with Suzanne at one time, Emma knew that. Her betrayal had hurt him, and Emma didn't know if he was over it even to this day.

What if he was remembering the Suzanne he knew

when they were dating and first married? What if he thought they could make another go of it, that things would be different the second time around?

The very idea that she might lose him to his ex-wife sent a chill through her bones that settled around her heart.

If only he would take her in his arms and tell her she had nothing to worry about. That he loved her and felt nothing for his ex any longer.

But he couldn't tell her something he didn't feel. He might want her physically, care for her as a friend and the mother of his unborn child, but he didn't love her the way a husband should love his wife.

And that's what scared her the most. Because if he didn't love her, there were no emotional ties to keep him with her, and the chances of his being lured back to Suzanne were that much higher.

She did her best to hide her fears, to pretend everything was all right and not let him know she died a little inside every time his ex-wife's car rolled up the drive.

The baby growing in her belly was the only thing keeping them together, and even though he'd told her he wanted to do the right thing, give their child a name and the stability of a two-parent family, she knew perfectly well that if he decided to take Suzanne back, he could divorce Emma and still be a decent father.

He'd wanted to be with her when he didn't think he had any other options. But his ex-wife was definitely offering him other options. Two rather large, bouncy options that any man would be reluctant to pass up.

Emma heaved a disheartened sigh and set her mug of once-hot, decaffeinated tea on the kitchen counter. She'd wasted enough time today staring out the kitchen window at the barn, watching for any glimpse of Mitch as he went about his workday and wishing things could be different.

She had work of her own to do. And as long as she was still married, she might as well make the best of it.

Grabbing a banana from the bowl of fruit in the center of the table, she headed for Mitch's office...which was quickly becoming *her* office, since she was the only one who used it these days for anything more significant than piling more papers on the desk.

She plopped down in the wheeled leather desk chair and clicked on the computer, then took a bite of banana and started sorting through stacks of file folders while the system booted up. The files were bright orange, red, blue, yellow...she loved color and one of the first things she'd done after taking over Mitch's accounting and records was to replace all the boring manila folders with new, brighter ones. It also made organization easier, since she could co-ordinate all of Mitch's sales in red, purchases in yellow, bills in blue, et cetera.

Following her own system, she set aside the items she'd already worked on and tried to separate out the things that still needed to be done. As she twisted in the chair to set aside a stack of completed work, a large brown envelope slid off the desk and onto the floor.

She'd never seen it before, but that wasn't unusual. Mitch often laid "to do" stuff on the desk or on the small corner table just inside the door for her to deal with later.

The mailer was unsealed and unmarked, with no names or addresses to clue her in as to its contents. Reaching inside, she pulled out a sheaf of papers and began to scan the neat, printed words.

Mitch's name within in the paragraphs of legalese didn't concern her, since she figured it was just another piece of ranch business. Perhaps the sale or purchase of a registered steer.

But when her father's name caught her eye, her eyebrows knit and she slowed her quick skim to go back and read the document word for word.

The more she read, the sicker she felt. Her stomach cramped, and bile began to climb its way up her raw throat.

Oh, my God. No, it can't be true.

But it was right there in front of her, in black and white. And even though her vision was growing cloudier by the second, she wasn't mistaken in her understanding.

The document was a legal codicil to her father's will, leaving the Double D to Mitch upon Wyatt Davis's death.

And all Mitch had had to do to earn this prime inheritance was marry her.

Thirteen

Emma lurched to her feet, dodging furniture on her race for the kitchen, making it just in time to vomit into the stainless-steel sink. With her head spinning so fast she felt like she might pass out at any moment, she ran water to rinse the basin and her mouth and splash her flushed face.

Dear God. Her father had sold her like one of his brood mares. And Mitch had taken her on not because he loved her, not because he wanted to be married or wanted another wife, but because he stood to gain just short of a hundred acres of land that connected directly to his, as well as several head of cattle and horses.

She clutched the edge of the counter, letting the tears run down her face unchecked. In a flash, Mitch's first proposal and later his determination to marry because of her unexpected pregnancy came back to her.

The emotionless pitch, the press for responsibility, respectability.

Oh, he might have wanted to do right by his child, but she was sure her father's generous offer made it a much easier pill to swallow.

Her breath was coming in gasps, her lungs seizing painfully with each inhale and exhale of oxygen. She turned, still holding tightly to the countertop to keep from sliding to the floor, still blind to her surroundings. She heard the wracking sobs filling the room, but couldn't even register that they were her own.

With her arms stretched out on either side of her body, she took one lurching step after another, making her way to the staircase and up to the second floor.

She had to get out of here, had to get away before she went crazy. She couldn't be in this house another minute, knowing her marriage was a fraud…more than she'd ever believed possible. Knowing that Mitch had lied to her, betrayed her…*bought* her.

Stumbling into the guest bedroom, she grabbed an empty overnight bag from the closet and carried it with her to the bathroom and into Mitch's room, tossing in items she thought she might need to get through the next few days. Her toothbrush, some bras and panties, a couple of shirts and pairs of slacks. She didn't know where she was going, but she could buy whatever else she needed once she got there.

One thing was certain—she was never coming back to Mitch's house. She was taking herself and her child and getting as far away from him as possible.

Let Suzanne have him. Let the devil take him. She really didn't care as long as she never had to look at his lying, deceptive face ever again.

She wasn't going to her father's place, either. As far as she was concerned, he was just as guilty in this betrayal as Mitch.

How could he do this to her? Her own father!

Bag in tow, she hurried down the stairs, wiping her cheeks with the side of her hand. The screen door banged against its frame as she pounded across the porch and jumped in her car. She twisted the key in the ignition, barely waiting for the engine to sputter to life before putting the vehicle in gear and stomping on the gas.

Gravel spun up behind her rear tires, leaving deep tread marks along the drive. But she didn't slow down, didn't look back.

She was leaving Mitch Ramsey in her dust—literally and figuratively. Forever.

With a slight limp to his right leg, Mitch ambled slowly from the barn to the house. He'd had a minor run-in with an eight-hundred-pound bull this afternoon, but he counted himself lucky he was only sore instead of sporting a few broken bones—or a broken neck.

When he opened the front door, he expected to find Emma in the kitchen. It was almost dinnertime, and usually when he came in from the barn she was busy cooking and setting the table.

She would look up from whatever she was doing and smile at him. Ask about his day and how the new colt was doing. Then she would tell him supper would be on the table by the time he got back from his shower.

It all made him feel very…domestic, comfortable, safe. Instead of being a trial, having Emma in his house felt right. Having her in his bed felt even better.

He didn't want to think too much about that, about how well she fit into his life. Having her around was definitely a plus, and he didn't get that sick, panicky feeling in his gut anymore when he thought about being married again. With a kid on the way, no less.

But she wasn't in the kitchen and he didn't smell anything baking. Maybe she was in the office or upstairs taking a nap. Lord knew the pregnancy could make her tired and out of sorts from time to time.

As he kicked off his boots and passed through the living room, he thought about the fact that things would be just about perfect if his ex weren't making a royal pain of herself. No matter how many times or ways he tried to make it clear he wasn't interested—he was married again to another woman, for God's sake!—Suzanne just wouldn't take the hint.

A part of him suspected she wasn't hanging around so much to win him back as because she was hoping to tap back into his financial support. When she'd run off with her rich boyfriend, she'd no longer needed his paltry income. And she hadn't been eligible for alimony because she'd remarried so soon.

He thanked God every day for that small blessing.

But now Kevin Burnes had filed for divorce and Suzanne was about to be left penniless.

Of course, with him being married to Emma—and having no interest whatsoever in a reconciliation—Suzanne would never again have access to his bank account.

So now she had switched gears and was attempting to guilt him into giving her money. But Mitch had wised up to his ex-wife's manipulations—finally—and he had no interest in getting involved with her again in *any* way.

Besides, he had a family to provide for now. He couldn't waste his time, energy or money on a woman who had cheated on him and then dumped him the minute someone better came along.

Something Emma would never do.

His brow creased as he passed the office. The door was wide open, but Emma wasn't inside.

He started up the steps, ducking his head into the bedrooms before making his way to the bathroom. She wasn't there, either.

Still, he wasn't worried. She could have taken a drive over to her father's place or might just be out back, sitting in the sunshine. He'd look more thoroughly after he got out of the shower.

Twenty minutes later, he was damp but clean and dressed in fresh clothes. The house was almost eerily silent. There were no footsteps, no clanking of pots and pans as Emma worked in the kitchen, none of the inattentive humming he'd grown used to.

He padded down the stairs to the front door, glancing outside and noticing for the first time that Emma's car was missing. Well, that was it, then. She'd gone over to her father's or run into town for something at the store. He was surprised she hadn't left a note the way she usually did, but it was no big deal. She'd be back soon.

After an hour passed, his stomach was growling so loudly he made himself a sandwich and considered calling Wyatt to see if Emma was there. He didn't want to come across as too protective or controlling, though, so he waited.

Two hours later, the sun began to set and Mitch admitted that he was starting to get worried. It wasn't like Emma to take off without telling him. It wasn't like her not to call and let him know where she was or how long she'd be, especially when it started to get late.

Picking up the cordless phone, he hit the speed dial number for her father's house and listened to the ring on the other end while he paced though the house like a caged animal. Wyatt picked up on the third ring.

"Hel-lo?"

"Wyatt, it's Mitch. Is Emma with you?" he asked, cutting right to the chase.

Silence filled the phone line for several seconds and then Wyatt said, "No, I'm afraid she isn't. Is something wrong?"

"No," Mitch answered, cursing himself for causing Emma's father any premature upset. He should have called a couple other places first. "I'm sure everything is fine. Emma wasn't here when I came in from the barn and I didn't find a note. But I'm sure she just went out for milk or something. She probably got cornered by one of the town gossips and is still trying to make an escape."

He laughed, trying to lighten the mood of their conversation, but he didn't think Wyatt was buying it.

"Anyway, give me a ring if she stops by, but I'm betting I'll be calling you back in a few minutes to tell you she just pulled up the drive."

He said goodbye and punched the disconnect button, letting his arm drop to his side as he considered where else Emma might be. It was unlikely she'd gone to his folks' place without him, and he didn't know any of her girl-friends' numbers by heart.

"Dammit." He let his chin fall to his chest, pressing two fingers over the bridge of his nose where a headache was beginning to pound.

Where the hell could she be? It was one thing to visit a friend or run into town for a while. But she'd been gone for four hours now, and that was only since he'd come in from the barn. God knew how long she'd been gone before that.

An arrow of fear stabbed his heart, stopping him in his tracks. What if something had happened? What if she'd gotten sick or hurt? What if she'd started to cramp, gotten worried about the baby and didn't think she had time to find him before going for help?

He never should have left her alone.

Pivoting on his heel, he raced to the office, desperate to find phone numbers for all of Emma's friends and acquaintances. He would start with her obstetrician and call everyone in the phone book, if he had to, until he tracked her down.

Dropping down on the seat of the chair, he started searching the desk, opening and closing drawers in search of her address book. His hand bumped the computer's mouse and the monitor suddenly came to life. Which only increased his concern, since Emma tended to turn the computer off whenever she wasn't using it.

He hadn't found a paper address book, so maybe she kept her contact information on the PC. His hand was on the mouse, scrolling around to find his options when his elbow knocked a pile of papers to the floor.

He swore, long and harsh, leaning over to pick them up without taking his attention from the computer screen. As he tossed the papers back in the center of the desk, he caught a glimpse of the top page out of the corner of his eye.

They seemed familiar, and he paused for a moment to look at them more closely.

His chest grew tight and a sinking feeling began to slide through his gut when he realized what they were. It was the legal document Wyatt had given him right after he'd married Emma. The addendum to his will, leaving the Davis ranch to Mitch in the event of Wyatt's death.

They'd both signed it, and Wyatt had been as pleased as a cat who'd just dropped a dead rat on his owner's bed. While Mitch had been more uncomfortable, never thinking his agreement with Emma's father was really appropriate.

And now he knew his uncertainty had been a warning. He should have turned Wyatt down. He should have backed out of their deal when he'd had the chance or burned the damn papers the minute he got home.

He sure as hell shouldn't have left them where Emma might find them.

Because she had. She'd found them and read them, and now she thought he'd only married her for a parcel of land.

Nothing could be farther from the truth, but she didn't know that.

How could she, when he'd done everything in his power to keep her at arm's length?

His shoulders slumped and he scrubbed his hands over his face. God, he'd really messed things up.

And the worst part was that he'd hurt Emma. Something he would never do intentionally. He'd rather cut off his own arm than hurt her.

She was one of the only people in his life who hadn't said "I told you so" after Suzanne's betrayal and abandonment. Everyone else had acted like he was the world's biggest pushover. But not Emma. She hadn't criticized or made him feel like a fool, she'd simply been his friend and supported him, regardless of his decisions or mistakes.

He had to find her. Had to make her understand before he lost her.

The desk chair rolled back and hit the wall as he pushed to his feet, his long strides eating up the floorboards as he headed for the front of the house. He grabbed his cell phone and the keys to his truck, then yanked open the door. His hand was already on the screen when he lifted his head and found himself staring into the heavily mascaraed eyes of his ex-wife.

"Dammit," he bit out. "What are you doing here, Suzanne?"

He didn't have time to deal with her right now. And on top of that, he just plain didn't want to.

"What do you think I'm doing here, silly? I came to see you."

Her overly sweet voice grated on his nerves. It always had. He didn't know why he hadn't realized it before now.

Deep down, a lot of things about his ex-wife bothered him. Her bleach-blond hair. Her tight clothes. The way she hit on every man in a ten-mile radius, even after they'd married. Her Tammy Faye Bakker makeup job and cheap, cloying perfume.

Maybe his family was right—he was the biggest pushover in the known world.

Or he had been. But not anymore. He had his head on straight now and wasn't going to be fooled by a pair of big boobs and a false grin.

He pushed the screen door open, forcing Suzanne to take a few quick steps back. Her car salesman smile slipped for a moment before she caught herself and pasted it back on.

"Where are you running off to in such a hurry?" she asked, mincing to keep up with him in her too-tight, too-high heels as he crossed the yard to his truck.

"None of your business," he said, yanking open the driver's side door and climbing inside.

"Let me make something perfectly clear. I don't want to see *you,* Suzanne," he told her, not bothering to beat around the bush. "We're divorced and have been for four years. We've got nothing to say to each other. I'm not sorry you left, and I'm not interested in getting back together."

"But, Mitchy—"

"No. No buts," he said, finally meeting her pampered hazel eyes. "I'm married to Emma now. I love her and we're having a baby. You're not welcome here, Suzanne, so don't come around anymore." He turned the key, listening to the big V-8 engine roar to life. "If you do, I'll call the sheriff and have you hauled away for trespassing. And if you think I'm joking...try me."

With that, he put the pickup in gear and peeled out of the yard, leaving his ex to come or go or rot, for all he cared. He just wanted to find Emma, *pronto,* and bring her home.

He'd told Suzanne he loved Emma, and it was absolutely true. He couldn't believe he hadn't figured it out before now.

That's why he'd been willing to marry her, even after the fiasco of his first marriage to Suzanne. Not because Wyatt asked him to or offered his land in exchange for wedding vows to his daughter, but because he'd been in love with Emma the whole time.

Oh, wild horses couldn't have dragged such an admission out of him. He wasn't sure he'd even realized it, consciously. But somewhere, deep inside, he'd known.

The question was, could he convince Emma of that before he lost her forever?

Flipping open his phone, he punched numbers with the side of his thumb while steering with one hand and trying to keep his eyes on the road. When his mother picked up, he got straight to the point, asking if she'd seen or heard from Emma. She hadn't, but promised to call him if Emma showed up.

Then he dialed his brother, hoping he was still home instead of off on another one of his high-powered business trips.

"Ramsey," Chase answered.

"Emma's missing," he said without preamble, knowing his brother would recognize his voice. "Is she there with you?"

"God in heaven, Mitch. When are you going to cut out the jealous, suspicious crap? You never used to be like this.

And it's starting to tick me off that you think I'd ever hit on or sleep with your wife…or any woman you were interested in."

"Chase," Mitch muttered between clenched teeth. "Shut up. I'm not asking if Emma is in your bed. I trust her a little bit more than that. And I trust you, too," he added, realizing it was the truth.

Emma would never cheat on him the way Suzanne had. She didn't have it in her. He suspected he'd known that all along or he never would have married her in the first place. Not even after he found out she was pregnant.

And if there was anyone he could trust as much as Emma, it was Chase. As brothers went, he'd gotten a good one.

"I'm calling because I'm worried about her, and I thought you might know where she was. I thought she might have come to you to tell you what a jerk I am."

"What kind of jerk are you?"

"The first-class, dumb-as-an-ox kind."

Chase chuckled, but his amusement fled as soon as Mitch told him about the deal he'd made with Wyatt Davis and the papers Emma had found in his office.

"Geez," his brother said with a long, drawn-out whistle. "Just when I thought you couldn't screw up any bigger than letting that blow-up doll, Suzanne, get her claws into you."

"Yeah," Mitch agreed, feeling his face heat with shame and embarrassment. "Not two of my finer moments, I'll give you that. But I love her, Chase."

"Who, *Suzanne?*"

The horror in his brother's voice made him chuckle, despite the concern coursing through his bloodstream.

"No, not Suzanne," Mitch told him with complete conviction. "Emma. I'm in love with Emma, my wife, and I don't want to lose her over some stupid agreement I made with her father that I never even cared about. Will you help me find her?"

"You know I will. Give me an idea of where to look."

Mitch didn't have the first clue, not if she wasn't at her father's. But he asked Chase to help him make some phone calls, and they divvied up areas of Gabriel's Crossing to search.

Then he hung up and began to pray. That he'd find Emma, and she and the baby would both be safe and healthy when he did. That she would give him a chance to talk, to explain, to beg forgiveness before she gave him the boot.

And that she would believe him when he told her he loved her.

Fourteen

An hour later, Mitch spotted Emma's car in the parking lot of the Dew Drop Inn on the outskirts of town, and stood on the brakes. His truck fishtailed for a second before he regained control.

He pulled in beside her at an awkward angle and jumped out. It was tempting to just start pounding on doors, or to take a guess that Emma's room would be the one directly in front of where she parked. But he couldn't be sure and didn't want to cause a scene or do anything to scare her unless he had to.

Marching to the motel lobby with its neon Vacancy sign in the window, he asked which room his wife was in, then had to provide proof of his identity before the teenager working the counter would tell him.

Lucky he hadn't burst through the door he'd first wanted to, because it turned out she was two rooms down. He found the number and lifted his fist to knock.

When no one answered, he rapped again. "Emma? Emma, it's Mitch. I know you're in there. Open the door. Please."

"Go away."

His heart swelled at her response and a wave of relief washed through him. She was here and she was all right.

But just as quickly, his stomach clenched at the sound of tears in her voice.

He laid his palm flat on the flimsy wooden panel and rested his forehead on the ridge of his knuckles. "Emma, honey. Open up. Please? I want to talk to you."

"Well, I don't want to talk to you. Go away or I'll call the front desk and tell them you're harassing me."

A muscle along his jaw ticked as he gritted his teeth in frustration. How was he ever going to apologize and make her understand if she wouldn't even let him in?

"Dammit, Emma, open this door right now or I'll kick it in. All I want to do is talk to you. If you don't like what I have to say, I'll leave."

Silence met his plea.

"All right, here goes," he said, taking a step back and readying himself to follow through on his threat. "One…"

Still nothing.

"Two…"

He heard a muffled "Fine" and then the chain on the other side jingled. The door opened with a squeak and Emma stood there staring out at him, her face pale, her eyes red and swollen from what he suspected were hours of crying.

Her obvious misery hit him like a punch to the gut, and he wanted to fall to his knees right then and there and beg forgiveness.

She crossed her arms, emphasizing the sexy swell of her breasts and the rounded paunch of her adorable pregnant belly.

"Are you all right?" he asked, needing more than anything to know she and the baby were okay. Then he shook his head. "I know you're not all right. I know you saw the papers for the agreement I made with your father. But I mean physically. Are you and the baby okay?"

"We're fine," she said grudgingly. "But I'm not coming back with you. I'm leaving. I'm filing for divorce and taking the baby, and I never want to see you or my father again."

He knew it was her hurt and anger talking, but her words stabbed straight through his heart.

"Don't do that," he said, his own voice low and scratchy with desperation. "Please, just listen to me."

Reaching for her wrist, he moved forward, forcing her to walk backward farther into the room. He kicked the door closed with his booted foot, telling himself he deserved her wariness when she pulled out of his grasp and shot a fearful glance over his shoulder at her only mode of escape.

"I know you hate me right now, and you have every right. I hate myself for what I've put you through. But I'd like a chance to explain. Please."

Her arms went back across her chest and she took a defensive stance a few feet away. "There's nothing you can say that will ever make up for what you and my father did."

Moisture gathered on her lashes, twisting his insides.

"You're absolutely right. You can't know how sorry I am about that. But you have to believe me when I tell you that I don't care about your father's ranch. He came to me with this bizarre proposal to leave the Double D to me in his will, as long as I became part of the family by marrying you. And I don't think he did it because he was in some all-fired hurry to marry you off. He was more concerned about the land ending up in the wrong hands, afraid you wouldn't want to run things after he passed.

"And I agreed because…" He took a deep breath to slow his racing pulse and garner courage for what he was about to say. "Because I love you."

He'd expected her to doubt him at first, but he hadn't expected the snort and eye-roll that accompanied her skepticism.

She sniffed and grabbed a tissue from the bedside table to wipe her nose. "Right. I'm supposed to believe that the man who accused me of cheating on him with his own brother and then wouldn't touch me after we were married was *in love* with me."

"Would it help if I told you I'm an idiot?"

"No. I already knew that."

A smile tugged at the corners of his mouth. Moving slowly so he wouldn't spook her, he stepped forward and took her by the arms, steering her in the direction of a worn vinyl chair.

"Sit down for a minute. Please."

For a moment, she looked like she might argue but then did as he asked. He lowered himself to one knee in front of her so they were eye to eye.

She was so beautiful, so precious to him, and he'd royally screwed up his chances of keeping her.

If he lost her now, he didn't know what he would do. Cry like a baby. Stop breathing. Crawl into a hole and die of loneliness. All those options held some appeal, since living without her would be no life at all.

"I'm an idiot for a lot of reasons, but the biggest is that I let Suzanne's betrayal make me think I could never trust a woman again. Which is complete hogwash. I could always trust you. I knew it, even if I wasn't willing to admit it.

"I didn't think I could handle the pain and humiliation of marrying another woman only to have her cheat on me, too. And the best way to keep something like that from happening, I thought, was to shut down, cut myself off. Pretend I didn't want or feel."

He wrapped one hand lightly around her wrist, feeling the pulse beating there, rubbing his thumb back and forth across the delicate veins beneath her skin.

"But I did want—I wanted you. And I did feel—I felt so many things for you, they scared me. *That's* why I agreed to your father's asinine plan, Emma. Not because I was interested in the land, but because I wanted you and didn't know how else to get you, keep you. Your father's offer gave me an excuse to marry you without having to admit that I felt something for you.

"And then when you told me you were pregnant…" Covering her expanding stomach with his free hand, he let his head fall forward until their brows met. "God, I was so happy. But I was petrified, too. I'd done such a thorough job of cutting myself off from my emotions, I wasn't sure I could turn them on again enough to raise a healthy, happy child. But I wanted to try. And it seemed like the perfect opportunity to bind you to me. Legally. Forever."

He leaned back, searching her damp, lovely blue eyes for some sign that she was listening and might be willing to forgive him.

"Don't be angry with your dad, baby. Please. His intentions were good, even if he went about them in a very bad way. And don't hate me, either. Please. I love you so much, it feels like my heart is going to explode if you leave me.

"I know I don't deserve it, and I have no right to ask, but give me a second chance. Come home with me and let me prove to you that I'm telling the truth. We'll tear up that damn codicil, burn it in the fireplace. Then we'll go over to your father's and do the same with his copy. And I told

Suzanne to leave us alone or I'd have her thrown in jail, so she shouldn't bother us ever again."

Seconds ticked by while he kept his gaze locked on her face, his chest tight with panic and the effort to draw air into his lungs.

"You hurt me, Mitch." Her bottom lip trembled and tears spilled over her lashes to run down her cheeks. "You really, really hurt me."

Gathering her close, he wrapped his arms around her and let his fingers tangle in the fall of her hair. "I know, sweetheart. I'm so sorry. I never meant to. I'd rip out my own heart before I'd hurt you on purpose."

She sniffed against his shoulder and he felt a small shudder roll through her fragile frame. He squeezed her even tighter, afraid that if he let go, if he loosened his hold for even a minute, she would slip away from him again.

"I'd like to tell you I'll never hurt you again, but I've still got that idiot thing going for me, so chances are, I will. The best I can do is promise you that I'll try not to. And if I do, you can tell me. You can hit me, beat me, yell at me. Just don't leave me."

He ran his hands through the hair at her temples, loving the soft texture of it against his skin. Then he gently kissed one corner of her mouth, followed by the other.

"Don't leave me, Emma. Stay with me and be my wife, my lover, the mother of my children. Help me run the ranch and show the folks of Gabriel's Crossing that even though I was stupid enough to hook up with the wrong woman once, I finally wised up and married the right woman. The only woman I could ever love."

She pulled back a little, and for a moment he was afraid she was going to turn him down. That his words meant nothing and he was going to lose her, anyway.

"Do you really love me?" she asked in a low voice.

He answered immediately, relieved to finally be able to express his feelings for her. "More than my own life."

"Would you really have married me, even if my father hadn't made that ridiculous offer? Even if I hadn't gotten pregnant?"

"Yes. It probably would have taken me a while to figure out that that's what I wanted, though—" he made a face "—since we've already established that I'm not the brightest bulb in the lamp when it comes to that sort of thing."

A soft smile started to curl her lips. "No, you're not. I've been in love with you since I was a little girl, and you never once looked at me like you might feel the same."

He pulled back, stunned by her admission. He didn't know what to focus on first—the fact that she'd said she loved him or that she'd had feelings for him longer than he'd ever imagined.

"Did you just say you love me?" he asked, wanting to be one hundred percent sure.

She nodded, lifting her own arms to fan her fingers through his hair and across his scalp. "Since we were kids. Then you went and married that bimbo and broke my heart."

Her grasp on his head tightened and she gave him a little shake. "No more bimbos," she told him sternly. "No more stupid deals with my father or anyone else, and no more pretending you don't care about me. If we're going to make this marriage work, then you have to be honest and open with me and stop punishing me for your *ex*-wife's behavior."

The hard knot of worry that had taken up residence in the pit of his stomach began to loosen as her meaning sank in, and his grin felt like it was going to split his face.

"Yes, ma'am."

"And you have to tell me you love me at least once a day. Twice if you do something idiotic."

He laughed, enjoying the vibrating sensation in his chest and moving up his throat. It had been too long since he'd laughed, too long since he'd been truly happy.

"Yes, ma'am." He would tell her a dozen times a day, if it would make her happy. Hell, it would make *him* happy.

"So will you come home with me?" he asked, not ready to completely abandon his fears until he heard her say the words.

"Yes, I'll go home with you. *After* we stop at Pop's to rip up those damn papers."

He chuckled again and hugged her close, pressing his lips to her ear, her throat, her cheek until he reached her mouth.

"Deal," he whispered and sealed it with a kiss.

Epilogue

The Dixie Chicks crooned about wide open spaces over the stereo speakers set up on either side of the big white gazebo in the center of the park, while couples danced and children chased each other through the grass, screaming and laughing. Everyone in Gabriel's Crossing had come out for the Fourth of July celebration, bringing their best covered dishes and dressing in red, white and blue from head to toe.

Emma smiled at Ida Mae Fisher, who was telling her yet another story about one of her fifteen grandchildren, and nodded at what she hoped were appropriate intervals. But her gaze scanned the crowd, looking for two familiar faces.

Her husband, who had gone off about an hour before to play a game of horseshoes, and her three-month-old daughter, who was being passed around like a bowl of mashed potatoes at Thanksgiving dinner.

It was the baby she was most concerned about. Amelia was so little, still a newborn, practically, and Emma didn't deal well with having her daughter out of her sight. Never mind that it had been her mother-in-law who'd taken the baby from her arms or that the woman had raised two children of her own.

She was a nervous, overprotective mama, Emma thought. So shoot her.

Two large, masculine hands snaked around her waist, locking in the middle and making her jump. She tilted her head back to find Mitch's gray eyes and grinning lips only inches away.

"Good lord, you scared me," she said, giving his arm a light swat.

"Ida Mae," he drawled in that whiskey-smooth voice that made her spine go soft and tingly, "would you mind if I borrowed this pretty young lady for a minute? She's needed over by the dessert table."

The older woman's eyes crinkled at the corners and she waved them away. "Of course not. You two go on. I'll finish telling you about little Dwight Allen later."

"Oh, goodie," he whispered in her ear, keeping his tall body pressed against her back as he turned with her and walked them both in the other direction. "I'll be sure to get you back for the rest of that story."

She chuckled. "That's all right. I can live without knowing how they got the kernels of corn out of his nose. Thank you for rescuing me, by the way."

Instead of leading her to the long picnic table weighed down with cakes, cookies, brownies and pies, he steered her away from the festivities toward the field of parked cars.

"You're welcome. I really did need to talk to you, though."

Her amusement fled in a rush, replaced by an immediate flicker of fear. She stopped in her tracks and twisted to face him, forcing him to halt, too.

"What's wrong? Is it Amelia? Is she sick? Did she get hurt?"

"The baby's fine," he answered patiently before she could break away and go in search of their daughter herself.

A second later, he'd neatly maneuvered her between two vehicles so that her back was against the passenger side door of his big blue truck. He leaned in and took her mouth, kissing her until her toes curled and her bones began to melt.

When he lifted his head, they were both breathing rapidly and she'd forgotten what she was worried about only a moment before.

"There. Now will you stop worrying about Amelia?"

"I'm a new mother. It's my job to worry."

His face split into an understanding smile. "I know. And you're very good at it."

She raised one eyebrow.

"At being a mother, I mean," he added quickly. "Not the worrying part."

"That's what I thought you meant," she said, letting him off the hook with a grin of her own.

"So what do you say we sneak away from the party and go home, where we can be alone for a change and fool around like teenagers. There's a new litter of kittens up in the loft I've been meaning to show you," he added as extra enticement.

Her blood warmed at memories of their first night together, in the loft of her father's barn, and at the thought of being alone with him again. Really, truly *alone*.

Since Amelia's birth, it seemed like their house had been overrun first by well-wishers dropping in to bring gifts and get a glimpse of the new baby, and then by

Emma's father and Mitch's parents, who were playing their roles as grandparents to the hilt.

And after everyone else finally left, either Amelia still needed their almost constant attention or they were just plain exhausted.

"I'd love to," she said.

They'd been at the town picnic three or four hours already. She was more than ready to go home for some peace and quiet. And if she was lucky, maybe a little cuddle time with her husband.

"Let me just collect Amelia and we—"

Mitch covered her mouth with his own and kissed her into silence once again.

Mmm, she rather liked his method of shutting her up. If he ever tried it during an authentic argument, she'd probably have to deck him, but as an every day mode of hushing her up it was certainly something she could get used to.

"When I said 'alone,' I meant it," he explained when he broke off this time. "Just the two of us. My mom's going to keep Amelia for the night."

Emma shook her head, already suffering the first twinges of separation anxiety. "Oh, no. I couldn't—"

"*Yes,*" he stressed, "you can. You need to. We both need to."

Before she could protest further, he brought two fingers up to her lips. "Amelia is going to be fine. Mom and Dad are thrilled about having her all to themselves, and you know they'll take nothing but the best care of her. I already put the car seat and diaper bag in their car, and I made them swear that if they needed anything, they'd call. I'll keep my cell phone on me at all times," he added, wiggling his eyebrows suggestively. "I may even set it on vibrate."

"Very funny." Biting her lip, Emma looked back over

her shoulder at the throng of people, not seeing Theresa and the baby, but knowing they were there somewhere.

"Come on," Mitch cajoled, his hot breath fanning over her cheek and neck as he lowered his head to nibble at her throat. "Say yes."

Her maternal instincts warred with the lust and need coursing through her veins. Finally, common sense won out.

Amelia would be fine for one night. And she really did miss being alone with Mitch, just the two of them, to do all the naughty, sexy things that had brought them together in the first place.

"All right," she acquiesced, her fingers curling into the firm muscles of his upper arms as his tongue did wicked things to the lobe of her ear.

She could feel the tilt of his grin in the curve of her shoulder, and then he gave her a tiny nip before straightening to meet her gaze.

"Have I told you yet today that I love you?" he asked.

As always, those three words coming from him made happiness burst inside her.

"Yes, you did. This morning, over breakfast."

"Hmm." His eyes narrowed as he studied her. "Well, I'm going to say it again, just in case I've done something stupid, or do before the day is out. I love you."

She chuckled, wrapping her arms around his neck and lifting up on her toes to reach his mouth. "I love you, too. But don't worry, you've been a very smart man lately."

"The smartest thing I ever did was marry you."

The conviction in his voice and sincerity shining in his eyes made her want to weep. She tugged him close and kissed him to let him know just how proud she was of the changes he'd made, leaving all of his hang-ups and insecurities over his ex-wife behind him.

And then he was shifting her to the side, opening the truck door and lifting her onto the seat. A second later, he'd rounded the hood and climbed in behind the wheel.

Emma smiled, taking in every detail of her husband's profile as he drove them home faster than the law allowed.

They'd come so far in one short year, overcome so much pain. But she wouldn't change a minute of it, because in the end, she'd gotten everything she'd ever wanted.

She'd gotten Mitch.

* * * * *

New York Times bestselling author
Linda Lael Miller
*is back with a new romance featuring
the heartwarming McKettrick family
from Mills & Boon® Special Edition.*

Sierra's Homecoming
by Linda Lael Miller

*On sale December 2007,
wherever books are sold.*

Turn the page for a sneak preview!

Sierra's Homecoming

by

Linda Lael Miller

Soft, smoky music poured into the room.

The next thing she knew, Sierra was in Travis's arms, close against that chest she'd admired earlier, and they were slow dancing.

Why didn't she pull away?

"Relax," he said. His breath was warm in her hair.

She giggled, more nervous than amused. What was the matter with her? She was attracted to Travis, had been from the first, and he was clearly attracted to her. They were both adults. Why not enjoy a little slow dancing in a ranch-house kitchen?

Because slow dancing led to other things. She took a step back and felt the counter flush against her lower back. Travis naturally came with her, since they were holding hands and he had one arm around her waist.

Simple physics.

Then he kissed her.

Physics again—this time, not so simple.

"Yikes," she said, when their mouths parted.

He grinned. "Nobody's ever said that after I kissed them."

She felt the heat and substance of his body pressed against hers. "It's going to happen, isn't it?" she heard herself whisper.

"Yep," Travis answered.

"But not tonight," Sierra said on a sigh.

"Probably not," Travis agreed.

"When, then?"

He chuckled, gave her a slow, nibbling kiss. "Tomorrow morning," he said. "After you drop Liam off at school."

"Isn't that…a little…soon?"

"Not soon enough," Travis answered, his voice husky. "Not nearly soon enough."

0807/51

MILLS & BOON
Desire 2-*in*-1
On sale 17th August 2007

Heartbreaker *by Diana Palmer*

JB Hammock was a bachelor through and through...but could sweet, caring Tellie Maddox be the one woman who could finally hook this heartbreaker?

Scandals from the Third Bride *by Sara Orwig*

Katherine Ransome had never expected the man who jilted her to try to woo her a second time. Would she trust Cade Logan with her heart...again?

❧

The Intern Affair *by Roxanne St Claire*

Executive Cade McMann had his eye on his intern, Jessie Clayton, but seducing her could expose a secret that could unravel their relationship...and the family dynasty.

Forbidden Merger *by Emilie Rose*

When tycoon Liam Elliot falls for Aubrey Holt, the one woman he can't have, their secret affair sends more than the bed sheets up in flames.

Mini-series – The Elliotts

❧

The Morning-After Proposal *by Sheri WhiteFeather*

Dylan Trueno vows to protect Julia Alcott, on one condition – she becomes his wife. Will she succumb to her desires and his dutiful proposal?

Executive Seduction *by Kristi Gold*

Corri Harris' steamy affair with her boss was everything she'd hoped. But as things got hotter, would Aidan O'Brien toss her aside or was he in it for keeps?

Available at WHSmith, Tesco, ASDA, and all good bookshops
www.millsandboon.co.uk

MILLS & BOON®
Blaze®

Scorching hot sexy reads...

4 brand-new titles each month

Available on the first Friday of every month
from WHSmith, ASDA, Tesco
and all good bookshops
www.millsandboon.co.uk

GEN/14/RTL10

0807/064a

2 NOVELS ONLY £4.99

On sale 17th August 2007

Bestselling novels by your favourite authors back by popular demand!

Princess Brides

Featuring

The Princess is Pregnant!
by Laurie Paige

&

The Princess and the Duke
by Allison Leigh

MILLS & BOON
Spotlight

0807/064b

2 NOVELS ONLY £4.99

On sale
17th August 2007

Secrets

Featuring
Two Little Secrets
by Linda Randall
Wisdom

&

Taming Blackhawk
by
Barbara McCauley

Available at WHSmith, Tesco, ASDA, and all good bookshops
www.millsandboon.co.uka

MILLS & BOON
Spotlight

0807/009/MB103

Mediterranean Men

Let them sweep you off your feet!

Gorgeous Greeks

The Greek Bridegroom by Helen Bianchin
The Greek Tycoon's Mistress by Julia James
Available 20th July 2007

Seductive Spaniards

At the Spaniard's Pleasure by Jacqueline Baird
The Spaniard's Woman by Diana Hamilton
Available 17th August 2007

Irresistible Italians

The Italian's Wife by Lynne Graham
The Italian's Passionate Proposal by Sarah Morgan
Available 21st September 2007

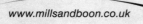

www.millsandboon.co.uk

*Romancipation

ro·man·ci·pa·tion *noun*
The freedom for women to love whom they choose
whilst retaining their own space and identity

Maggie is living the life she's always wanted.
Her career is taking off and, thanks to Japanese
straightening technology, her hair is lying down.
Maggie even has a funny, caring boyfriend – but
there's one problem: he wants Maggie to move in.

Maggie's not sure she's ready to move from "me" to
"we"… As she examines the relationships around
her, Maggie has to decide: is she ready to face her
fears and embrace her own romancipation?

Available 17th August 2007

MIRA

In the heat of the desert, two women find love in the arms of their Arabian princes

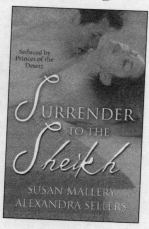

THE SHEIKH'S SECRET BRIDE *by Susan Mallery*

Malik Khan, Crown Prince of El Bahar, had been determined to possess Liana Archer from the moment that he saw her. But should Liana trust the man who could give her anything – everything – but love?

SHEIKH'S TEMPTATION *by Alexandra Sellers*

Sheikh Arash Khosrari was the only man who had ever touched Lana Holding in one night of unbridled and electrifying passion. But would the obstacles in their path be enough to take the heat out of their white-hot desire?

Available 7th September 2007

FROM INTERNATIONAL BESTSELLING AUTHOR LYNNE GRAHAM

Three powerful and intense stories of three
friends who each find themselves a Latin tycoon
to love. A secret son, an affair with the boss
and an end to a paper marriage in:

The Frenchman's Love-Child
The Italian Boss's Mistress
The Banker's Convenient Wife

Available 3rd August 2007

www.millsandboon.co.uk

M&B

FREE

2 BOOKS AND A SURPRISE GIFT!

We would like to take this opportunity to thank you for reading this Mills & Boon® book by offering you the chance to take TWO more specially selected 2-in-1 volumes from the Desire™ series absolutely FREE! We're also making this offer to introduce you to the benefits of the Mills & Boon® Reader Service™—

★ **FREE home delivery**
★ **FREE gifts and competitions**
★ **FREE monthly Newsletter**
★ **Books available before they're in the shops**
★ **Exclusive Reader Service offers**

Accepting these FREE books and gift places you under no obligation to buy; you may cancel at any time, even after receiving your free shipment. Simply complete your details below and return the entire page to the address below. You don't even need a stamp!

YES! Please send me 2 free Desire volumes and a surprise gift. I understand that unless you hear from me, I will receive 3 superb new volumes every month for just £4.99 each, postage and packing free. I am under no obligation to purchase any books and may cancel my subscription at any time. The free books and gift will be mine to keep in any case.

D7ZEE

Ms/Mrs/Miss/Mr...Initials ....
BLOCK CAPITALS PLEASE

Surname ....

Address ....

....

....Postcode ....

Send this whole page to:
The Reader Service, FREEPOST CN81, Croydon, CR9 3WZ

Offer valid in UK only and is not available to current Mills & Boon® Reader Service™ subscribers to this series. Overseas and Eire please write for details. We reserve the right to refuse an application and applicants must be aged 18 years or over. Only one application per household. Terms and prices subject to change without notice. Offer expires 31st October 2007. As a result of this application, you may receive offers from Harlequin Mills & Boon and other carefully selected companies. If you would prefer not to share in this opportunity please write to The Data Manager at PO Box 676, Richmond, TW9 1WU.

Mills & Boon® is a registered trademark owned by Harlequin Mills & Boon Limited.
Desire™ is being used as a trademark. The Mills & Boon® Reader Service™ is being used as a trademark.